A KNIGHT TO CALL MY OWN

Sherry Ewing

Kingsburg Press
SAN FRANCISCO, CALIFORNIA

Kingsburg Press
P.O. Box 475146
San Francisco, California 94147
www.KingsburgPress.com

Publisher's Note: *A Knight To Call My Own* is a work of fiction. Names, characters, places, and incidents are a product of the author's imagination. Locales and public names are sometimes used for atmospheric purposes. Any resemblance to actual people, living or dead, or to businesses, companies, events, institutions, or locales is completely coincidental.

Cover Photo: *God Speed* by Edmund Blair Leighton (1852–1922). This media is in the public domain in the United States. This applies to U.S. works where the copyright has expired, often because its first publication occurred prior to January 1, 1923. {{PD-US}} This work is in the public domain in the European Union and non-EU countries with a copyright term of life of the author plus 70 years. {{PD-old-70}}

Cover Design: Mari Christie at www.MariChristie.info
Editor: Barbara Millman Cole
Book Layout ©2013 BookDesignTemplates.com

A Knight To Call My Own/ Sherry Ewing. -- 1st ed.
ISBN 13: 978-0-9905462-7-6
ISBN 10: 0990546276

For my sister-in-law Barbara

*A truly gracious and amazing lady who found her own
knight in shining armor in the arms of my brother.
He is one lucky man and so are we
to have you in our family!*

Love you, Barbie!

Acknowledgement

To Tricia Linden ~ critique partner extraordinaire and a true sister of my heart. Thank you will never cover everything you do to help me make my books reach that next level!

To my wonderful and supportive family~ thank you for always believing in me.

To my editor Barbara Millman Cole ~ I appreciate all you do to give my readers a quality book to enjoy

And last but certainly not least:

To the lovely ladies of my Street Team ~ Thank you for your continued support and for everything you do for me so that other readers can find my novels.
I appreciate all your efforts on my behalf.
I'm so happy you're all with me on this incredible journey!

ONE

Berwyck Castle
Spring, the Year of Our Lord's Grace 1180

B EAUTY'S THUNDERING HOOF BEATS RESOUNDED, as the horse galloped across the strand, and left no doubt as to the urgency of her rider. Clumps of wet sand marked Lynet's passage and gave evidence to just how far she had traveled. The distant voice of her guardsman calling her name was all but lost between the powerful roar of the ocean waves crashing into the shore and the dissonant emotions that filled her mind, causing tears to flow freely down her cheeks.

Transferring the reins of her mount to one hand, Lynet wiped the moisture from her eyes to clear her vision. Gasping for air, she tried to calm her racing heart, but 'twas to no avail. Heart-broken, she had saddled her horse and had left the safety of the castle walls hoping against hope her frantic flight would offer some form of solace to settle around her very soul. But 'twas of no use. Nothing would cure this pain of lost love. She would need to reach deep down inside herself in order to find a way to move on.

Tugging on the reins, she brought Beauty to a sudden halt then slid from the saddle to the soft sand beneath her feet. The horse was well trained and stood where she had left her whilst Lynet walked a short distance towards the ocean's edge. Any energy she still may have had left her in an unexpected rush of defeat as her knees buckled beneath her, and she fell to the beach in a heap of despair, her outstretched arms and opened palms braced against the ground to keep her balance. Lynet's chest heaved whilst she tried to fill her lungs with breath.

After a moment, and in an attempt to gain what little composure she had left within her, she shook the sand off her gloves, only to discard them, afore she plopped herself down to sit in a very unladylike manner. Having lost her wimple somewhere along the way on her hectic flight, she pushed her long blonde tresses away from her face.

Her fingers trembled as she reached inside her cape and pulled out the parchment she had crumpled into a ball. She smoothed it out as best as she could, knowing he had written the words himself and had spent good coin to ensure she received his missive. Afore she had read the letter the first time, she had held such hope the words he had written her would be the ones that she had long awaited. Alas, this too was a bitter disappointment she should have expected after all these years with nary a word from him. His long absence, and now this unambiguous message, confirmed her worst fears. All had tried to warn her, but she had wanted so much for him to realize on his own that he could come to care for her. 'Twas not to be.

She knew she should not read his words again, but she scanned them all the same, wanting desperately to believe there was some hidden meaning she might have overlooked. Unfortunately, for her peace of mind, they did not change. Fresh tears fell from blue eyes that rivaled the clear sky above her whilst she pondered these far too few words afore her blurry vision.

Lynet,

I have but recently learned you continue to hold out hope that I would one day come for you. Alas, 'twill not be so. As I told you years afore, I have nothing to offer a fair lady such as you.

I beg of you, sweet lass, to find yourself a bonny lad to call your husband and live a happy life. 'Tis my fondest wish to know that you live a life filled with the love of a good man, whomever such a man shall be.

Your Servant,
Ian

Lynet sniffled and wiped her nose with the back of her sleeve. Taking a deep breath, she carefully folded the document and placed it back inside her cape. If she were smart, she would toss the parchment into the ocean waves and never think on Ian's words again. But she could not force herself to even consider such an act, knowing this would be the last bit of remembrance she would have of the man she loved all her young life.

Rubbing her eyes, she resolved her heart to forget her youthful infatuation with a knight who clearly did not love her. *Love!* Mayhap, 'twas just a foolish girl's hope that her love would be returned. A woman full grown would have resigned herself, years ago, to make a match with an acceptable suitor and leave the thought of love to the bards who weave such nonsense.

She stood with a new resolve, firmly in place, to harden her heart so she might never be hurt again. She was, after all, a score of years and should have been wed ere now with bairns about her within her own hall. 'Twas not as if her sister's husband had not brought the finest men afore her both from England and Scotland. She gave a weary sigh, knowing 'twas far past time she put away her fanciful thoughts of chivalry and a man who would love her for herself, not her wealth. Marriage was one of convenience to bring further lands and monies into one's possession. She would no longer leave any place in her heart for love! Surely 'twould be a waste of time to believe in such drivel. Love and marriage did not go together. 'Twould be best to forget such fanciful notions of actually loving the man she was to marry.

Placing her hood about her head, she turned to Beauty and realized how foolish she had been to travel unaccompanied as far as she had. Berwyck Castle rose high above a cliff far off in the distance, and 'twould take some time to return to the safety within its boundaries.

She had just put her foot into the stirrup, when she glanced up at the sound of another horse galloping in her direction. Swinging her leg over the saddle, she quickly adjusted her gown and cape to reach the dirk she kept hidden at her side. She was about to kick her mare into motion to ensure her escape, when she recognized the rider and heard, with relief, the sound of her name carried on the wind.

Her guardsman came abreast of her with a look of disapproval upon his face. 'Twas clear the man was not pleased at her actions this day.

"You will be the death of me, my lady, if you so much as ever think on leaving Berwyck again without a proper escort," the man berated her.

She solemnly gazed upon the guard afore her. He was a handsome man of a score and ten with dark black hair and eyes the color of an aquamarine sea. Having been appointed captain of her guard when she was at the young age of ten and four, the knight beside her had spent many an hour following her about to ensure she remained safe and out of mischief. She hoped he would understand her vexed mood. "I seek your pardon, Rolf, but I needed some time unto myself."

"Bah! There are plenty of places you could have found such solace within the safety of the keep and castle walls!" he complained bitterly. "Think you our Lord Dristan shall forgive me so hastily that I let a mere girl of such tender years escape my notice?"

"I shall speak to my sister's husband on your behalf. 'Twas hardly your fault I left the keep as I did and in such a hurry," Lynet returned with a toss of her head.

Rolf rolled his eyes at her words. "By God's Bones, 'twill only make it worse, my lady! I am already destined to be in the lists 'til the midnight hour for such a lack of duty. You, of all people, know the repercussions of failure under Lord Dristan's watch."

"Aye, Rolf, I know, and again, I must needs seek your pardon," Lynet exclaimed. "I will still endeavor to make all aright with our liege lord."

"Then let us away, and make haste. My fate is already sealed one way or the other."

Lynet bowed her head, since there was no sense in furthering the argument between them. "Lead the way, Rolf. You shall have no more trouble from me this day."

He gave her a look of pure skepticism. "That, Lady Lynet, remains to be seen."

They quickly traveled the beach, retracing the path upon which Lynet had recently fled. Her captain remained watchful from years of training to be leery of the unexpected ambush. She supposed 'twas foolish to leave the grounds of Berwyck unattended as she had. If she had been captured, the price of her ransom would indeed be high, for most knew of her worth, be she wed or not. Her dowry was quite substantial, even if she were not under the protection of the Devil's Dragon of Berwyck. Most would not so much as dare take something, much less someone, under his care, and yet, there were most certainly always the foolish at heart who would not think twice in doing so, if 'twould fill their coffers with the riches she would bring.

They slowed their mounts as they neared the open barbican gate. Was it just her imagination, or did she receive several disappointing looks from those high above who guarded Berwyck's walls? She gazed upward to stare at the heavy metal spikes of the portcullis as they rode beneath them and she shuddered whilst thinking of the death trap awaiting an unwelcome visitor.

Bringing her horse to a halt in the outer bailey, she waited patiently for a lad to come to take the reins and lead Beauty to the stables. Ever efficient, she did not sit there long afore two young lads came running towards her and her guardsman.

Rolf dismounted and promptly came to her side, raising his arms to assist her from her saddle. She gladly accepted his help, resting her hands firmly on his broad shoulders. As he began to slowly lower her to the ground, their eyes locked to one another for the briefest of moments when she became level with his gaze. His stare was intense and quite unexpected causing her heart to flutter softly like the wings of a small bird in flight. Heat flushed her face since she had never thought to be the recipient of such a look, especially from her captain. She blinked, breaking the spell between them as he set her unsteadily on her feet.

He cleared his throat, causing Lynet to realize she continued to hold on to his arms for support. She hastily muttered an apology and dropped her limbs uselessly to her sides. Embarrassed to the core of her being, she refused to look at him again 'til she felt the slightest pressure of his fingers beneath her chin. She raised her eyes to once more meet his and saw a tentative grin form on his face.

"I know 'tis not my place, Lady Lynet, but Ian is a fool for not seeing what he would gain by taking you to wife," Rolf said with a sincere heart.

She scoffed at what she presumed to be reference to the wealth she would bring to her marriage. "Oh aye!" she responded sarcastically. "He is indeed a fool to throw away so much coin to fill his coffers, even if *I* come with such an agreement."

"I was not referring to monies, my lady."

"Were you not?"

"Nay, I was not. Any man with sense in his head can see coin matters little where you are concerned, not to mention he would be blessed to have you at his side."

Rolf's words consoled her injured pride, making Lynet blush whilst her face once more became heated at his words. Silently, she wondered for the first time if Rolf held a certain affection for her. She had never thought of her guardsman in such a manner, most likely because her heart had always belonged to Ian. Still, she could not boldly speak her mind to inquire if he spoke his own feelings. Instead, she voiced the next thought that popped into her head.

"Why do you not just address me by my given name, Rolf? You know I have asked this of you more times than I can count," she whispered sweetly.

He gave her a small nod of his head. "You know the answer, my lady, if you but search your heart," he replied respectfully.

He did care for her! Silence stretched between them, and she pondered how she could have been so blind. Sadly, she understood that she had hurt his feelings, but, 'til now, had been unable to offer him anything more than friendship. She thought of how Rolf had pulled her out of more reckless scrapes than even she cared to admit over the past several years. He had always been there, hovering near at hand, since Dristan had won Berwyck in the name of the king and had appointed him as her captain. If there were a fool in her midst, it surely must be herself.

Rolf's name was called, and its sound took her out of her musings. Looking up towards the lists, she noticed how Dristan was beckoning to his knight whilst his captain, Fletcher, stood anxiously with his sword resting upon his shoulder.

"I must go," Rolf scoffed, "I have a long night ahead of me."

"Aye," she returned softly. "I will still have speech with Dristan if you but wish it of me."

He turned his gaze to her once again, and Lynet thought she would burn on the spot from the intensity of his eyes leveling on her body. "Nay, you will not, my lady, but perchance, you may take pity on me by providing me with something to quench my thirst, once I return to the hall."

Rolf did not wait for the opportunity to hear her answer, but bowed low over her hand and took his leave of her. She watched him go and pondered her stupidity. *How many other broken hearts have I left in my wake with my refusal to wed over the years?* There was no reply forthcoming inside her head, and, mayhap, she would never know for sure.

Lynet turned to make her way into the keep 'til she too heard her name called from the lists. Returning her gaze back towards the sound of men training, she noticed her liege lord crooking his finger for her to join him.

She gave a weary sigh and, with much trepidation, put one foot in front of the other. 'Twas time to pay the price for her waywardness and the trouble she had caused this day. She would not make another mistake as to actually put off the inevitable, for the Devil's Dragon demanded reparation for her insubordination. She might as well get it over and done with so she could once more begin to ponder the direction her sorry life would now lead.

TWO

The Drunken Bard Tavern
Edinburgh, Scotland

BOISTEROUS LAUGHER FILLED THE OVERLY crowded tavern as men banged their cups upon heavy oaken tables whilst awaiting them to be filled, yet again. Serving maids busily went about their business, trying as best as they could to replenish their customers' ale, without too much abuse to their already bruised backsides. An outraged squeal of protest, as a playful slap landed squarely on one pretty maid's bottom, only caused another round of loud guffaws.

A scuffle broke out whilst yet another set of intoxicated louts attempted to lay claim to the same maid who worked the inn for a bit of coin. She was rudely tossed aside as one of the ruffians took his chair and slammed it upon the head of the other. Splintering wood flew in multiple directions, whilst complaints were bellowed from those nearby, as the two combatants continued their fight on the floor. 'Twas only at the shouting of the barkeep, informing his patrons they would be paying for any damages incurred, that the two rose and took the matter outside to be settled where things of this nature should be resolved in the first place.

"Now, this is a tavern more to my liking!" roared Turquine as he lifted his mug and drained its contents. "I like my inn to have some flavor and not be so meek and civilized like the last one we visited."

"Ale!" called his brother Taegan. The serving maid hastily filled his cup, but with a wink of her eye, she plopped herself right down into his lap. His hearty laughter filled the room as he began to nuzzle her neck much to her approval.

Ian held out his own tankard as another serving wench answered his call. When she came up to him, she leaned forward practically spilling out of her gown. He did not mind the view she freely offered him for she was well endowed. With a promise in her smile, she wound her arm around his neck and settled herself in his lap 'til a most unladylike shriek rent the air.

Another woman rushed over and stood shaking her fist in outrage. "Eh now, sod off! Ye know I's 'ad me eye on this one!" She gave the girl a hard push 'til Ian's arm snaked around the irate wench's waist, bringing her closer to his side.

Ian chuckled as they began to bicker between themselves. "Now, now, ladies, enough of all that. There are more pleasurable ways to spend the eve. I think there is more than enough of me to go around." He gave each a quick kiss on the cheek, which seemed to pacify at least one of the maids. The other looked as though she was not of a mind to share what she had laid claim to. "What of you, Thomas? See something you like?" he asked bringing both women closer upon his legs.

Thomas scanned the room, but only went back to his ale. Putting down his full tankard, he turned his attention back to

Ian. "I suppose one of us should remain sober and alert to the dangers that surround us," he muttered.

Taegan only laughed and reached out to thump Thomas on his back. He got a meaningful glare for his effort. "Danger? What danger? We are but enjoying a bit of sport, are we not lads?"

Thomas snorted in disgust. "Standing on Scottish soil dressed as English knights is nothing to jest about. I am surprised we have not been knifed in our sleep already for coming this far north."

Turquine downed his ale and slammed his tankard upon the table. Standing, he made a striking figure as he all but preened, showing off his impressive form. "What say you, Ian? Think you any of these Scots would be up to the effort to have a go at it with one lately of Dristan of Berwyck's guards?"

Ian laughed, watching his comrade strut in front of the fire, much like a fancy peacock with his tail feathers fanned out to catch the attention of its mate. "None would dare, Turquine," Ian responded loudly. "Have another cup, and let us enjoy our sport this night. I do not relish testing the patience of any who may be foolish enough to take up your challenge."

Ian took no further notice of his traveling companions, since he had two women to better occupy his efforts. He took turns giving each his undivided attention and whispering the words most women wanted to hear afore they were bedded.

'Twas the harsh sound of a sword being released from its scabbard that caused Ian to unceremoniously dump both wenches to the floor. He stood quickly with his sword ready in his hand. 'Twas an automatic reaction from living many a year on the road, keeping danger at bay. It tended to ensure one's safety and ability to survive yet another day.

Thomas held two men off at the point of his sword, whilst Ian eyed them both warily 'til he noticed the tartans wrapped around their bodies. He may not recognize the men, but the plaid they wore with obvious pride was one he had not thought to see any time soon. *What the hell are they doing this far south?* Replacing his sword, he placed his hand upon Thomas's shoulder. "Hold, my friend," he said firmly, waiting 'til he felt Thomas relax his stance.

Retaking his seat, Ian hardly gave a second notice of the two women, who were still in the process of picking themselves up off the floor. He waved his now empty tankard at them. "Be good lassies, and bring food and refill our cups," he ordered them. Ian inwardly continued his assessment of the two Scots, who still waited to gain his attention, as he subconsciously drummed his fingers on the hilt of his sword.

"Well?" Ian asked the strangers, hearing for himself the sarcastic tone in his voice. "What do you want from us?"

One was clearly braver than the other, since he stepped forward, although he eyed Turquine and Taegan cautiously when they moved closer to Ian's side. "We could not help but over hear yer conversation. Be ye, Ian MacGillivray, lately o' Berwyck?" he inquired.

Ian flinched. The achingly familiar brogue brought unwanted memories of his childhood rushing into his head. Ian was momentarily lost whilst unwelcome visions assaulted his mind of when his older brother had all but thrown him out of the only home he had ever known. He could still see his mother standing in the doorframe, pleading with him to beg his brother's forgiveness. As leader of the clan, his brother's word was law, and as younger brother, 'twas not Ian's place to question the running of the lands, no matter how poorly a job his sibling had been doing. Even as the younger son, he would have been blind to not have taken note how his brother was already governing the estate into the ground.

Hatred burned in his veins for a past life he could not change. He felt once more the bitter sense of betrayal, as though 'twere but the eve afore when his life had been torn asunder. He blinked his eyes when they began to blur with memories that should remain in the past. The last thing he needed was to look a fool and shed a tear for the pain of his youth caused by his bastard of a brother!

Ian shook his head, trying to dismiss his thoughts, but 'twas not as easily done as he would have liked. "Aye, I am he, but what concern is it to you, may I ask?" he questioned harshly.

"I told ye 'twas him, Angus, although he looks more like a bloody Englishman than a member o' our clan!" the other Scot sneered, pounding the man in front of him on the back. "Sounds like one, too..."

"Shut yer trap, ye fool!" the first Scotsman said. "Me apologies, me laird, fer this buffoon o' a companion. Connor and I have been searching many a month tae find yer whereabouts."

A gruff laugh escaped Ian afore he could hold it back. "Laird? Eh gads man, you have the wrong MacGillivray, if you address me as laird!"

"No disrespect intended, fer I would not gainsay yer words, but if ye are in truth Ian, lately of Berwyck castle, then we have the right man," Angus replied. He began reaching inside his shirt but the sound of swords being drawn once more halted his movements. Angus held up his hands in surrender afore carefully pulling out a well-worn piece of parchment. He handed the missive to Ian. "Mayhap, this can put the matters aright. 'Tis from yer mother, me laird."

Ian held out his hand for the document. "My mother?"

"Aye, me laird. The Lady Fiona gave explicit instructions tae give this tae none other than yerself."

"I see." Ian unfolded the parchment and began scanning the words afore his eyes. His brow furrowed in anger as he read. He had little sympathy knowing his brother was dead, leaving the clan without a leader. They had never been close, and, as a ruler, he had been a tyrant. He was not sure how the people had been fending, if his mother's dire words were not a falsehood. Fields had been left fallow with little coin to purchase seedlings. Livestock had been stolen by neighboring clans with no one to take control of ensuring they remained on MacGillivray land. "How did he die?"

"Ambushed, me laird, whilst returning from Inverness," Angus answered.

"And my Uncle?"

Angus hesitated and took a sideways glimpse at Connor afore answering. "He is attempting tae take o'er as head of the clan. 'Tis why yer mother sent us posthaste tae find ye."

Ian handed the parchment to Thomas who began perusing what had been hastily written by his mother's hand.

Thomas guffawed. "'Tis nice of them to pick out a bride for you, Ian, especially not knowing you would ever return."

Turquine leaned over Thomas's shoulder so he, too, could see how fate was changing the course of Ian's life. "Just where did you say your home is, Ian?"

"I do not believe I ever mentioned it, men." Ian took a sip of his ale remaining silent in his thoughts 'til he felt a nudge from Taegan. Setting down his tankard, he at last answered him, although he did so hesitantly knowing just how far home truly was. "'Tis far north, on Loch Ness, and 'tis called Urquhart Castle."

Taegan began to squirm where he stood. "Not sure if, us being English and all, we will fit in with all those Scots, Ian. No offense..."

Ian gave a snort, knowing how he felt. "None taken, my friend. Besides...I have not said I will be returning, now, have I?"

"But me laird, the clan needs ye!" Connor interjected loudly.

"Needs, me?" Ian ran his hand through his hair whilst his eyes raked the two Scots afore him. He let out his heavy breath. "Aye, I suppose they may at that, but Urquhart has not been a home to me for many a year. I will not be told I must needs marry some lass I know not, just to appease the elders of a clan who did not claim me as their kin! I will not be used as some bargaining tool, just to bring peace between our neighbors."

Ian stood and strode to the hearth where he rested his arm on the mantel. Staring into the red glowing embers of the fire, the image of a fair young lassie with flowing blonde hair came to the forefront of his mind. Her name whispered across his memories. *Lynet.* Just thinking her name brought a smile to his face whilst he remembered the innocent lass he had left behind. These memories were unexpected, and yet, with thoughts of her, they became welcoming all the same. If he must take a wife, why could it not be her? At least the decision would be one of his own choosing.

"Ye will come?" Angus asked with hope ringing in his voice.

Such a question startled Ian to think his face must have shown his answer afore he could verbally give it. "Aye, I will return home," he began, but held up his hand to halt any further words from Angus who clamped his mouth shut with a snap. "I must needs travel south to Berwyck first, for I have a matter to resolve there. You may travel with us. Be prepared to leave come the morn."

The two Scots left their group and went back to their ale, whilst Turquine and Taegan returned to their sport. Thomas took a seat next to Ian. They each grabbed their tankards and took a long pull then wiped their mouths in unison with their sleeves.

"She may not wish to marry you, you know, especially after the note you recently sent her," Thomas offered.

Ian was taken aback. "How did you know where my thoughts were leading?"

Thomas shrugged. "What other reason would take you to Berwyck? Besides, I was of Amiria's guard, if you care to remember. 'Twas not hard to miss the infatuation a certain young girl had for her sister's captain."

Ian grinned at Thomas's words and continued to drink his fill. Confident Lynet still cared for him, he turned his attention to the food laid out afore them and began to eat with a hunger he had not known he even had. As he enjoyed what was left of the eve, it never occurred to him the lady herself might not be all that pleased with his offer of making her his wife.

THREE

LYNET RUSHED ACROSS THE OUTER BAILY, clutching the herbs the castle's healer, Kenna, had asked her to fetch. She had taken extra care to ensure they had been crushed completely in the mortar she still held, and, with other needed ingredients, she had formed the concoction into a sticky paste. 'Twas a procedure she had executed many times over the past six years whilst under Kenna's tutelage. She could have performed such a task with her eyes closed. Knowing who the recipient was to receive her administrations caused her to run faster to reach his side.

She saw a group surrounding his body when she neared the lists. He barely looked injured, for he sat propped up against a tall oak as though he had not a care in the world. 'Twas not 'til she drew closer that she saw the grimace on his face. Unable to miss the injury to his arm, Lynet gave him a small grin for reassurance and plunked herself down near his feet. Peeking at him through lowered lashes, she saw he watched her every move. Still...she was unsure if he was appearing ill from the wound or the berating he was receiving from the company around him.

"You fool, Rolf!" Amiria yelled shaking her fist at him. She returned her sword to its sheath afore she continued her tirade. "How could you be so careless?"

"Bested by a woman!" Bertram interjected with a laugh, as others joined in on the merriment. "He will not live this one down anytime soon."

Fletcher leaned forward into the circle to confront the man who was currently in the process of cursing at his fellow guardsmen. "I hope whatever you were thinking on was of great worth. You will be working double time in the lists come your recovery."

Rolf's gaze flew to Lynet's. "'Twas of the greatest worth," he replied with a hushed tone.

She tried to hide her surprise at the gentleness of his words, whilst he looked upon her searching her face. Someone cleared his throat, allowing her time to tear her attention from Rolf's sea-green eyes and begin unfolding cloth to use as a bandage. She could see a foot being tapped impatiently in her peripheral vision, its owner trying to gain her notice.

Lynet was not sure she should dare ignore such an unspoken plea. Raising her face, she saw her liege lord towered over her with a mighty frown that could only be meant for her. Arm's folded over his massive chest, she saw his anger brewing in his fierce demeanor whilst it simmered there at a low boil ready to erupt. He held his rage in check, but 'twas only just below the surface of the calming hand of his wife who tried to placate him, if such a feat was humanly possible. He was not called the Devil's Dragon without reason. How her sister Amiria was able to tame such a beast was still a mystery to her, but perchance they balanced one another. 'Twas apparent by the glare he leveled upon her, however, that she had once more infuriated this man looming above her.

"We will have speech, Lynet," Dristan demanded of her.

"But, my lord...Rolf needs tending."

"Kenna will see to it."

Amiria's voice reached out to her husband. "Perchance, now is not the time, Dristan."

"'Tis well past time if you dare ask me," he bellowed, whilst his gaze swept the men who lazily stood about as if they had time to spend at their leisure. "Well? There is training that must needs be attended to, lest you would care to continue well into the eve, instead of fill your cups with ale when the call to sup is announced!"

The men scattered like fallen leaves taken up in disarray from the force of a wild and gusty wind. With one last pleading look at her sister's retreating form, Lynet rose, wiping her hands on the apron tied at her waist. No help would be found this day from her sibling. Dristan took her elbow firmly in his hand, and she all but ran to keep up with him. He led her to a garden bench, but she chose to stand her ground when she faced him. He was not pleased. In no way could she misinterpret his mood.

She watched, as he struggled to keep his fury under control. Apparently, her face once more exposed more of her thoughts than she would have liked, since she knew without a doubt she had erred yet again. "Rolf is a good man," she declared softly, for she knew where this conversation was leading.

Dristan's voice cracked like thunder in his frustration. "Aye, he is a good man but one who has nothing but the strength of his arm to offer you."

Lynet shrugged. "Mayhap, that is all I am in need of."

"You know nothing, Lynet, of what you are in need of. He is but my vassal. As such, Rolf is subject to the laws I set in place."

"I thought he was your friend, or am I mistaken?"

Dristan began pacing back and forth in front of her. 'Twas a true testament that he was annoyed with her since he could not stand still. "Aye, he has been a friend these many years but that does not mean he is entitled to wed with a noblewoman. He has no title, no land, and could die on the morrow upon the battlefield, leaving you a widow. Is this the life you wish to lead? A dead husband, buried in the ground, whilst you still have children to raise? Or perchance, becoming some washer woman trying to scrape out some meager existence whilst you reside in some run down hovel you will call a home?"

"'Twould never come to that. Rolf would never allow it. Besides...I could do far worse than to wed with Rolf," she replied with a toss of her head, "like marry some titled man who only wants me for my dowry so he can enrich his coffers. At least Rolf is honorable and appears to care for me."

"Care for you?" Dristan objected in concern. "Did he declare himself to you without my permission?"

Lynet felt foolish for speaking her mind in front of the one man who had tried to do what he thought was best for her these past many years. "Nay, of course not. Even he would not dare to proclaim such to me without your leave."

Her words seemed to calm her liege, for he nodded his head towards her. But his visage suddenly changed, much to her dismay. 'Twas as if he made a decision of great import. "'Tis far past time for you to wed. I have only myself to blame for failing in my quest to see you settled with a husband of worth and a keep to ensure your safety."

"Husband of worth? I do not need someone of such ilk, but a man who will love me!" Lynet groaned, knowing she did not like where this discussion was heading. "Please, Dristan, my situation is not so dire as yet. There is still time for—"

"Nay!" he interrupted her by halting her words in mid-sentence with a raised hand. "I will no longer cater to your wishes to find a suitable mate on your own nor sit idly by watching you become a spinster. I know I promised Amiria I would allow you time to find a man you could come to love, but I will be damned if I continue to let the two of you twist me around your fingers so I concede to your wishes!"

"'Tis not like that, my lord." She watched as one black brow lifted to mock her words. "Well, mayhap, 'tis a little, but, 'tis no reason to rush into the matter of seeing me wed," she protested, stamping her foot for good measure. She could tell by his stance she would not win this contest of wills between them.

"We shall host a tourney and invite those whose suit is worthy of you," he continued speaking as though he had not heard her complaints. "At the end of the games, the winner shall have your hand in marriage, and Father Donovan will perform the ceremony. My mind is set. Resign yourself to your fate, little sister." He left her abruptly.

She stood in numb silence with her mouth hanging open. Completely stunned, she realized 'twas the first time she could remember that Dristan had not listened to the import of her opinion, as though he valued her thoughts. Rejected, she slumped down on the bench, barely feeling the cold stone beneath her. Her world quickly crashed down about her, whilst her worst fears became a harsh reality. She promised herself she would not cry, but 'twas almost an impossible task, knowing she had just become nothing more than a useless pawn played in a game ruled only by men.

FOUR

ROLF FLINCHED AS KENNA FINISHED tying the bandage about his injured arm. He flexed his fist testing the strength of his limb. Satisfied 'twould not become a useless stump, he rose from the ground and held out his hand to assist Berwyck's healer.

He was amazed at the firmness of her grip, for such a slight woman, but more surprised when she did not release his hand. He made a quick grab for her as she swooned into him. Others may have thought the woman merely fainted but he knew better. Kenna had the sight, and he feared what she would tell him of the vision she was having concerning his future. Was it just his imagination, or did he feel as though his fate was just sealed as it unwillingly pounced across his soul?

Keeping his hold securely upon her, he lowered her down onto the ground. Her eyes, hidden behind closed lids, moved rapidly as her vision played afore her mind with images only she knew for certain. Rolf knew she would reveal what she thought was of import, once she came back to him. Though he was not sure he would care for her words. Already his heart felt heavy with what he feared she would foretell.

The sound of running footsteps signaled Rolf of Kenna's husband Geoffrey coming to her aid. Geoffrey was followed closely by Dristan, who came to stand afore him. The scowl his lord tossed in his direction did not bode well.

Geoffrey knelt at his wife's side, not daring to touch her. Years of living with her had brought with it the knowledge that for her husband to do so would vault Kenna into another direction she was not meant to take. Geoffrey had interrupted her visions several times in the past, and the outcome had been worse than her merely being tired after her ordeal. Rolf was not sure he could be as patient as his friend had been over the years. To watch Kenna sometimes in agony whilst her visions haunted her was not something he would ever get used to.

She began to rouse as her eyelids fluttered open. With a shaky breath, she looked around her and gave her audience a weak smile. "All is well," she whispered softly.

Geoffrey shook his head as he helped her rise unsteadily to her feet. "Are you sure, Kenna?" He placed a kiss upon her temple causing her to smile.

"Aye," she replied. Her gaze roamed over Rolf's face and he could see the sorrow fly fleetingly across her green eyes. "We must have speech."

Rolf nodded his head and took hold of her arm. Dristan waved Geoffrey off to the lists afore he turned his attention to the pair afore him. "You will see to her 'til she is recovered," he muttered between clenched teeth.

"Aye, my lord."

Rolf stood there in silence whilst he watched Dristan take his leave. Unwilling, he at last looked down upon the woman who would ruin what little hope he had held for his future. He knew what she would say even afore the words left her lips.

"She is not for you," Kenna said placing her hand on his forearm. "I am most sorry."

He felt, more than saw, her touch as she patted his arm, he supposed, to show some form of comfort. He laughed inwardly. He should have known his feelings for Lynet and his desire to make her his wife would not come to fruition. But he had held such hope.

"There is no reason you must needs be sorry, Kenna. 'Tis hardly your fault you confirm my worst fears."

"Lord Dristan would never allow such a union anyway, Rolf. I hate to say this, but even if he agreed to your suit, the king would not be pleased you wed above your station in life."

"King Henry would have no reason to believe I would not remain a loyal subject if Lynet and I were to marry."

"Perchance 'tis so, but what compensation to his coffers would it gain the crown if he were to accept your petition?" she asked softly.

Rolf raised his eyes heavenward. "I have enough coin to see Lynet would never want for anything she desires, if this is what you ask. If I must beggar myself afore the king, then 'twould be worth any price I must pay for Lynet to become my bride."

"Then, mayhap, all will work out after all. 'Twill be up to you to change your future, Rolf. My visions are just those...visions. On occasion, although rare, they have been known to be wrong." She gave him a despondent sort of smile afore she picked up her satchel containing the supplies she generally stood in need of to heal Berwyck's people. He followed her gaze as it swept across the lists to the lone young lady sitting forlornly on a bench. "Go to her," Kenna said as if reading his mind. "I think she is in need of you."

He felt as though his boots were filled with a hundred stones, for his tread was heavy with trepidation. Every step drew him nearer to her side, and yet the closer he came to her, the further he felt her slipping from his grasp. Lynet must have felt his presence, for, when he came to stand in front of her, she raised her tear streaked face to his. His breath caught in his chest to see the anguish she was feeling. 'Twas obvious her meeting with Dristan had not gone well.

He held out his hand to her and she took it with no hesitation. "Come with me."

"Where are we going?" she asked, as she began drying her face with her sleeve.

"Anywhere...as long as we can have a private word together," he ordered roughly, still feeling the effects of Kenna's premonition that Lynet would never be his.

Her hand in his, Rolf's mind flew in a hundred directions where he might find some form of concealment for them and still ensure Lynet's reputation remained unscathed. There were not many choices in a castle the size of Berwyck. The best place would be her chamber, but his sense of chivalry surpassed the need for discretion. He settled for the stable, although, 'twas hardly the optimal location for the discussion he had in mind.

The moment he closed the door, he immediately turned to her, placing his uninjured arm upon the wood so she could not escape his reach. He was daring much, but he was tired of watching her from afar.

"What is amiss?" he finally demanded of her when the silence continued to stretch on between them.

Her breath caught in her throat, and she stifled back a cry. "Everything!" she answered hotly. "My life, as I have known it, is over, Rolf."

"Surely you exaggerate. It could not be as bad as that, Lynet."

She looked at him with startled eyes. He realized he had at last spoken her given name, as if the two of them had already come to an understanding between themselves.

"You have no idea what has happened," she declared, clearly miserable with whatever was tormenting her.

"Then tell me what has you so upset. I do not like to see your tears," he said softly. Her lips parted, and for the briefest of moments, Rolf thought of bending down to taste her kiss. Their eyes met and were held to one another. He began to lean forward, but she must have known where his thoughts were taking him.

She ducked underneath his arm, and, sadly he watched whilst she distanced herself from him. She went to a nearby stall and supported her arms against the door. "Where do I start?" she cried out in her misery as she laid her head down on her arms.

"You start at the beginning, my lady, where every story commences."

Anger flashed in her tear filled eyes. "He means to auction me off to the highest bidder, Rolf!"

He was surprised at her words, for they were so unexpected. He closed the space between them 'til he stood behind her. He took her arm and turned her. She refused to look at him, 'til he took his fingers and raised her face. "What nonsense is this you speak of?"

"'Tis Dristan. He proposes a tourney, and the winner will become my husband. How can he do this to me?"

He swore. She did, as well, 'til her face fell in frustration. Throwing herself into his arms, she began to cry in earnest. 'Twas the last thing he expected, and yet, it seemed the most natural thing in the world when he gathered her into his embrace. She fit there so perfectly, or so he thought, whilst he began whispering words to comfort her.

"Would you favor my suit?" The words left him in a sudden sense of urgency to hold on to the hope, as long as he was able, that Lynet could be his. He felt her jerk against his chest. She began to hastily disengage herself from his arms.

"He has already said he would not grant you permission to pursue my hand, Rolf."

"Could you come to care for me, Lynet? I have enough coin and you would want for nothing I assure you." Her mouth moved wordlessly whilst she seemed to try to find some form of response. Mayhap, Kenna was right, and Lynet was not for him. "Forgive me. 'Twas unfair for me to ask such of you, especially when I bear no title."

She shook her glorious mane of blonde hair, and he watched as it swirled around her head. "'Tis not that I do not care for you, Rolf. 'Tis just that, 'til most recently, I never thought of you in any way other than as my captain."

"I understand."

"Do you?" she almost begged him with her eyes to recognize what she was going through. "It matters not how with time I may have come to form some affection for you in my heart, Rolf. Our Lord Dristan will never allow our relationship to be other than what it is, a captain to guard his lady. Nothing more...nothing less."

"I will make him see reason—"

She held up her hand to silence his words. "'Tis impossible, and I dare not give even the smallest measurement of hope you could steer Lord Dristan from his course regarding the path my life will now lead. I will wed, and 'twill be to a man not of my choosing. 'Tis not for me to find true love and a knight to call my own."

Lynet sobbed, and, afore he could halt her with a kind word, she ran from the stables. Rolf let her go, but in doing so, he pledged to himself he would do all in his power to change Dristan's mind. 'Twas either that, or run away with Lynet. Even as the thought fleetingly swept across his mind, Rolf could feel the scorching heat from the Devil's Dragon leveling on his form. Dristan would follow him to hell and back for daring such an offense. He would not be lenient for taking such a liberty with his charge, no matter the feelings Rolf had for her. There must be another way than to infuriate his liege lord and still have Lynet as his bride, he mused. The alternative would not be a good way to die.

FIVE

IAN REINED IN HIS HORSE and took in the sight afore his eyes. He never thought he would miss a place as much as this fortress he had called his home for many a year. He felt his companions come abreast of him as they awaited him to move on, yet still, he bided his time and drank in the view in front of him.

Berwyck Castle...mayhap, 'twas not the physical place he had yearned for, but rather, those who resided within its protective walls. He rested his forearm on the pommel of his saddle like some melancholy lad in his youth. But he cared not what the other men thought of him whilst he took a moment unto himself.

Memories assaulted his senses of a beautiful lass he had had no right to fall in love with, but fall in love with her he had. She was beautiful beyond measure to any other; strong willed and stubborn to a fault; a fiery temper along with a calming demeanor, if she so wished it; and she could wield a sword better than most men of his acquaintance. Yet, her affection went to another, and he did not fault her for that. Nay, she was happy with her choice in a husband, and he was glad Amiria had found love.

As he put his horse into motion, his thoughts wandered to the youngest woman of the MacLaren clan. She had been a docile young girl of only ten and four summers when last he had seen her. Ian still remembered sitting in Berwyck's garden after Amiria and Dristan had wed. He had been filled with despair of losing the one woman he would have taken to wife if circumstances had been different. Lynet had been so young that day when, with pleading clear blue eyes, she had spoken her heart to him. Her childlike kiss, given so freely afore she had fled his side, had surprised him.

Memories continued to assault him as he remembered Berwyck being under siege, yet again. Many a knight had fallen, but one had been felled by Ian's own hand who had dared to touch the lass Lynet. He had saved her that day, and he had then foolishly given in to the moment by kissing her most thoroughly. By doing so, he had given her some measure of hope he would return for her, although such an act had never crossed his mind. He had not seen her since, except briefly, as she had waved farewell when he had left Berwyck, he thought, forevermore.

Crossing a river, they entered the village adjacent to the castle grounds. 'Twas a flurry of activity, more so than the usual happenings of its inhabitants.

"Berwyck must be preparing for a celebration," Thomas proclaimed. "I wonder what the occasion is."

Taegan gave a look of longing at the nearby tavern. "I just want a cup of cool ale in my fist to take the taste of the road from my mouth."

Turquine laughed cheerfully. "So what else is new, brother?" You always want ale to meet your undying need to quench your unending thirst!"

Ian laughed with the men 'til they came to the outskirts of the village. Any further thoughts of merriment left him as he observed the sight afore him. Although the distance from the village to the walls of the keep was some ways away, the usually empty space was filled to capacity. 'Twas not hard to miss the tents set up surrounding the castle walls. From the looks of it, he would say Dristan had gathered all from near and far to partake in whatever event they were to socialize. Perchance his timing of returning to Berwyck was not at its best, and yet he had no alternative. He must needs return north immediately to assume his rightful position of laird of Urquhart, afore his Uncle and others usurped his inheritance...at least whatever was left of it.

They reached the barbican gate amid cheers from the guards high above, who stood at their posts. Word quickly spread of their return, and as lads came to take their mounts, Ian saw Killian making his way to their side. 'Twas good to see the man who had been an integral part of his training 'til he was appointed captain of Amiria's guard.

They greeted each other with a hearty pounding of each other's back in welcome. If the truth must be told, Ian had missed the older man, and his counsel, these many years.

"'Tis good tae see ye, laddie!" Killian beamed.

"Laddie?" Ian chuckled. "Will you never think on me as anything other than a boy, Killian?"

"Nay! Since I taught ye everything ye know about wielding that claymore o' yers, I earned the honor o' calling ye anything I wish, me boy!"

"Eh gads! 'Tis no wonder I stayed away so long."

"Ye have been missed, Ian, along wit' the rest o' ye," Killian stated looking over the group. "We are a might tight fer lodgings, but I am sure we can squeeze ye in somewhere in the Garrison Hall. Who is this wit' ye?"

Ian gave a muffled laugh. "It seems my fate has changed, my friend, and I have become laird of Urquhart, now that my brother has met his demise. Angus and Connor of Clan MacGillivray found me and my company in Edinburgh. I am to head north once I leave here."

"Well...'tis interesting news and good fortune, Ian. Have ye been issued an invitation from Lord Dristan tae come compete in the tourney, now that ye own yer land?"

"An invitation? Nay, I have not received such an invite, nor has there been time for information of this nature to be known to only but a few," Ian laughed. "'Tis not as though I have not proved my worth in other competitions over the years without need of having permission to enter games of this sort. What is the difference in this contest over any other when there is gold to be won, along with the favor from a pretty lady?"

Killian stroked his beard and perused Ian over his bushy brows. "Then ye have not heard what yer prize will be."

"I have heard nothing, Killian, since I did not even know Dristan was holding a tourney."

Killian threw his arm over Ian's shoulder and began steering him towards the Garrison Hall. "Then ye may find it in yer best interest not tae compete, lest ye wish tae find yerself wed at the end o' the games, laddie boy."

Ian's step faltered, and he turned to look into the amused face of his longtime friend. He knew the answer afore he even voiced his question. "And just who, may I inquire, will be the lucky bride?"

"Who else would be eligible at Berwyck?" Killian chided. "'Tis the Lady Lynet, of course. Best get yerself cleaned up a mite tae make a good impression...that is if'n ye want yerself a bonny bride, along with the rest of the gents who have come tae claim her!"

God's blood, this is not what I had planned! Ian followed Killian into the Garrison Hall in bemused silence as he realized that, perchance, taking Lynet to wife would not be such an easy task, after all.

Merciful heavens. Will this man never cease his babbling? Lynet stifled a yawn as yet another suitor stood afore her. She had lost count of those men she had been introduced to this past se'nnight. She felt her sister kick her shin beneath the table, and she tossed Amiria a glaring frown. Then she consciously forced another smile to her lips. Her sibling's strike was a painful reminder for her to at least attempt to show some interest, but 'twas of no use. She would rather soon forget this whole humiliating predicament she found herself in.

She tried to pay attention, really she did. But what was there of merit in yet another knight full of himself, especially whilst he looked down his aristocratic nose at her, almost as if to see if *she* was worthy of *him*? She eyed him wearily. It took her no time at all to come quickly to the conclusion, yet again, there was nothing noble in this one's character she could define, other than he claimed to be some distant kinsman of her father's family.

The man all but preened in front of her, trying to display his dashing good looks. Aye! Sir Broderick of Lorn was a handsome fellow with blonde hair reaching to his nape, and yet, she had seen his kind at least a dozen times this day. She watched him bow to those at the raised dais and was thankful this latest bit of torture was at last at an end.

"I shall compete," Broderick smugly announced. "I look forward to collecting my prize."

His words hung in the air like a death sentence. She caught his eyes skimming over her 'til they lingered on her bosom. *Is that a leering grin beginning at the corners of his mouth?* Lynet's brow rose in indignation that he would dare such an offense. He only gave the briefest of nods and left, calling for wine.

Lynet tried to remain calm, but her anger, along with the silent sour words lingering in her mouth, were about to be her undoing. She leaned forward on the table to peer at her liege lord. Amiria sat back with her own grim expression, allowing Lynet a better view of her husband. She knew he felt her gaze when he looked at her from the corner of his eyes, but he offered no words of solace. If anything, his demeanor showed nothing other than a coolness she knew would get her nowhere.

She opened her mouth to give a bitter retort to his silent avowal, only to have Dristan halt her words with his steely stare.

"You will not sway me from this course, Lynet, so do not waste your words on me," he declared folding his arms across his chest.

Amiria patted his arm. "You must admit, my lord, the selection you bring afore her leaves something to be desired."

"They are all titled, hence they are all worthy of her," Dristan retaliated.

Lynet put her hand on the table, bringing herself as close to the pair as she could without putting her arm in their trencher. "Worthy of me? You would have me wed one of these fools? Wed, to spend my life catering to the whim of some selfish lout? To someone who only cares for the monies I bring so he can clothe himself richly or purchase another steed to fill an already overflowing stable? Someone who will only see me for my beauty and parade me around at court like a pretty bauble he has acquired?" she hissed.

"They are not all of such temperament," Dristan huffed.

"Ugh!" Lynet threw up her hands, ready to run screaming from the keep. "Do not be blinded by what you think you see, for they are what I claim. The remaining few are either too young, or too old, my lord."

"Then you have nothing to worry about from those who will not hold their own against a seasoned warrior, or did you forget the conditions of the competition that only the man who is triumphant at the end of the games will win your hand?"

"You condemn and sell me into a life of servitude. I will be chattel to one of these fools and you care nothing for my feelings." Lynet stifled back a sob.

"All will work out as it should, Lynet. Of that, I have no doubt." Dristan reached for his goblet and stared at her over its rim.

She peered at him trying to determine what his expression meant, for he had a strange look upon his face, as though he held some secret. "Not if I am to marry any of these sorry excuses for men who have come looking for glory. By the time the next two se'nnight's are over, you will have nothing left of your larder."

"Let me worry about my larder, Lynet."

Exasperated with the conversation, she sat back in her chair and returned her attention to the goings on within the hall. All were merry with thoughts of their victorious win, especially one mountain of a man. She vaguely remembered being introduced to the burly brute the day afore. He was Scottish, for sure, and from the Highlands, if her memory served her aright. Giving a heavy sigh, she became once more disinterested in the happenings in her own hall. With wine and ale flowing freely, few would be in any condition to compete. Mayhap, that would be in her favor.

She noticed Rolf making his way through the room and her breath caught at the sight of him. He had dressed in his finest, and the dark blue tunic fit him well. He made his way confidently to stand afore the dais and gave a low, polished bow, performed with a courtly flourish. A soft smile at last lit her features as he arose to stare at her with twinkling merry eyes. He was devilishly handsome and had a grin upon his face like a boy who had just received a well-deserved treat! *What is he up to,* she wondered?

"Rolf," Dristan said nonchalantly, and looked as if he was trying to hide his own smile.

"My liege," Rolf replied with another courteous nod. He may have answered his lord, but his eyes held only unto her own. A flicker of hope pounded within her heart that perchance all was not lost.

"All is in order?"

"Aye, my lord."

Dristan nodded towards his knight. "Then come and sup with us. I give you leave to sit next to Lady Lynet."

Her mouth hanging open in a very unladylike manner, she watched as Rolf made quick work of lessening the space between them 'til he sat next to her. He began filling the trencher afore them with the choicest of meats so they could partake of the meal. He waited politely 'til she took a piece of venison and started to chew afore he delved into his meal. Taking a sip of wine to loosen the meat that seemed to stick in her throat, her heart picked up its pace 'til she thought surely everyone in the room would be able to hear its rapid beat.

She could stand the silence between them no longer. "Lord Dristan heard your petition?" she whispered for his ears alone.

"Aye." 'Twas a simple, yet annoying statement, which told her nothing further of the information she was dying to know as he continued to eat his fill. She watched him discreetly from the corner of her eye for several minutes 'til she could stand it no longer. Underneath the table, she gave him a none-too-gentle poke in his ribs with her finger. His brow lifted as he began wiping his hands, since he had finished his food.

"And..." she prodded for him to continue.

Rolf shrugged his shoulders. He took his chalice in hand and began twirling the stem casually between his fingers afore he took a long slow sip of his wine. She began to drum her own fingers upon the table, a clear indication she was impatient. It seemed as if she waited an eternity afore he finally answered her. "I am here next to you. Should that not speak for itself?"

She sighed inwardly in relief, knowing Rolf would do everything within his power to win her hand. For the first time in weeks, Lynet felt as though a heavy weight had been lifted from her weary shoulders. They began to converse with a lighthearted banter. 'Twas nothing out of the ordinary of what their conversations had been over the years, other than he was seated to her left in a place of honor. The placement would have normally been given to her husband, and there were several men about the room who stopped what they were doing to observe the pair with narrowed eyes. She mentioned they were being observed, and yet, Rolf only laughed, as though she had nothing to worry about.

But worry she did, along with the fate of her heart. Yet, 'twas naught because of the men she had already been introduced to, nor the handsome one sitting comfortably by her side. Where but moments afore she had visions of her life with Rolf and what that would entail, those images quickly shattered into a thousand fragments as she watched another make his way through the hall, as he had done so many times in her past. She could not believe who her eyes beheld. For Ian...of all the people Lynet least expected to see...had come home!

SIX

FROM THE FURIOUS GLINT IN HER EYES, Ian could tell Lynet clearly was not pleased to see him. He would need to quickly remedy that and see if he could win her favor. Ian bowed low to those seated at the table afore him. When he rose, he suppressed a frown, seeing Rolf seated next to the woman he had not seen in many a year. *A woman!* Aye...for surely she was a small lass no longer. If Lynet had been beautiful in her youth, he was not sure what verbiage would now do the lady justice. To say she was simply stunning, would surely be considered a sin.

He tore his gaze from Lynet to see her sister Amiria staring at him with an amused smirk on her own beautiful visage. Her violet eyes sparkled with a mischievous twinkle, as if she knew where his thoughts had led him. Her husband, on the other hand, did not look as pleased. Apparently, their friendship over the years only went so far, especially where Lynet's heart was concerned.

"We have not seen you in these parts for many a year, Ian," Dristan stated the obvious. "What brings you back to Berwyck?"

"A matter of grave importance, my lord."

Dristan rose from his chair and made his way to stand afore him. "And what, pray tell, could be of such import you would disturb our festivities?" he muttered quietly.

"I think you are well aware of what is of such import." Ian ran his hand along the nape of his neck. "I did not know when I traveled here I must needs compete in a contest to win her hand."

"Such is the conceit of man," Dristan grumbled wisely. "Mayhap, a contest is just what is in order to see just how far you are willing to go to have her."

"I would have preferred the alternative."

"Aye, I suppose you would have, at that." Dristan moved so Ian's view of Lynet was blocked. "Do not hurt her any more than you already have with your absence these many years or you will answer to me. Do you understand my words, Ian?"

"'Tis the farthest thought from my mind, my lord." Ian nodded in Lynet's direction. "May I?"

Ian felt Dristan's gaze rake over him 'til Dristan gave his assent with the briefest of nods...if that is what the barely perceptible movement could even be called. *One barrier has been breached, and now, on to the next,* Ian mused. He strode forward 'til he was afore Lynet, who quickly glanced at Rolf. 'Twas painfully evident to Ian his old comrade was no more pleased to see him than was the beauty seated to his right.

"Lynet," Ian said with a smile that rapidly faded at her words.

"'Tis Lady Lynet, to you," she scoffed.

"My apologies, my lady," he said stiffly. *So, this is the game she wants to play, is it?*

Her head rose slightly whilst she looked down at him from her raised position. "We did not expect you to grace us with your presence, Ian."

"Laird." He did not take his eyes from hers whilst her gaze traveled to his own amused ones.

She appeared startled. "Pardon me?"

"As well, you should," he said with a mocking grin. He had purposely left his mantle on, but now whipped it off his body. Holding out the garment, Connor came behind him and took his cloak. Ian watched as Lynet let out an alarming, startled gasp. His green and blue plaid reached down to his knees with a sash pinned at his left shoulder by a brooch symbolizing his clan. He bowed afore her, once again.

"It seems the heavens have smiled down upon me, my dear, Lady Lynet. I stand afore you as Laird of Urquhart Castle and of the Clan MacGillivray."

He watched in amusement as she tried to hide the tremble in her hands as she reached for her cup, and he saw she took a moment to recoup her wits from her shock. "I see." Her reply was barely audible, but she recovered quickly. "May I then be the first at Berwyck to offer my congratulations on your good fortune, Ian...Laird MacGillivray," she corrected with a gracious nod of her head.

He smiled at her trying to find the young girl hidden behind the eyes of the woman he had unwittingly hurt. Unfortunately, he could only see the face of a woman scorned. "You are not the first to offer such felicitations, but I welcome them all the same, especially from someone so lovely."

Her brow arched, giving him a glimpse of perchance her fiery nature, but afore she could form some kind of a smart retort, the minstrels chose such a moment to begin tuning their instruments. Rolf stood, yet afore he, too, could make such an offer, Ian held out his hand to the lady who commanded both men's attention.

"Lady Lynet, I beg the honor of the first dance," Ian bade, "especially since Rolf here has already had the distinct pleasure of dining at your side. You do not mind, do you, old man?"

Rolf grumbled underneath his breath, but stepped aside when Ian came around the dais to reach her side. "Shall we, my dear?"

"I am *not* your dear," she replied coolly. She tentatively placed her hand in his. He caressed its back with his thumb, attempting to put some warmth into her freezing limb. "Please excuse me, Rolf. I shall return shortly." Lynet offered him the briefest of smiles, afore Ian whisked her away towards the center of the room.

Other's joined them, taking their places side by side 'til they began the intricate steps of the dance pattern to a lively tune. Much to Ian's dismay, the fast-paced dance did not leave time to have even the briefest of conversations. He would need to find a way to improve the situation 'til it became one in his favor.

Lynet's mind raced as she tried to find some balance to her world that was tearing her in different directions. After all these years, he at last showed up at Berwyck. Their hands met in the middle of a circle only to break apart with another turn. He eyed her with heavy lids, as though seeking an answer to a question only he knew for sure. 'Twas as if he but waited all these years to come and claim her. Lynet, however, knew differently.

She tried to think rationally, but 'twas of no use. Her world once again tilted, turning her emotions upside down, just knowing Ian was here...at Berwyck...in this room...dancing with her. Her traitorous heart leapt in earnest when they came together as they danced. How she remembered longing for such a happening to occur in her younger days.

His smiled broadened, as if he had read her thoughts. Even the hint of emerald green she saw hidden deep in the hazel of his eyes seemed to cry out for her to remember their color. Those sparkling eyes were a painful reminiscence of when he had rejected her at the tender age of ten and four summers. She attempted to harden her heart, for she would not be made such a fool of again.

The music came to a close. She could only manage to stand there with her chest heaving as she attempted to breathe normally and kept wondering how she could escape his presence without appearing rude and incurring Dristan's wrath. Afore she could take flight, Ian gently took her elbow and began guiding her from the hall. Others attempted to stop their progress and keep them from leaving the chamber, but Ian managed to brush aside those who would ask for the honor of her next dance.

She barely felt the turret stairs beneath her slippered feet as they began their steady climb to the upper floors housing Berwyck's family. Up they went 'til they reached the third landing, and she suddenly began to wonder at his ploy. *Surely, he does not expect to go to my chamber now, does he?* Alarm flashed briefly in Lynet's eyes as he did, indeed, steer her towards the right and down the passageway.

"Where are you taking me?" Her voice shook with her distress. Ian gave her a look that almost shouted she should know better than to think he would harm her.

They continued onward, passing her doorway, and Lynet finally let out her breath in relief. 'Twas only a momentary reprieve, for he opened the door to Amiria's solar, sliding the bolt into place behind them once they entered.

She put as much distance between them as she could. Looking around the room, Lynet quickly came to the conclusion there was not much space in the chamber, and she began to feel as though the walls were closing in on her. He advanced. His plaid swayed about his muscular legs that were no longer encased in tight fitting hose. Her eyes darted to find someplace to rest upon other than his handsome face and spectacular body; a body that radiated such a heat as she had never felt afore. He reached out for her hand and took it.

Her breath left her with a rush of excitement that practically blinded her to anything other than Ian's warm skin. Scorching hot awareness to his every move raced up her arm at his touch, and she felt as though her very blood was on fire. She felt herself losing a battle she had no idea she was even in. She needed to get away from him quickly, and yet, with this fleeting thought, he brought her closer. He lifted her chin so she had no alternative other than to stare upon his face.

She tried to calm her nerves and strengthened her resolve to not give in to this man who had broken her heart. *God's bones, but no man should look so beautiful,* she mused. For beautiful he was, in her mind, even more so than she had remembered him. He had always had such an effect on her, and it mattered not that he was older than she. For as long as she could remember, he had been the man she had fallen in love with at such an early age. The heart knows what it wants, and their age difference was not a concern, at least not for Lynet.

Ian ran his finger down one of her cheeks. She shivered in delight as her body naturally responded to the subtle caress. "We have not much time for speech, Lynet," he whispered tenderly.

She saw his lips moving, but her feeble attempt to pay attention to his words failed her as panic of being alone with him began to set in. "What?"

He looked on her with an amused expression. "Dristan...he will come in search of us," he answered. "I but wished to speak with you privately so we could come to an arrangement."

"An arrangement?" Her eyes narrowed when she became suspicious of his motives for being here. *Does he honestly believe he can just lay claim to me as easily as that?*

"Aye."

He does! Merciful heavens, did she appear to him as some simpleton, or merely a naive fool who would willingly come to him after a crook of his finger?

Lynet pulled out of his arms and stood behind a chair, as if this simple act of putting such an inconsequential piece of furniture between them in itself would protect her from his advances. "Surely, you jest, or did you not witness the spectacle outside our gates?" She was doing everything within her power not to let her temper flare out of control.

"Nay, I do not see the matter as something to jest about," Ian replied, taking several steps towards her. "I would have thought you to be happy to see me after all this time, or am I mistaken?"

"I would have been happier if I had seen you afore you sent that bloody note!"

"I had nothing to offer you at the time 'twas written, Lynet. Surely, you can understand my plight and reasoning for sending such a missive."

"I waited for you for all those years, and you wrote me but a few lines. A few lines, Ian!" Her fingers balled into fists at her side. Although, in truth, she would have liked to have beat them against his chest to drive the point of her frustration into his thick skin. How could he not know what his absence had done to her poor little heart?

"I told you at my leaving not to wait. Nothing changed over the years, and 'twas not 'til recently that I was told I should write so you could go on with your life."

"You did not even write of your own accord?" she shouted at him and began shaking with fury. She turned towards the fire to mask the anger that was about to get the best of her, but she could not keep the words from pouring out her mouth as she turned to face him once more. "Who told you to send me such a missive?" The words rushed from her pursed lips whilst uncontrolled rage wracked her frayed nerves.

"There was only one who would share such information with me, since she had recently come from Berwyck," Ian answered. "I do not see how this makes any sort of difference other than, at the time, I thought 'twas only right to do you such a service."

"Who?" Lynet said between clenched teeth.

"'Twas the Lady Katherine de Deveraux, Riorden's wife. Was she mistaken by hinting you still held an undeniable fondness for me?"

"Nay, she was not mistaken," Lynet whispered. Recent memories flooded her mind as she remembered unburdening her soul to Katherine. She had first come to the castle with Riorden, who was a lifelong friend and comrade of Dristan's and had been the captain of his guard. Looking at the couple, one did not need Kenna's gift of sight to see how much they were in love, although they had had a rough course to overcome to find how deep that love truly was.

Katherine had returned several months later, alone and distraught, thinking her husband had forsaken her and had turned to another. Heavily along with child, Riorden had at last found her, once he learned his wife was actually alive and not dead at the bottom of the Coquet River near their home of Warkworth. Lynet could only surmise Katherine had most likely felt she was doing Lynet a favor by confiding to Ian. She supposed she could forgive the lady such a trespass. The timing of his return, however, could not have been worse.

"And what of now, Lynet," Ian continued. He sought to pull her to him, but she brushed off his attempts and folded her arms about her. He gave a heavy sigh.

"Now?" She cried out with a muffled laugh, showing how truly distressed she really was. "Now, my laird, you are far too late, or did you forget I am at present only a prize to be won to the highest bidder?"

"I am sure I can convince Dristan to halt this nonsense of finding you a husband amongst those who may want to win your hand," Ian declared. "Besides, I must needs marry, else the elders of the clan plan on ensuring they choose a bride for me."

"Oh, do they now?" she huffed. "And, I suppose, you think I would at least be biddable and thankful to become your wife more so than any other of your acquaintance?"

"Why should my bride not be, at least, someone with whom I am familiar? At least, I know you."

"Ha! You do not know me, else you would have been here long ago and not kept me waiting six long years to see you again!"

He advanced on her 'til she felt the wall pressed against her back. With nowhere else to turn, she held him back by firmly placing her hands upon his chest. Touching him was a huge mistake, for there was nothing but hard muscles beneath her fingertips, as solid as the stones behind her!

"Tell me you are not happy to see me, sweet Lynet." The huskiness in his voice was almost her undoing, yet again.

She lifted her eyes to meet his. *Damn! Mistake number two!* She would not give him the satisfaction of knowing just how much she had missed him. "I am *not* happy to see you!" she retorted meaningfully. Lifting her chin a notch, she prayed the expression she gave him was a defiant one. His chuckle led her to believe she had failed in her quest to appear indifferent to his charms.

"Perchance, you should tell your eyes that, little one, for your gaze tells me your lips speak a falsehood." His grin was surely from the devil himself, as it broadened whilst she attempted to mask her feelings for him. His deep laughter rumbled in his chest, only giving evidence she had completely forgotten her hands were still pressed upon his granite-like torso. She let go quickly with the feeling she had been burned.

"Go back to the Highlands and marry some other witless girl. I care not who you wed, as long as 'tis not me," she yelled, pulling herself from his arms and making her way to the door. She slid the bolt back and opened the door, only to come face to face with a very angry brother-in-law.

"Is there something amiss here?" Dristan demanded.

"Nay," Lynet cried out in frustration, "nothing is amiss. Ian and I are finished here. Let the damn games begin!"

She did not wait for his response, but ran down the corridor to her chamber. Flinging herself face down upon her bed, she allowed the tears of her frustration to finally spill forth like the churning waves of a turbulent sea. 'Twould be hours later afore she came to the sad realization she had not even acknowledged

Rolf's presence or concerned look whilst he had been standing next to their liege's side.

SEVEN

'TIS BEEN SOME TIME SINCE we have all been together," Dristan drawled to the men gathered in his solar.

"Hear! Hear!" The men agreed with him as they lifted their tankards and sipped the cool bitter ale to toast their brotherhood. Ian was no different in his regard for those gathered within the chamber, since he had trained and fought beside these men, many years ago. There was only one difference today than what had been found in the past. Rolf, who Ian had once considered a friend, peered angrily at him over the rim of his cup. 'Twas painfully clear, Rolf was no more happy to see him than Lynet. He would not be surprised to find himself up against the man in the coming days in order to win the lady's hand. He appeared as determined as Ian to have Lynet for his bride.

Conversations filled the room as those who had been traveling told their tales to those who had stayed behind as Dristan's guard to defend the keep. Laughter came from many as Taegan and Turquine retold stories of their conquests with the fairer gender 'til the sound of the door opening had all heads turning in its direction.

Surprise registered on many faces when Amiria's twin brother Aiden entered, followed closely by the youngest member of the MacLaren clan. At ten and four, Patrick had grown since Ian had last seen the youth. He, too, had been gone from Berwyck's domain whilst he served Riorden de Deveraux as his squire. That Riorden entered the room with his own commanding demeanor directly behind the boy only gave evidence to Ian that the event to follow in the coming day's affected all who had once lived within the security of Berwyck's walls.

Riorden's group strode purposefully to Dristan with little regard to the rest of the men within the room. Their speech immediately became an extremely heated discussion, with Lynet being the topic of concern, as their voices rose in volume. Ian silently viewed the scene playing afore his eyes 'til they turned as one in his direction. He was not sure why Riorden was glaring at him so, but Aiden's scornful sneer was certainly understandable, despite the fact he had guarded the younger man's back for many a year. 'Twas obvious Lynet's brother planned on having words with him.

Aiden took a step forward, but was halted as Riorden put a hand upon his shoulder. After a brief and silent exchange between the two men, Riorden came afore Ian and began looking him up and down. Ian supposed, given the fact he was wearing the colors of the MacGillivray clan, and not the normal clothes of a knight, Dristan's former captain was somewhat surprised.

"So..." Riorden began. "I have heard tell, you have most recently come into a title."

Ian shrugged, as though 'twas nothing. "News travels fast, it seems," he drawled offhandedly. "I did not expect such tidings to reach Warkworth so speedily."

'Twas Riorden's turn to give a casual shrug, along with a short amused chuckle. "We were already on our way here to witness this farce Dristan seems determined to play forth. We did not learn the news of your good fortune 'til we arrived, but a few minutes ago."

"We?"

"My wife Katherine travels with me, along with Nathaniel and Ulrick, although they will now return to their duties here at Berwyck. They will be up shortly, once they see my wife and son settled."

"May I offer my congratulations on your heir, Riorden? It appears good fortune has smiled upon you, as well. I am pleased all has worked out for you," Ian offered his well wishes with a small smile.

"Aye. We may have hit a few bumps along the way, but I am most fortunate to have such a woman as my Katherine to grace my life."

"She seemed a most astute young woman when we had speech at Bamburgh last year. God has indeed blessed you, to bring a woman such as Lady Katherine to your side."

"You do not know the half of it, nor just how far she has come, my friend." Riorden's laughter erupted, and yet, Ian could not for the life of him decipher what the jest might be. "But tell me, why are you—"

Riorden's conversation was interrupted by a discrete rap upon the solar door. Afore any could answer, the lady of their musings poked her head inside the chamber. Without so much as a by your leave from Dristan, she gave a wave in their direction and boldly walked into the room.

All conversations ceased upon her entrance, but she gave it no mind whilst she made her way to her husband, who leaned down and placed a kiss upon her forehead. She appeared as if she did nothing out of the ordinary, and Riorden did not seem upset she interrupted the men. Ian hid his shock, however, to see another woman dressed in hose and tunic, much like Amiria continued to prefer. There were not many women of his acquaintance who would dress so daringly.

Wrapping her arm around her husband's waist, she peered about her and gave the men a smile that lit up the room as though the sun had appeared afore them to brighten their day. "Wow! There's a lot of testosterone in here, isn't there?" she murmured. "And aren't the lot of you just such handsome devils, too!" She took another glance around the chamber and suddenly appeared almost shy when she espied Dristan's captain. "Hello, Fletcher," she said softly.

"My lady," Fletcher replied with a slight bow, keeping his eyes fixed on Katherine.

Ian watched her blush afore she recovered herself and leveled those aquamarine eyes on his own sorry form. "Lady Katherine, a pleasure to see you, again," Ian said with a nod of his head, feeling the need to say something when she continued searching his face.

"Ian, you're just the person I came looking for," she finally replied afore turning to Dristan. "My Lord Dristan, how nice to see you. I'm sorry for interrupting your meeting with the men, but you don't mind if I steal Ian away for a few moments before I join the ladies, do you?" she asked.

An almost comical look flashed upon Dristan's features afore his face returned to a mask of irrelevance. "Not at all, Lady Katherine."

"Where is the babe?" Riorden asked his wife in concern for their son.

Katherine patted his arm. "James is just fine, hun. There's no need to worry about him. Amiria has taken him to be coddled by the other ladies in her solar. I will join them directly, but first, I wish to have a chat with Ian." She turned towards Ian. "Shall we?"

A sense of déjà vu assaulted Ian's senses, and he felt as if they had had this conversation afore. 'Twas not too far off the mark, since the last time he had speech with this particular lady, she had been heavily along with child. He offered her his arm, as any gentleman would do, but instead of attempting to find a quiet corner in the solar, she surprised him by beckoning him out the door. He followed her lead down the corridor 'til she came upon an oval shaped alcove with a window. The mason of Berwyck had cut into the stone wall a large enough seat where soft cushions had been placed for a person's comfort. A soft breeze blew in from the open shutter that allowed a view to the ocean far below.

Katherine sat and made a motion for Ian to join her. As he settled himself across from her, he waited for her to say what she had on her mind. She only perused him with a gentle smile set upon her lovely face. He began to wonder if she, mayhap, had the sight as Kenna did.

"I didn't expect to see you," she quietly began, "at least, here, of all places."

"My circumstances have changed since last we met," Ian commented, as he thought on her oddly strange speech. "You are not from the area, are you, my lady?" he blurted out.

She gave a muffled giggle that she quickly hid behind her hand and turned, he supposed, to collect her thoughts by gazing out the window.

After several minutes of observing the view afore her, she turned back to him. Her face gave no hint of her momentary lapse of composure. "I've always loved the ocean. You can find such a calming effect and solace watching the waves crash into the shore, don't you think?" she said with a sheepish grin.

Ian hid his own smile, since 'twas hard not to notice Lady Katherine avoided his question by changing the subject. "I do not believe this is why you brought me out here, my lady. However, if you would care to speak of meaningless things, would you now like to have speech about the weather...?" Ian's voice trailed off, as Katherine's bubbling laughter rang out once more.

"My, my, but you are perceptive, aren't you, dear Ian? Very well, let's get right down to the heart of the matter, shall we, and cut to the chase?" she stated matter-of-factly. All traces of humor had now left her visage, and she gave him a stern look.

"My lady?" he asked, perplexed by her terminology.

"Never mind," she whispered, evading his concern, yet again. She leaned forward slightly towards him. "Do you love her?"

He was taken aback at the straightforwardness of her question, for 'twas not one he thought she would ask. "Do you not think your query too forward, my lady?" he grumbled awkwardly, knowing there was only one woman she referred to.

Katherine shrugged her shoulders and leaned back against the wall. "I guess it probably is. But given how many men have come to claim her, I don't really think you have a whole lot of time on your hands to figure out how best to proceed, unless you've already formulated some kind of plan."

"I have not given it much thought," Ian replied, raking his hand through his hair.

"Ugh! Maybe you should, before it's too late!" She started mumbling to herself about pigheaded men and how the whole gender, no matter the time, were completely clueless. Ian was not sure how to respond, so he waited 'til she finally stopped her tirade. "Well? Have you at least spoken to Lynet?"

"I am afraid, I am not in favor with the lady," Ian replied, "at least at this particular moment in time".

"Time...yes...funny thing about Time is—"

"I hate to interrupt you, Lady Katherine, but is there a point to our conversation?"

Her brows drew together as she all but scowled at him. "Men...sometimes you just don't have any hint about what is important," Katherine fumed. "You can be so stubborn!"

"My lady, what part of this conversation am I missing?"

"Never mind," she huffed. "Did you tell her how you feel about her?"

His patience at an end, Ian rose, leaned an arm upon the wall, and looked out on the waves crashing into the shore, as if, true to the lady's previous words, the sight could miraculously calm his fretful soul. It had no such effect. "My Lady Katherine, I have not told Lady Lynet how I feel about her, because I barely know the young woman she has become. She was a mere child when last we met. Since I was so much older than she, with nothing to offer, I did not think of her as anyone else but a pretty lassie I remembered with great fondness, who was also Amiria's little sister. I, however, am in much need of a bride, and I have come here seeking her out to offer her marriage. I had no idea, to win her hand, I would have to be victorious in Dristan's public competition."

"Please, for the love of God, tell me you didn't just waltz back here expecting to scoop Lynet up and immediately run off with her to wherever you'll now call your home?"

Ian let out a curse, for that was precisely what he had had in mind, not that he had intended to say such aloud. "More or less. As I stated, I had not thought too far ahead, other than to travel to Berwyck."

Katherine shook her head sadly. "Then it's no wonder you're out of favor with the lady. I wouldn't be very happy to see you, either, under such circumstances. Hopefully, you'll find it in your heart to have at least some small measure of affection for the girl, if you hope to marry her. There's nothing worse than trying to be with someone who doesn't love you."

"You sound as if you are speaking from experience."

"I am."

Ian reached over and took her hand then gave its back a brief kiss. "The tournament is to begin two days hence. Do you have any advice to give someone like myself, something I could do in order to change the lady's mind and current feeling towards me?"

"Well...to tell you the truth, I do, Ian," she answered softly.

He waited for what she could possibly offer as guidance, but she only continued to stare at him, as though waiting for him to possibly come to the same conclusion on his own. He could not stand the silence any longer and at last spoke up. "And what exactly should I do to earn the lady's heart?"

"There's only one thing you need to do, Ian, and it's really quite simple."

"And what is that, my lady?" he asked in puzzlement.

She gave him a sly smile whilst her eyes twinkled mischievously. Laughing, she at last gave him his answer. "You must win!"

EIGHT

ROLF STOOD SILENTLY on the narrow parapet, gazing into the darkness of the night. He could not see far enough to espy the vast ocean, but he could hear the sound of the surf pounding ruthlessly into the shore far below him. Normally, such a sound would fill him with wonder at the power of the sea, but not this eve. Tonight, he was ill at ease on what the coming days would bring, or not bring, should he fail in his quest. He still held a small sum of hope that Kenna's vision would not come to pass.

He did not have to turn his sight far to witness the goings on of life at camp. Tents filled the area surrounding Berwyck's walls of those who also hoped to win the fair Lynet. The smell of campfire smoke and the fire light from the torches on the battlement walls filled the air. The fumes and smells made his nose twitch, causing him to sneeze. Muffled laughter and speech was barely audible from those who were still awake, each man bragging of his own singular prowess, and how he, too, would have the young bride at the end of the games.

He lifted his head heaven bound to stare at the thousands of stars splashing across the moonlit sky. Closing his eyes, he gave a silent plea God would answer his request. 'Twas a heartfelt prayer he offered up to the heavens, and yet as Rolf gazed once more upon the open skies above him, he felt nothing giving evidence that his petitions would be met. Apparently God did not make bargains with mortal men when it came to falling in love and what the heart desired...more is the pity.

Hearing the hinges of the turret door squeak open, Rolf turned to see who would be coming up to the rooftop at such a late hour. Most had already made their way to their chambers hours ago to rest afore the games began. Slumber, however, eluded Rolf, especially when he was wound so tight. The games could not begin soon enough for him to take out his frustration upon the field.

A splash of wispy material caught his attention when the unmistakable figure of a woman appeared through the turret portal. The instant she emerged from the shelter of the doorway, a gusty breeze caught her gown, and all but floated around the vision afore his eyes. 'Twas almost as if God himself had sent him an angel in answer to his appeal. She attempted to gather the garment around her and at last made some progress when she pulled a tartan around her head, clutching the plaid at her breasts.

Rolf watched her progress across the battlement walls with interest. His placement concealed in the shadows, she obviously did not see him standing on the parapet. So engrossed was she to reach the wall herself, she stumbled, letting out a startled gasp when her foot caught on the last step. Crying out in alarm, she began to sprawl face forward, causing Rolf to swiftly close the remaining distance between them. He caught the young girl in his arms afore any harm could befall her.

Her flowery scent was the first thing to assault his senses, and he did not need to see her face to know just whom he held in his arms. His limbs seemed to have a life of their own as they offered her the support she stood in need of as she regained her balance. He took a step nearer 'til both her hands came up and pushed hard against his chest. He stood firm in his resolve to keep her at his side. His hands slid to her waist as he inched her even closer into his embrace.

"How dare you," she shrieked in outrage. Her face rose to meet his 'til recognition set in. "Rolf?"

"Good eve to you, Lynet."

"What are you doing out here in the middle of the night?"

He gave an amused chuckle. "I could ask you the same question. Perchance, could you not sleep, either?"

"Nay, I could not, and my chamber was stifling. I had enough of my tossing and turning. I decided I needed some fresh air."

"I understand your plight completely, my lady." Rolf watched her face whilst she apparently came to the realization he was holding her far too close. Her hands moved from his chest and went instead to his arms.

"You should not be holding me thusly. 'Tis not seemly. What would someone think if they came upon us?"

"Mayhap, they would think there was no longer any need for a tourney and your hand was already spoken for," Rolf murmured. There was no mistaking the feeling of contentment that was racing through him whilst holding her close. "There is no need to worry about the guards, for they are busy at their watch, so they will pay us no mind. Besides, I believe I like the way you feel in my arms and would like to keep you here as long as you would allow it."

A small smile lit her lips. "I should return to my chamber," she whispered softly, and yet, she made no effort to leave. Instead, she began caressing the fabric of his tunic.

"Stay with me," he insisted.

Lynet gave the briefest of hesitations afore replying. "Only for a moment or two, but then, I must depart."

Rolf gladly seized the opportunity she granted him and turned Lynet so her back rested against his chest whilst they peacefully stared out towards the sea. She gave a brief sigh. He interpreted such a sound as one of pleasure, for the scene between them was one of intimacy two lovers might share at some midnight rendezvous. He tightened his arms around her waist and forced, to the back of his mind, the uncanny premonition the felt that this would be the only time he would ever hold this woman in his arms.

The silence stretched between them whilst both were lost in their own thoughts. Rolf's were about the coming days of battle and strategic maneuvers necessary in order for him to win each competition. He could only surmise Lynet's were filled with horrific images of who she may be forced to wed at the completion of the games. As if her thoughts were spoken aloud, he felt her shiver and knew 'twas not from the cool night air.

"Lynet," he quietly broke the quietness surrounding them, "about the morrow..."

She quickly turned to face him, bringing her fingertips up against his lips. "Shh...please do not speak of it, Rolf, I beg of you."

Taking her hand in his, he began to caress it with his thumb. "We may not have another opportunity to have speech, my lady, and therefore, I feel the urgency to speak my mind."

"I do not know what more can be said that has not already been spoken between us. I cannot bear the thought of the coming days, nor how I will manage to endure through this farce that determines my life."

"I only wish I had spoken sooner to Lord Dristan. Mayhap, none of this would be happening if I had done so."

"'Tis of no consequence now, Rolf, since we cannot, in truth, turn back the hands of time. Nothing can change the course of what is to come," she said forlornly.

"You must know, I will do all within me to win your favor at the end of the games, Lynet."

"Aye...I know you will."

Her words, though barely audible, went straight to Rolf's heart as if a bolt had pierced it. She shuddered again and tentatively laid her head upon his chest. He was pleasantly surprised she would dare to honor him with such a display of affection, and he took advantage of it. The golden length of her cascading hair seemed to call to him as though it actually gave voice for him to touch the curling tresses running down the length of her back. He gave in to the guilty pleasure afore him and began stroking her hair. 'Twas as soft as the petals from a winters rose that had somehow endured the bitter frost.

"I must go," Lynet whispered, raising her head.

Their eyes locked. Time had seemed to be their enemy moments afore, yet now it stood completely still. Her lips parted. Any further words she may have uttered were silenced as Rolf followed his instincts and lowered his mouth to her own.

Lynet should have expected this to happen when she had stated she would stay with him. But nothing in her score of years had prepared her for the sensation of her very first kiss as a woman full grown. She would have thought such a momentous event would send her heart flipping end over end, but 'twas further from the truth than she cared to admit, even unto herself. Although mildly pleasant, such a kiss as this did not make her want to profess her undying love to the knight who would offer her everything she desired if she could but learn to love him.

Perchance, she did not put enough effort into such an endeavor, for how was she to know how this kissing business was accomplished, having only experienced it once afore as a young girl with Ian, haphazard and brief as that had been. She took a step closer. Rolf must have taken this as a sign of encouragement. He deepened their kiss, and Lynet quickly became aware of two startling revelations. For one, Rolf had far more experience than she herself did when it came to kissing and certainly knew what he was doing. The second was far more disappointing to her peace of mind. She abruptly realized, if they were to marry, she would be settling into a relationship where they may have found a common accord, but Lynet would never truly love him deep within her heart. They both deserved much better than such a fate as that.

"I hope we're not interrupting..." an annoyed voice called out from behind her.

Shame flooded through her, down to her very toes, as they swiftly broke apart. To be caught in such a compromising position such as this and by *him,* of all people! She turned to see none other than Ian himself making his way up the last of the parapet steps, followed closely by her brother Aiden, who strode menacingly towards Rolf with a clenched fist.

"I should call you out for taking advantage of my sister!" Aiden bellowed, wedging himself between her and Rolf. "What the devil were you thinking to touch her so?" Rolf threw both his hands up, obviously not willing to fight her brother in front of her.

"'Tis wretchedly obvious he was not thinking at all, Aiden," Ian drawled, taking her elbow. "Come, Lynet. I will escort you to your chambers."

"Nay! I will go nowhere with you, Ian," she professed in embarrassment whilst trying to wrench her arm free with little success.

Aiden whirled around, glaring at her 'til she snapped her mouth shut. "You will go with Ian to your chambers. You have enough to worry about in the coming days with all the rabble outside our gates vying for your hand and should get your rest whilst you may," her brother ordered. He made sure his words were abundantly clear, giving evidence he was not pleased with her behavior.

Her emotions torn between the three men, she watched as Aiden made to usher Rolf from the battlement wall. 'Twas clear her brother had no qualm about leaving her alone with Ian. But she knew otherwise and what this could mean to her already tattered heart. Ian was by far more dangerous to her wellbeing.

"Rolf," she called, stepping towards him although Ian's grip kept her from getting any closer to him. "I will see you on the morrow." He gave her the briefest of nods as acknowledgement afore leaving with Aiden, who continued his lecture as they did so.

Lynet stood in silence as she watched the turret door shut with a resounding slam. She made the blunder of looking up into Ian's stormy face once they were alone. His visage was furious with possibly a hint of jealousy hidden in the depths of his eyes. 'Twas hard to tell what the man was pondering inside his head, but she knew she would not have to wait long afore he spoke his mind. When he did, it caused her to inwardly cringe.

"You will not meet with him by yourself again, Lynet." He enunciated each word with clenched teeth, giving confirmation to the anger he was holding in check. "Do I make myself clear?"

Her own rage exploded to the surface like blinding, white-hot lightning. "Who do you think you are that you assume you can just order me about and tell me what to do?" Courage to stand up for herself raced through Lynet, for she would not let him see how he affected her so. Her reckless and traitorous heart skipped a beat with his nearness. Damn the man's soul to hell. How she hated him!

"I will tell you who I am, lass. I am the man you will forever bow down to and call husband come the end of these games," he roared ferociously, like a wounded animal.

"I will neither bow down to you, nor any other man, you worthless cur," she shouted right back at him.

Ian grabbed her arms, giving her a shake 'til she felt her teeth rattle. "You will submit to me, you stubborn woman. Do you not even realize when you have met your match?"

She lifted her head at him with narrowed eyes. "Aye, as a matter of fact, I do, for he just left with my brother!"

"He is only the captain of your guard, Lynet. He has no right to lay claim to you as his future bride," Ian retorted hotly, "nor to steal your kisses in the moonlight."

"That did not stop you from loving my sister when the same held true of your position. What makes you think you are a better man than Rolf to hold my affection, or that you can do a finer job of kissing me? I enjoyed his lips on mine and will kiss him anytime I should choose to do so," she snickered, tossing him a defiant glare that all too quickly fell from her features. With one glance upon him, she might as well have slapped his face, considering the look he gave her. She knew she had pushed him too far.

He said not another word, but made fast work of guiding her down from the lofty parapet walkway. Her slippered feet barely touched the coldness of the stones beneath her, so rapid was their hasty decent down the turret stairs. When they came to the portal of her chamber, Ian backed her up against the solid wood with his arms resting on either side of her, as he had done but recently. There was no escaping him.

They stood, just the two of them, listening to the crackling sound of the lit torches in the passageway. Far more troubling to her way of thinking was her heaving chest as she attempted to gain her breath. She could no longer stand her submissive stance of looking down at her feet, so she raised her eyes to meet his.

When would she stop making such stupid decisions as actually looking at the man, not that she had anywhere else to gaze, given his close proximity. The firelight from the torches in the wall sconces brought out the red of his hair. She would have sighed at the sight of it, but would not give him the gratification. His heavy lidded, hazel eyes took on a light of their own and seemed to search into her very soul. She gulped and watched a gleam enter those knowing orbs whilst a discerning grin formed on his mouth. A mouth that was rapidly closing the distance between them!

"Do not dare—"

Her words were cut off as his mouth quickly took possession of her own, for possess her he did, with just the slightest first brush of his lips. She gasped when a turbulent wave of searing heat radiated throughout her entire body. But, such a profound encounter only allowed him to further plunder her senses as his tongue began to frolic with her own. *Sweet Jesus, what in the world is he doing to me?*

She felt his hands cup her face 'til he tilted her head, allowing him better access to her mouth. An unexpected moan escaped her. 'Twas, apparently, what he had wanted to hear from her. The sound surely only confirmed his own damn suspicions that she had told a lie when speaking of the effect of Rolf's kiss. She was certain such a revelation pleased him.

His hands began a slow descent as they roamed down her back 'til he cupped her bottom, bringing her up hard against his solid frame. She quaked in response to such intimacy between them. Her shock did not stop his arm from winding around her waist, keeping her firmly in place as he continued to devour her last shreds of reality. The disbelief of feeling his firmly muscled body pressed up against her own sent any sense of prudence to remain indifferent to him fleeing from her mind. How could one keep a hold on any form of rationality when all she could suddenly feel was the unmistakable form of his manhood pressed intimately against her?

She was lost, and she unexpectedly cared not. Nay...all she could recognize in her feeble attempts to remain level headed was the fact that any control of the situation she may have had up to this point had vanished as soon as Ian had kissed her. Her arms made their way up and around his neck to playfully finger his shoulder length hair. She mimicked what he was doing to her mouth, letting him teach her what he liked. She must have done something right, for she heard his own groan of pleasure whilst he tightened his grip upon her.

Was it just her imagination, or did her body seem to mold itself to his own, as if they had been made for one another, even whilst his hands roamed freely over her backside? And yet, she did not complain, or even make the slightest protest. This was how it felt to finally be in his arms. She had dreamed of this moment for so long, she was almost waiting for someone to come and wake her, for surely she must be dreaming. She reached out and clasped the nape of Ian's neck as she urged him onward in this journey he was taking her on. 'Twas sheer bliss...bliss 'til she felt herself being rudely yanked from his embrace.

Lynet gazed around with passion filled eyes to see who had interrupted them, but there was no one near, except the man who had proved his point that Rolf was not the knight for her. Aye! The deliberate burning glare in those obnoxious hazel eyes told her he knew exactly what he had done to her, and he was glad for it, the bastard.

Ian leaned down from his towering height so they came almost nose to nose. "Lesson number one, Lynet, is never lie to me again. Rolf is a good man, but he will never be able to make you feel the way I can. I will be victorious at the end of the games, and you will be my wife. *You...are...mine.*"

He gave her but an instant for the words he proclaimed to register in her brain, which surely had been turned to mush. Afore she could even mange to form some limited response that would most likely be garbled jibber-jabber, Ian gave her a quick kiss upon her already tender lips, opened her door, and gave her a gentle push through the portal. Once she was inside, Ian closed the door behind her.

Feeling completely numb, with her feelings a jumbled mess, Lynet could go no further into her chamber. Instead, she leaned back against the wooden door, trying to somehow control and still her racing heart. It took every bit of effort she had left in her just to turn her body and lift her arm in order to slide the bolt into place. Her ear pressed to the door, she listened intently for signs of Ian's departure. She held her breath with the knowledge he, too, lingered just on the other side with only an obnoxious piece of wood now separating them. She heard it then...the unmistakable sound of his footsteps receding down the corridor to seek his own slumber.

With his departure, her breath left her in a swift rush afore her trembling legs crumbled beneath her. Sliding helplessly to the floor, her hands shook as she fingered her sensitive lips. Aye, she had indeed been most thoroughly kissed, and by one who knew, inevitability, she had enjoyed every instant of their encounter. Surely he had branded her as his own with the scorching warmth of his touch. She may as well call Father Donovan and get their marriage over and done with. May God above help her and give her strength for what was to come with that insufferable man she so wanted to hate.

Hate him, or love him...she was not sure which she wanted to believe more. Either one was just as bad. For what truly mattered where her heart was concerned, was that Lynet recognized she was in big trouble.

NINE

LYNET'S FEET BARELY TOUCHED the turret stairs beneath her as she held on to the red wrap around her shoulders. She was late and knew for a certainty she would incur Dristan's wrath for not being in her place on the platform erected for the family at the start of the games. How she had managed to obtain even a wink of sleep was beyond her comprehension. She had tossed and turned upon her bed for hours, thinking on Ian's kiss afore she had thrown the coverlets from her to do something more constructive with her time.

She had a firm resolve this morn when she had risen after only a brief two hours of rest. Her brow furrowed thinking on that insufferable man. Ian was overly confident she would simply fall in love with him after just one kiss. Of that, there could be no doubt, but she was determined she would prove him wrong. She would not succumb to his charms so readily and become such an easy conquest. Nay, she would not!

With thoughts of Ian's kiss seared into her heart, she pushed down the notion she would belong to him at the end of the games, no matter that she had wished to be his wife for almost her entire life. There was another who was equally ready to take on the role of her husband, and Lynet was sure that, with time, she could somehow manage to love him.

Silencing the small voice inside her head telling her she was making a horrific mistake, she kept onward in her quest to be the mistress of her own fate. Racing through the Great Hall, she took no time to grab even a bit of cheese to break her fast. She did not want to miss the opportunity of sending Rolf off to battle for her hand without a small token of her affection. Aye, the embroidered red ribbon she held tightly in her hand billowed behind her in the soft morning breeze as she continued her flight through the inner bailey. There was no time to lose if she was to bestow this token to the knight who deserved her loyalty after all he had done for her over these past many years.

Through the portal of the inner bailey, she saw him sitting tall and handsome upon his black as night steed. The mighty warhorse practically pranced with pride as it carried its rider, who held a banner with one hand and the reins with the other. Yet, she was wasting precious time staring at him, the little she had, and her common sense that she must needs hurry had her rushing through the tall gate to reach the outer baily wall.

Rolf was already riding out towards the postern gate, along with the other knights who thought to make her their lady wife. If she had stopped for even one instant, she might have been impressed by the display of colorful standards that flew in the air for the entire world to see. There were many who would be competing this day, but only one now drew her attention as she rushed towards him.

"Rolf!" She called out his name and watched as he pulled back upon the reins to halt his steed. His grin widened whilst she shortened the distance between them, moving forward to stand in the middle of a staircase which led down to the outer baily.

He maneuvered his horse 'til the animal became parallel with the steps to the back entrance of the keep. 'Twas just what she needed in order to gaze upon him, eye to eye, given the additional height the stairs afforded her.

"My lady," Rolf murmured with an appreciative glance at her attire. "You are most lovely this day. The yellow of your gown is like a fresh breath of summer sunshine to brighten my day."

Lynet blushed upon hearing the compliment, adjusted the shawl she had around her shoulders, and gazed at him shyly. "I have something for you. I was up all night working on it that I may bestow it on you and place it upon your arm."

"You would honor me with a favor?" he asked, waiting for her response.

"Aye," she declared with a simple acknowledgment and a slight smile. His brow rose as if in a silent question as to the wisdom of her choice. Lynet did not have long to wait to hear what she feared would come from his lips. This man knew her so well.

"Is there not perchance another who you would rather give such a token to, my lady?" he questioned honestly whilst keeping their gazes locked, one on the other. "Not that I would complain such a gift was placed upon my arm as long as your favor was freely given."

Lynet began to squirm under his close scrutiny and averted her eyes to fumble with the ribbon. Hiding the heaviness of her heart, she raised her face. The confidence that had briefly filled her just moments ago, now left her shaking with her decision to press forward to wed Rolf, should he be the victor in the games. "Nay...there is no other," she proclaimed holding out the favor.

"See how I have embroidered it with your colors so no other would question my choice in a champion knight? It even matches the shade of your cloak."

"'Tis in truth Dristan's colors, my lady, as you well know, since I have no other place than Berwyck to call home," Rolf said solemnly.

"Aye, I know that, of course. And yet, I would still tie this upon your arm if you would but allow me the privilege," Lynet said breathlessly. She looked over Rolf's shoulder to see another who watched her intently. Her heart began its erratic beating with his nearness and knowing he gazed upon her, yet she refused to allow Ian to change her resolve. "Will you allow it?" she asked returning her full attention to Rolf.

"I would be a fool to gainsay you and say you nay, Lady Lynet," he answered, holding out his arm to her. "You do me a great honor."

She finished tying the ribbon, but still lightly touched the chainmail on his arm. "Nay, 'tis I who am honored by your acceptance of such a meager offering for one who would go into battle for my hand. You will be careful, Rolf, will you not?" she asked with a slight tremor in her voice. She would hate to see anyone hurt because of her.

"But of course," Rolf said, taking her hand. He held it gently afore leaning forward to brush his lips across her skin.

She gave a slight shiver. 'Twas not, however, from the gentleness of Rolf's display of affection, but in response to the blazing hot glare from Ian afore he stepped into the stirrup and lifted himself up onto his white, ivory-maned horse. 'Twas as if he knew of the ploy she played. Yet to her, 'twas not a game of chance, but her future that was at stake.

Lynet had not realized her eyes continued to linger on Ian 'til she felt her arm drop as Rolf let go of her fingertips. Her attention once more on her captain, she saw a fleeting look of sadness within his eyes afore he masked the emotions in a cocky grin of self-confidence.

"I look forward to claiming several dances this eve after I win my matches, my lady," he declared, and, with a jaunty salute, he kicked his horse into motion, setting off for the tournament.

Lynet watched Rolf go with a soft smile that quickly turned into a frown when a voice came within her hearing, closer than she anticipated. She turned to see Ian take the very place that Rolf had occupied but an instant afore.

"Have you no favor to bestow upon your future husband, my dear Lady Lynet?" Ian's voice all but mocked her.

"Aye...I just gave him one," she replied with a saucy flip of her hair. Hazel eyes met blue whilst she attempted to catch her breath. How could one man leave her so lacking for air from just the briefest of glances?

Ian looked her up and down with an appreciative gaze then gifted her with his own handsomely roguish grin that had her heart beating frantically, once again. "Nay, you did not. But, 'tis of no consequence. You shall soon learn that attempts to make me jealous will not work on me."

"I did no such thing," she said, aghast he had read her so openly.

"Aye, you did, but those are the games children play, and seldom do they achieve what the heart of an adult desires."

"What do you know of what my heart desires?" She drew the wrap closer together to attempt to hide her trembling hands. Surely, even he could hear the rapid betrayal of her beating heart, as it all but cried out for the man afore her, much to her dismay.

Ian brought his horse closer to the stairway. "Mayhap, I should show you yet again as I did last eve?" he whispered huskily, sending a wave of desire coursing through her.

"I think not," she retorted hotly as a blush began to creep up her cheeks. *Damn the man's soul to hell.*

"Another time, perchance, since I must needs go and begin winning my bride," Ian proclaimed.

With a tug on the reins, he, too, began to make his way from her. Confusion suddenly consumed her 'til worry that he might be severely injured came to the forefront of her mind. "Ian...wait," she called out. Surprised she summoned him to return to her, Ian quickly turned his mount in her direction.

Lynet watched in maidenly delight when Ian maneuvered his steed to stand afore her. With a click of his spurs, the animal put one of its legs forward and bowed his head afore rising. Ian hardly looked like a Scottish laird this day, as he was once more garbed as a knight of the realm. He had always been handsome to her eyes, but he was even more so, now that she had the opportunity to see him through the eyes of a grown woman ready to fall in love. Ian raised his hand over his chest and gave his own short bow, as well as could be managed with the weight of his armor. "My lady," he said afore once more returning abreast of the stairs. "I am your most humble servant."

She bit her lip with indecision for just an instant afore whipping the shawl from her shoulders and tying it on Ian's arm. "This does not mean I favor you above others," she declared, trying to find some way to justify her actions that two different men would be wearing a small token of her affection.

"If you say so," Ian said, smiling afore he took her hand in his and laid a gentle kiss upon her fingertips.

Afore she could give him a sharp retort of any kind, he left her there alone, stumbling for words to say to him inside her head. Knowing she, too, must needs make her way to the field, she proceeded no farther than down the few stairs afore another prevented her from following after the two men who wanted to claim her heart. She stared at the young lord in her path, trying to hide the contempt she felt for this particular individual.

"You have erred greatly to give your favor to anyone other than myself, let alone that you gave out two," Broderick of Lorn sneered at her with a curled lip. His distaste of what she had done was clearly plastered on his handsome face, and she knew a life with this particular man would be spent catering to his every whim.

Lynet lifted her head defiantly. "You are not my husband, nor master, that I must needs answer to you," she spat out, not caring who heard her words that barely contained her fury.

Broderick's nostrils flared whilst he clenched and unclenched his fists. He then did the unexpected by blatantly staring at her body, as though he were undressing her right there in the courtyard with his eyes. "Mayhap, not yet...but you will be mine by the tourney's end."

Lynet's limbs quaked beneath her gown as he left her. In those brief, few instances she looked upon Broderick, she witnessed an evil side to the intimidating man that she did not ever want to witness again.

Trying her best to compose herself, she came to realize she was clutching at the stone winged dragon upon the railing of the stairs. The mouth snarled forever open, and if the etched eyes could condemn her for giving her favor to two different men, then the demon was doing just that. She wagged her finger at the carved beast, as if it had spoken aloud her own foolish thoughts.

"Do not look at me like that," she sneered afore picking up the edge of her gown to run and find her place amongst the crowd. Each step told her she needed to pick one knight alone to cheer for. With her decision once more made, she choked on her choice and took her place next to her sister to gaze at the combatants for her hand. The sooner Rolf won, the sooner this fiasco would be over!

Rolf had not thought the hideous emotion of jealousy would ever consume him. Yet whilst he watched the young woman of no more than a score of years dance her way across the Great Hall, jealous he was. He was not the only victor this day, and 'twould take yet unto a full two se'nnight's afore he could be proclaimed the victor. He was so confident he would win Lynet's hand at the end of the games that he gave no further thought he could not also win her heart.

He fingered the edge of the ribbon she had lovingly made for him whilst he continued to gaze upon Lynet and her current partner. He had witnessed her moment of astonishment that he had chosen to wear her token this eve when they came to sup, although, how she could think that he would not, mayhap, told him more than he cared to admit, even unto himself. But don it he would, for she had given it to him, and he would pray 'twould remain intact, given the number of knights who attempted to tear it from his arm.

He diverted his attention from the fair maid long enough to witness Kenna's sad look whilst she watched him. 'Twas almost an open confession that could have been shouted from the rafters, for her silent look told him what he already knew within his heart, if he cared to but look deep enough. He refused to acknowledge he would lose this chance to have Lynet as his wife, no matter that Ian MacGillivray had the same deep commitment.

Rolf ignored the warning signs around him with a heavy sigh and once more looked upon Lynet and Ian as they danced in perfect accord. The young woman may have tried to remain indifferent to her partner, but Rolf easily saw behind her ruse. Each time she knew Ian no longer watched her, her eyes sparkled with happiness, like the jewels brightly shining around her throat.

The dance ended and the couple broke apart, to Rolf's great relief, although 'twas not long afore another took Ian's place. Rolf had already had the pleasure of his victory dance with Lynet so he knew there would not be another opportunity to have her in his arms. He was about to retire to his chambers when he noticed Lynet's current partner risked much, considering the placement of his hand.

Rolf was about to intervene on the lady's behalf when Dristan rose and took care of the matter himself. Mayhap, that, too, was for the best. He was afraid if he had had to deal with Lord Broderick, the man would be missing a much needed limb for having placed his hand lower than Lynet's waist. At least, that would have ensured one less man vying for her hand in marriage.

He took delight when the lady of his musing noticed him leaning up against the wall and waved. He returned the gesture with a slight nod of his head and was pleasantly pleased when she began weaving her way through the crowd to join him. A servant was passing by and Rolf reached out for a chalice of wine, which he offered to Lynet when she came abreast of him.

"My thanks, Sir Rolf. I am most parched," she whispered breathlessly.

He continued to gaze down upon her, but said not a word. Her flowery essence assaulted his senses, as if to mock him of what he would never have to call his very own. Still he could not, for the life of him, help himself from inhaling the scent of her and enjoying this brief moment to treasure for all of his days.

"Rolf?" His name echoed inside his head, and he realized she must have been speaking to him, but he was ignorant to what the lady had been saying.

Clearing his throat, he looked down into the bluest eyes he had ever beheld and was once more lost. "My lady?"

She gave him a slight smile. "I had asked if you are enjoying the festivities this eve."

He returned her smile with one of his own. "I am now," he replied and watched a most becoming blush rush up her cheeks.

She appeared as though she was struggling for something to say. 'Twas a first, since speech between them had never been difficult. "Rolf, I—" she began, only to have her words stumble into silence, once more.

Her unspoken words tore at his heart, knowing the cause. She did not need to speak them, for 'twas perfectly clear to whom her affections truly belonged. Yet, 'til she settled the matter between them, Rolf would continue to fight for her hand and hold out some small measure of hope she could still be his.

Lynet reached out and fingered the edges of the ribbon placed on his arm much as he had just recently done. "I am most pleased you still wear this, Rolf," she murmured. "You know I do care for you, do you not?"

Afore he could mutter some form of a reply, Dristan called to her, for another was ready to claim his victory dance. Lynet murmured a barely audible hasty farewell and departed.

With a heavy heart, Rolf left the festivities to retire. He may not have much of a chance to win the lady's heart, but by God, he would die trying, if he must.

TEN

"YIELD!" IAN CALLED OUT TO THE KNIGHT beneath the point of his claymore. He waited with his heart hammering inside his chest 'til the man at last nodded his confirmation Ian had won the match. A round of cheers went up from those seated in the stands, who had been watching for what seemed like hours whilst men continually hacked away at each other with their swords.

Ian lifted the visor of his helmet and made his way to bow afore Dristan and those surrounding him. His eyes lingered on the young woman who had barely acknowledged his existence in the past several days. Today was no different, as she all but ignored his presence. He took off his helmet and glared at her 'til she at last peered at him in a sideways glance. She flushed a becoming shade of red. He smiled at her obvious frustration to remain uncaring. With a blush like that painstakingly plastered on her comely face, he knew he had her undivided attention, whether she willed it or not.

His point made, he gave her a low courtly bow, despite the heavy metal encasing his body. "*My* lady," he said, loud enough that all within hearing heard the emphasis on his claim to the beautiful Lynet.

"Harrumph!" Lynet gave an off handed reply, all but raising her pretty, little, pert nose at him.

He chuckled whilst calling for ale and left the field 'til the next poor sorry excuse for a knight rose up to challenge him again come the morrow. The array of opponents had been falling like rain drops from the grey skies 'til only the best of the best now remained for him to fight to claim his prize. Since Dristan had made it perfectly clear these rounds were not to be challenges to the death, many had grumbled their complaints as they had fallen victim to better adversaries. From the sneers that followed him through camp, Ian had made plenty of enemies by advancing through the ranks to win Lynet's hand in marriage.

Ian bestowed a brief glance over his shoulder at Angus and Connor, who he knew guarded his back, as he made for his tent to take his ease. Although Killian had made room for him in the Garrison Hall, he preferred to be outside of the keep walls, not trusting himself to restrain the urge to throttle the very lady he was trying his best to win.

The little vixen! How many nights, as the victors celebrated in the Great Hall, had she all but told him with her eyes that she hated him? Their kiss, however, told him differently, and 'twas the reason he continued to maintain the advantage in the matches he entered. 'Twas sheer goading on his part each time he bowed down afore her as he won, again and again. He looked forward to the day when he would become the last man standing. There was no doubt in his mind Lynet would be returning with him to Urquhart.

Still, he had to give her credit in her resolve to attempt to prove to herself, at the very least, that she cared not for him. Ian had watched, one fair morning at the beginning of the games, when she bestowed yet another favor on Rolf's armor, as if the first one she had given him had not been enough. Once the deed had been accomplished, she had peeked directly at him through lowered lashes 'til he gave her a mocking salute. If she thought to make him jealous, she would shortly come to the realization she would not win at her game. She should have heeded the warning he had already given her that such a ploy would not be to her advantage.

She had done Rolf no favor that day, however. The ribbon, once placed in front of all those competing for her hand, had all but floated on the breeze, as if daring and waving a bright red flag at a charging bull to come and take it from his arm. Rolf had taken a fair beating that morn, and yet, he still remained one of several combatants to fight another day. As one of Dristan's guards, Ian would have expected no less of the man.

In the evenings, Lynet had been forced by Dristan to dance with those who had won their matches each day 'til 'twas quite clear the lady was not enjoying the music. Coming to claim her for a dance after she had just been partnered with her distant cousin, who apparently now called Lorn his home, Ian had bristled as she had started to leave him standing alone on the floor 'til he had made a grab for her arm. He had spoken not a word as he had all but dared her to continue her departure. She had chosen wisely that night, and he had been pleased to watch her breathing elevate each time their hands touched or came in contact with one another as they went through the pattern of the dance. He remembered, in mild fascination, when the pupils of her blue eyes had dilated, and he had known then and there she wanted him as much as he wanted her. His only wish had been to sweep her from the room, thoroughly kiss her stubborn pride from her lips, and have her admit she still cared for him.

"Me laird..." Angus's voice interrupted his musings, and Ian wondered how long the man had been holding back the flap to the entrance of his tent whilst his laird reminisced on a tiny slip of a girl.

Ian entered and went to a nearby pitcher. After pouring water into the bowl, he cupped his hands and splashed the cool liquid on his face to remove the sweat of a hard day's labor. Angus handed him a drying cloth, and he took it gratefully, along with a tankard of cool ale to take the dirt from his mouth. He gulped the spirits 'til the cup was drained. "Help me get this damn armor off," Ian drawled, as exhaustion began to seep from his body. Only now, away from the prying eyes of others, would he give in to the need for rest.

"I told ye we should 'ave brought a lad. Look at us...reduced tae the duties o' squire!" Connor complained. Ian shot the man a piercing stare that silenced any further words of complaint. "Sorry, me laird."

Ian grunted some form of reply and managed a sigh of relief as the armor that had been weighing him down all day was slowly removed from his body. The chain mail was to be removed next. Bending forward, he allowed the weight from the heavy links to do the work for him as the mail slid from his chest onto the floor. Any energy Ian may have still possessed drained from him as if water running through fingers. Angus lifted off the padding he had worn so the metal would not rub his skin, only to reveal a path of blood that had been trickling down his side for some time.

"Yer injured," Angus stated the obvious as he began poking the stab wound in Ian's side.

"That hurts, if you would but care to inquire," Ian declared with a hiss.

"'Tis going tae be hard tae hold yer lance and balance yerself in the saddle come the next event with a wound o' this nature."

"I am sure I will manage, given the price I would pay if I fail. At least, I have the morrow to rest."

Angus continued his torture of assessing the wound, much to Ian's irritation. "How did ye come by this, and fer how long has it been bleeding the life from ye?"

"'Twas from Broderick, that sniveling distant relative of Lady Lynet's. Apparently, the gent did not like the beating he was receiving and thought to even the odds."

"Well...he did a right fine job and knew just where tae slice ye between the plates o' yer armor. The wound needs tae be stitched."

"I am sure 'tis not the first time the wretch has behaved so cowardly, and 'tis one of the reasons we did not get along whenever he came to visit Berwyck. I never could stand a cheat."

"At least he has now been eliminated from the competition. I heard tell he was packing his gear and cursing yer name at the same time," Angus laughed.

Ian flinched, looking down at his side, and did not care for the look of the wound. Since he had not wanted to call attention to the issue of someone getting the better of him by calling for Kenna's aid, he had left the injury unattended throughout the day. 'Twas not the wisest choice. The edges of skin were jagged and an angry shade of red. 'Twould not surprise him in the least to see the gash becoming poisonous. "Bloody Hell! The bastard used a dirty knife."

"Aye, that he did, and 'twill become more infected than it already is if we do not take care o' the wound soon." Angus wiped his bloodied hands on a cloth and turned to Connor. "Go and fetch Berwyck's healer, else we will be planning a funeral, instead o' a wedding."

Angus pulled up a stool and motioned for Ian to sit. Lowering his tall frame, Ian sat, waiting for Kenna's aid in healing his injury. He did, after all, need to fight another day.

Lynet lightly held the arm of a man whose name she could not recall to save her life. He was of the Davidson clan in the north of Scotland. At least that much she knew. He made her uncomfortable with his enormous height and massive build. 'Twas as if she were walking beside a mountain that blocked the sun from the skies. She appeared as a child next to him and could not imagine spending her life with such a man.

"You would like the Highlands, my lady, and the lochs surrounding my home." The giant beside her spoke with the deepest timbre to his voice she had ever heard afore. Was it her imagination, or did it feel as though the ground actually shook with his speech?

"Aye, I am sure I would enjoy such a place," Lynet replied off-handedly as they walked the camp towards the castle's keep. She peeked at him from lowered lashes only to see a scowl of displeasure set upon his face. Although there was no mistaking the fact he was a handsome brute, she did not care for those deep set brown eyes settling on her body as though he were stripping the garments from her for all the world to see her naked. She raised her chin and spoke her mind. "Have I offended you in some way that you would look at me so?"

"You do not even remember my name, do you lassie?" he grumbled irritably.

"I am afraid not and must apologize for my lapse in memory," she murmured.

"'Tis Calum," he replied sourly. "You would do well to remember it, come the future, especially since you will become my bride."

She halted their progress, for she had had enough of arrogant men telling her what to do. "We shall see," she retorted with a shake of her head. Espying Kenna busily helping an injured knight across the way, she waved off her escort. "Please excuse me, my Laird Calum. I must needs see if I can be of use to our healer."

Not waiting for a reply, she cared not that she left the man standing alone, most likely glaring at her retreating form. She made her way through the throng of people who were busily making their way to their own tents after a day of revelry. The days had been long, and the complaints high from those who had fallen and no longer were eligible for her hand in marriage. She was overjoyed the majority of noblemen were no longer in the running.

She came to stand next to a man who was pleading his cause to Kenna, who continued to work on her injured patient.

"I understand your plight, good sir, but I must needs finish here afore I can attend to another," Kenna murmured, never raising her eyes to the man who sought her help.

"But the wound is deep, mistress, and me laird is in need o' yer help!" the man said forcefully.

Kenna at last looked up with an irritated and impatient sigh and met Lynet's gaze as she stood there in silence. "Would you be so kind, my lady, and see to the gentleman's wounds?" Kenna asked. "I know I should not ask such of you, but as you can see, I have my hands full at the moment."

"But of course I can help, Kenna. Just let me go fetch my medicine satchel."

"No need, Lynet." Kenna tossed her a bag of her own supplies. "Take these and see to this man's laird. I will send a boy to fetch what I stand in need of."

The man set a brisk pace, and Lynet all but ran to keep up with him. They did not go far 'til Lynet stood afore a spacious tent that had been erected on the outskirts of the main activity of camp life.

The tent flap was held open for her to enter, and she did so, allowing her eyes to become adjusted to the dim interior after being in the bright sunlight. She saw him then, sitting there on a stool waiting for her. Blue eyes met hazel from across the room whilst her breath left her when she realized exactly who was injured. She rushed to his side. All thoughts of the animosity she had been feeling towards him left her, knowing he was hurt.

"What an honor," Ian drawled carelessly. "The lady herself comes to aid a most humble servant."

"Hush, you fool!" Lynet ordered, almost forgetting her kinder thoughts but an instant afore. Kneeling down at his side, she called for more light so she could better examine the wound. "Why did you not stop your fighting so this could be attended to? 'Tis already festering."

"Aye, I know." Ian lifted a bottle of spirits to his lips and took a long drink.

"Well...why did you not halt the combat?" She probed deeper into the wound and heard him cuss. "Sorry," she muttered softly.

"You know the reason I continued on with the games, Lynet. 'Tis foolish of you to think I would allow myself to be beaten by some sniveling coward who thought to win the match by deceit."

"And did you?"

Ian shook his head, as if he was clearing his thoughts from the fiery liquid he drank. "Did I what, my dear?"

Lynet sighed and stopped momentarily to look up into his visage. "Did you win the match?"

His brow rose, as if he was surprised she would even ask such of him. "How could you doubt I would not become victorious in the end?"

She remained mute, for truly, what was there to say when the man had fought relentlessly just to win her hand, despite the injury he had incurred. She began making a paste to pack the wound and draw out the infection, but she could feel the heat of his stare. The look he cast her sent a small thrill through her, even though he was just so exasperating at times. She kept to her task and tried to force from her mind the view of him sitting so nigh with a smirk plastered on his handsome face.

Pulling out linen for bandages, she told Ian to raise his arms. Naturally, this brought her into closer proximity of the man she was determined to hate for rejecting her all these years. Her fingers brushed across his bronzed chest, lightly furred with a hint of red, as she began to wind the cloth around his torso. She could actually smell the spirits on his breath. She was so near, she almost forgot her mission 'til she reached the end of the bindings. After she tied the knot, he put his arms down. Lynet sat back on her heels and collected the medicinal ointment, herbs, and linens to pack away in Kenna's satchel.

Ian offered her his hand as she rose, sending currents of heat flowing through her veins at his touch.

"You should stay abed to ensure no fever sets in," Lynet said as his thumb caressed the back of her hand he still held.

He gave a brief laugh. "And miss the chance to sup with you this eve and claim my dance? Not a chance, little one."

She smiled at the endearment as he raised her hand to his lips. Their eyes met yet again whilst her heart once more leapt up into her throat. She cleared it, trying to find her voice. When she finally spoke, the sound came out as more of a croak, causing his own smile to broaden, knowing he had affected her so.

"Then if I cannot steer you from your course, I shall see you this eve, my laird." She noticed his eyes took on an almost wicked gleam. "What amuses you so?" she asked, trying her best to control her breathing.

"I but enjoyed the sound of you calling me *my laird*," Ian chuckled, still holding on to her quivering hand.

Her brow rose at his nerve to bring her error to her attention. "Did you now?"

"Aye, I did, my dearest Lynet."

She attempted to hide the smirk lighting her face, but knew she had failed when his laughter rumbled inside his chest once more. "Well...do not get used to it. I said your title in a lapse of good judgment on my part, I assure you."

"If you say so, but..." He let his words drop off, as though he knew she had once again spoken a falsehood. The look he tossed her told her he was completely amused with how uncomfortable she was feeling for her slip. "Sure sounded like an endearment to me."

He finally let her hand go, but Lynet could tell 'twas done with reluctance. "Since the morrow is the Sabbath, I will check on you after mass and stich your wound if no further infection is present."

Lynet did not wait for any form of reply. She practically ran from the tent whilst her heart continued its rapid flight. He was winning her slowly, but surely, and he knew it. Mayhap, 'twas time to admit defeat and give in to the love she had always harbored for the insufferable man!

Calum unfolded his arms from his chest and watched Lynet with interest as she left the MacGillivray tent and made her way to the keep. He was not pleased with the events that were fast becoming clear to him. His estates failing, he needed the girl's dowry to replenish his coffers, by any means necessary.

She cared for the man...that much was becoming abundantly clear. He had noticed her pleased expression, when she thought no one was looking, whenever Ian of Urquhart had been named victorious from the relentless matches he won. If he did not do something about it, MacGillivray would attain her hand, despite Calum's best interests to do the same. Aye, the MacGillivray laird was the biggest threat to his own plans to have the lass. Perchance, Calum needed to take a different tactic in order to see his own desires were fulfilled.

ELEVEN

O<small>NCE UPON A TIME, THERE LIVED</small> a beautiful princess," Lynet began 'til her nephew Royce started squirming in her lap. She gazed down at the boy, who did not appear pleased with the tale she was about to weave. "What is amiss?"

The boy crossed his arms over his chest in a way so reminiscent of his sire, Lynet did everything in her power not to break out in laughter and shame the lad. "Cannot you tell me the tale of the knight, and how he slays the dragon, Aunt Lynet? 'Tis one of my favorites."

"But, I told you that one just yester eve. Do you not want to know how the fair princess falls in love with her knight from his show of bravery?"

The boy shrugged. "Tell such a tale to my sister when she is grown. I am most sure she would enjoy such flowery words!"

Royce scurried off her lap to find something else to hold his attention in the solar. She was not surprised when he picked up his wooden sword and began making jabbing motions, as if he, in truth, were slaying a dragon of lore.

Lynet gave a deep sigh and went to the window to catch a hint of the sea breeze and calm her nerves. The night was dark, and, although she could not see far, she knew he was out there, just beyond her sight. Earlier in the day, she had been refused admittance to his tent and assumed he did not want to see her. She had asked Kenna to attend him in her place, since she could not convince Ian's guard to let her pass.

Leaning against the stones, she felt the rough edges against her back whilst she watched Amiria holding her infant daughter and Katherine holding her young son. Jealousy reared its ugly head, for she became most envious of the visions they presented. 'Twas apparent motherhood agreed with them both, and she only wished she, too, were married with a bairn or two of her own to raise.

She needed to get out of here and away from all the domesticity surrounding her of late. Given the fiasco Dristan had started, she did nothing but fear the worst in her future prospect for a husband. Mayhap, something to eat would lighten her spirits.

She opened the door to the solar to depart and saw Rolf stood there with his hand in mid-air, since she interrupted his efforts to bid entrance. Her eyes darted in dismay to the sling holding an injured arm. She knew, in that instant, her fate where Rolf was concerned had been sealed. From the look on his face, he was aware of it, as well.

Lynet closed the door quietly so they might take a brief moment to have speech. Trying to form some semblance of words to express her sorrow, she found none and at last looked up into her captain's face. There was a sadness there she had never thought to see.

"Oh Rolf!" she whispered and held her hand up to his cheek. He took her hand but briefly, afore letting it go. 'Twas apparent he had already resigned himself that he had lost any chance he may have had to have her as his bride.

"I am most sorry, Lynet," he began. "I have failed you."

"Nay, you have not, my friend. Has Kenna seen to the wound?"

"Aye. I fear I would not have been victorious in any case, despite my best efforts to make some claim on you. We both know I had already lost you prior to my injury."

Lynet took the wimple from her head, finding the cloth choking the life from her. 'Twas actually done so she did not have to fully gaze at him. She had the uncanny feeling Rolf would be able to read her face and the emotions she was trying to hide from him. "I do not know what you are talking about," she stated with a quivering voice, dropping her eyes to her shuffling feet.

She was not surprised when he took her chin between his fingers and gave her no choice but to meet his gaze. "Aye...you do, but that is of no consequence now." He took her hand and bent over it, kissing it lightly. Straightening to his full height, he moved past her and put his hand on the latch to Dristan's solar. "Ian is a good man and will make you a fine husband, Lynet."

The odd, startled gasp that escaped her halted his progress in opening the door. She watched his brow rise in a silent demand to tell him what had caused such a reaction. She took a step closer, as though she wanted to delay the inevitable. "Ian said much the same about you."

"Did he now?"

"Aye."

Rolf gave a slight chuckle afore his composure returned whilst he masked his feelings from her. "I am most surprised he would think I would be a good husband."

She shook her head realizing her mistake in not clarifying her words to him. "Nay, not about being a good husband, but how you are a good man."

He gave her a lazy, charming grin, and she felt as if a little piece of her heart died inside, knowing she had inadvertently hurt him. "Well...that would be more like what I would have expected from him." He leaned down and dared much by giving her a short kiss upon her forehead. "I pray you shall have all you ever desired in your life with him."

Afore she could form any reply, he was gone. She stood in silence, looking stupidly at the closed door, almost willing him to return to her side so she could explain herself. But what was there really to clarify? Rolf knew her better than she knew herself. With Ian's appearance and determination in the games, 'twas only a matter of time afore the Scotsman would become victorious. There were few who had not already fallen victim to Ian's steadfastness to win her hand. Even Rolf had known 'twas only a matter of time 'til Lynet would let her defenses fall and open her heart to Ian of Urquhart.

She descended the turret stairs with a heavy heart and made her way to the kitchen more resolute than ever to keep her mind off her troubles. She had just sliced several pieces of cheese and an apple when she became aware she was not alone. She was surprised to see one of Ian's guards standing afore her. She supposed she should be afraid to be alone with someone she was not familiar with, but nothing was further from the truth.

"Connor, is it not?" Lynet asked and saw his nod. "Is something amiss?"

"Aye, milady. 'Tis me laird. He be runnin' a fever."

Lynet began collecting various herbs from cook's supply. "Why did not you come fetch me sooner then?" she stated in anger.

"He would not 'ave it, milady," Connor explained. "Said he would see tae his own damn care, pardon me language."

"Never mind. Take me to him, and hurry!"

Lynet reached for a cloak hanging from a wooden peg near the door and settled the garment around her head and shoulders. She all but ran to keep up with the tall giant beside her, who took her elbow as he ushered her to Ian's tent. She did not wait for permission to come in, but quickly entered, making her way to the bed of furs Ian was resting upon. His head was burning with heat. She would have held some hope he was on the mend if such warmth was accompanied with perspiration, but his skin was dry to the touch. 'Twas not a good sign.

"Get some water boiling on the fire then send a lad to fetch cool water from the river," Lynet ordered and began pulling things from the satchel she had brought. She looked up and saw Angus had taken Connor's place. She nodded towards the man. "Come...help me turn him so I can remove the bandage."

They worked swiftly. Lynet cleansed the wound and liked not what she saw. Quickly coming to a decision, she reached over and put a dirk into the heart of the fire afore her. She made another paste from the herbs and gently placed the concoction into Ian's injury.

"We shall seal the wound," she stated, reaching for the dagger.

"Do you not need to remove the paste you just put into his side?"

"Nay, it will not harm him, but only help with his healing."

She watched the tip of her dirk as it turned a bright red. "The best course of action is to close up everything inside to kill the infection."

"He willna like it, milady," Angus uttered.

"I suspect as much, but you must help me by holding him down whilst I run the blade across his skin."

Angus got into position, and afore Lynet could change her mind, she ran the red hot blade across the whiteness of Ian's skin. He bellowed in rage and bucked like the wildest stallion. The smell of scorched skin fill the air. Yet, Angus remained firm in his resolve, and 'twas only a moment afore any strength Ian still held left him. He wearily collapsed on his makeshift bed, much to the relief of Lynet.

Connor returned, carrying a bucket of the frigid water from the river. From the looks of his boots and hose, he had attended to the task himself, since he all but left a puddle of water to mark his path.

Lynet took a cloth and dipped it into the bucket then laid it gently on Ian's forehead. She gave the guards a sideways glance and all but dismissed them. "Go find your rest men and have no fear. I shall not leave him unattended and will see to his healing. I promise, he will yet live to fight another day."

She worked far into the night, exchanging cloths when they became warm from the heat of his body. She tried to get him to sip on some broth, but he would have none of it. She at last gave up for the time being, seeing as she was making more of a mess of things without much of a result to show for her efforts.

Yet, still his fever raged on, far into the late evening hours. Lynet began to pray 'til her eyes became heavy from lack of sleep. She laid her head down next to this still man who had stolen her heart years afore. With loving thoughts filling her soul for Ian MacGillivray, she closed her eyes and fell fast asleep.

⚬❦❧⚬

Ian opened his eyes and peered above him with blurred vision. Opening his mouth, he attempted to lick his dry lips. He was parched and desperately in need of something to quench his mighty thirst.

"Wine," he called out, although the voice he heard sounded as though 'twas not his own, for 'twas raspy, at best, to his ears.

He felt a movement beside him and somehow managed to rise up on one elbow. Such a small effort on his part caused the room to spin inside his head. He closed his eyes to halt the movement that almost took the last of his strength. *Bloody hell, what is wrong with me?*

A calming voice came to him then, soothing his spirit 'til the wetness of cool water ran down his throat. He reached for the cup, attempting to gulp the contents, since his thirst was so great.

"Go easy now, Ian," the voice whispered to his soul. "You must needs take small sips, my love."

He laid himself back down upon the furs beneath him and leveled his gaze upon the woman who knelt beside him. She was a vision to be sure...an angel gracing his poor sorry form with her goodness and healing touch. Her golden hair framed her face like a halo, and he knew, without a doubt, a guardian from heaven was watching over him. Hesitantly, he reached out a hand to slowly cup her cheek. He was rewarded to hear her sigh most pleasingly, even as her own hand grasped at his.

"I am dead, then?" he mumbled.

Her smile reached her glorious eyes, and she placed a tender loving kiss in his palm. A truly loving gesture, but one he was not surely worthy of, from one of God's own.

"Nay...you yet live. I have prayed for you, Ian, and am most thankful your fever has broken."

"What happened to me?" Confusion wracked his brain whilst he tried to understand her words.

She did not bother to state the obvious, but laid a cool cloth upon his head. "You have not been well, my laird, and should have called me sooner."

His mind began to clear 'til his vision focused on the young lass afore him. "Lynet?"

"Aye...rest yourself 'til you are completely healed."

"You will not leave me?" he asked quietly.

She brushed a lock of his hair from his forehead that threatened to spill across his eye. "Nay...I will stay with you always, Ian."

Her declaration restored his faith in himself that he would call her his wife. Silence came between them with only the sound of the crackling fire for noise as its smoke rose up through an opening in the canvas above. He heard dripping water, and a cool cloth was placed upon his forehead. His eyes never left hers whilst she continued her administrations on his behalf. She lifted the bandage on his side and replaced it with a poultice that took the sting from his wound.

He finally found his voice. "I never forgot you, Lynet." His words lingered in the air, and he saw hope alight in her face.

"You need not say words you do not mean, Ian. The past is the past. Let any hard feelings I may have felt stay there. The only thing that matters is you are here now and must needs get well."

He pointed to a nearby table. "Would you bring me that small chest?" Ian asked quietly, finding a renewed strength with Lynet's nearness.

She retrieved the small box and brought it with her to sit down next to him. Folding her hands in her lap, she waited shyly for him with a blush upon her face. Ian pushed the box towards her. "Go ahead...open it," he urged. "The proof you seek is there for you to see I speak no falsehood."

Her hands shook as she flipped open the lid. He continued his perusal of her with much interest whilst she began taking various items out and carefully laying them upon the bed. She had almost reached the bottom when her hand halted and her mouth formed an O of surprise. She covered her lips with her fingers whilst tears shimmered in her eyes. "Oh, Ian!"

He knew what she had found, so he rose up and pulled forth an aged green ribbon from the bottom of the chest. 'Twas a favor Lynet had bestowed upon him in her youth. She had embroidered the token herself when she was no more than ten summers. The stitching was far from perfect, but he had not cared. He could still close his eyes and see her, as if 'twas but yester morn when she had asked to tie it to his arm. Her eyes had been such a brilliant shade of blue that summer day. He had been honored to receive his first ever token of affection from her, especially since he himself had been so young at the time and more or less full of self-worth. He had kept the ribbon with him always in remembrance of a pixie-like faerie who had followed his every move.

"You saved it?" Her voice was barely loud enough to hear. But Ian could tell she was pleased by his gesture of keeping this bit of remembrance from her childhood.

"Aye."

"I cannot believe you kept my favor all these years."

"How could I not?" Ian did not take his eyes from her as he made a large loop in the ribbon. Her breathing accelerated, as if she realized what he was about to ask of her. "Handfast with me Lynet, and let us put an end to this calamity to claim you in marriage by anyone other than myself. Handfast with me, and I promise you will not regret your decision."

"Dristan will be furious that we—"

He cut off her words and sat up clasping her cool hands in his own. "I care not what Dristan thinks."

"But everyone will be so disappointed in me. That I would use such trickery when the games have yet to be completed..."

"Dristan and your family will forgive us our trespass. I only care that you will agree to become my wife."

Her breath left her whilst she pondered his words. "For how long?" she managed to whisper.

"For as long as you would like to make the arrangement between us. I will leave the length up to you."

Tears welled up in her eyes, and Ian was not sure if they were tears of joy or of remorse. Her words confirmed they were the latter. "I could not bear to become your wife in every sense of the word, only to have our union mean nothing come a year's time if you so choose to end our marriage. What if there is a child? What would become of us then?"

He pulled Lynet into his arms, and her hands wrapped carefully around his waist. "Then we will make our marriage vows to last for always. We will handfast now 'til we can call Father Donovan to us and seal our union afore the holy eyes of God."

"But my family may disown me for such a lack of prudence." Lynet sat up, wiping the moisture from her eyes.

"Let me worry about your family. I will take care of everything, if you would just tell me you will agree to our joining, sweet Lynet."

He watched her emotions race across her face 'til her visage transformed to one of a firm resolve. "For once, I shall think of no one other than myself," she whispered, and she raised her eyes to gaze into his own. She smiled, and her happiness tugged at his heart. "Aye, I will have you, Ian MacGillivray, for my husband."

Ian's breath left him in a rush of excitement, and he leaned forward to brush his lips against Lynet's. "Angus! Connor! Get your sorry arses in here, and witness our union," Ian called merrily, giving her no choice to change her mind.

His guards entered as Ian took the ribbon and draped it over his wrist. Clasping Lynet's hand, he moved the favor 'til it rested around their joined limbs. With a nod towards his guardsman, Angus pulled the cords together and tied a knot, sealing their fate.

Angus cleared his throat and leveled his gaze on the suddenly shy woman. "Will ye take this man fer yer husband, milady?"

"Aye, I will indeed," Lynet said sweetly with a rosy blush to her cheeks.

"And Laird MacGillivray, will ye take this woman tae wife?" Angus inquired, yet again.

"Aye, most assuredly will I take her."

Angus remained serious in his words whilst he clasped his palm over the couple's tied hands. "The length o' the handfast will be the standard o' one year's time, me laird?"

Ian shook his head. "Nay...our union will be for a period of forever and a day."

Angus nodded his approval. "Speak yer vows then, tae one another."

Ian smiled into Lynet's sparkling eyes as they recited their vows together. "I take thee as my spouse, for today we are as one. Like the stars above, you shall be my constant light, a place I turn for comfort and security. Like the earth beneath our feet, our union will remain solid and true. I remain yours alone 'til death claims me, and, even then, my soul will find yours."

"Kiss yer bonny lass tae seal yer vows spoken this night," Angus said reverently.

Ian waved off his guardsmen as he drew his wife into his arms. Nothing had ever felt so right as to embrace this young woman and know she was his to hold for all time. He broke off their kiss, and she sighed in pleasure whilst she fingered the edges of the thread still keeping them bound. 'Twas a sight he would remember with great fondness, for many years to come.

Lynet broke their silence by beginning to untie the keepsake she had bestowed upon her knight so many years afore. She was beyond words of what had just transpired between them. Taking the favor, she carefully replaced the ribbon in the wooden chest and closed the lid.

"Come lie with me, Lynet," Ian urged, pulling back the coverlet for her to join him in their marriage bed.

She shook her head as rationality to his illness took precedence over the matters of her heart's desire to give in to his urgings. "Nay, I cannot Ian, at least, not as yet. I would not deny you your rights, as my husband, but you must needs regain your strength afore such an undertaking."

His chuckle rumbled deep within his muscular chest, even as her eyes devoured with yearning the expanse of his lightly furred torso. "You think a little thing like a dagger thrust could keep me from making you mine completely? 'Tis nothing but a small poke in my side, and surely will not hinder me in claiming you as my wife. Come...let me love you for what remains of the night."

Leaning down, she gave him a chaste kiss then watched when a frown appeared on his brow. She pushed on his chest, and he easily fell back upon the furs. "You are as weak as a newborn kitten, Ian, so do not attempt to flatter me with your prowess, and what you think you are capable of this night. We have the rest of our lives together," she whispered softly then kissed him quickly again and moved out of his reach. "Now rest yourself, for I will not have you be an ornery patient whilst under my care. I will return in a few hours, after I myself have rested and seen to my normal morning duties at the keep."

"You promise you will return?" Ian asked with sleepy eyes, proving her point he was far from being completely healed.

"Aye...nothing could keep me from your side," she answered honestly, tucking the fur about his shoulders. "Now be good, and go to sleep. I shall see you afore you even have a chance to miss me."

"I miss you already," he murmured quietly, closing his eyes as he reluctantly felt sleep claim him.

Lynet took a moment to look her fill at this man who was now her husband 'til she reached out to cup Ian's cheek. Brushing her thumb gently across the roughness of the stubble, she gave a brief smile and leaned forward to give him a soft kiss. He barely moved. Satisfied he took his rest, Lynet gathered her things and left his tent. 'Twas still many hours afore the dawn would break. If she hurried, she would still be able to catch a few hours of sleep herself and return to him after her morning ablutions and mass, come the break of day.

She began to hurry whilst humming a tune to herself, but carelessly did not pay attention to the shadows filling the night. 'Twas a mistake she realized only too late when she felt a sharp object slam against the back of her skull. Darkness began to overtake her. Her eyes rolled back in her head whilst she felt herself pitching forward. Her last thought afore she lost consciousness was the wrath Ian would surely feel when she did not keep her promise to return.

TWELVE

WHAT THE BLOODY HELL DO YOU MEAN she is missing? Who was the last to see her?" Dristan's bellowing caused several people in his solar to cringe with worry. There had been a long passage of time since any had heard so much displeasure coming from their lord.

All eyes turned in Ian's direction, as though he was, in truth, the culprit who had taken Lynet from the keep. "I can explain," he began, "She came to my tent–"

Slam! He stumbled back from the force of Rolf's fist making contact with his face. He should have seen that one coming. Yet, nothing prepared him for Rolf reaching for his throat whilst Aiden lunged around his tormentor's body to try and get a piece of him, as well. Rolf's murderous eyes blazed with fury as he squeezed tighter. Ian clawed at the hand around his neck. His head whirled as felt the room spin from his lack of air. 'Twas evident he was not completely well that he could not shake off his adversary, who himself was also wounded and fighting with only one arm! Obviously, he was still in need of Lynet's herbs and healing touch.

The chamber broke into chaos. Not that Ian cared at the moment if voices were raised loud enough to shake the rafters in the ceiling. No one seemed to pay any attention that his very breath was being taken from him. A scuffle broke out and furniture began to scrape against the stone flooring as 'twas moved. The higher pitched voices of the ladies in the chamber mingled with the deeper tones of their knights as they tried to calm the hot tempered men. Ian gasped for air and at last heard Dristan's bellow for Rolf to cease. Ian's face flushed with color as he gulped air into his burning lungs, now that his windpipe was no longer being crushed.

Rolf grabbed him by his tunic with his good arm, bringing them face to face. "I will kill you myself if you have harmed one hair on her pretty head," he threatened, giving Ian a shake.

Kenna came rushing to their side and grabbed Rolf's arm. He at last let go of his grip on Ian, and she turned her scolding eyes at him. "He has been gravely ill, Rolf, and should not be out of bed. You could at least hear his explanation, although, I can vouch for his illness." She began shaking her fist at the man, as though he were a misbehaving youth.

"You have been warned," Rolf pointed his finger in Ian's direction.

Ian pulled his tunic back down into place and brushed away Kenna's helping hands. "I am well, Kenna," he croaked and cleared his throat. "Stop fussing over me and leave me be!"

Kenna moved off to be consoled by her husband, but still muttered aloud about insufferable men. Dristan quickly regained control of his solar and ensured Amiria was once more settled in a chair near the hearth. That she took a dirk from her boot and was fingering its hilt whilst her violet eyes flashed angrily in his direction, gave Ian only a moment's pause. She, of all people gathered here, should know better than anyone that he would never harm her sister. Even Katherine had a perturbed look upon her features that showed she was displeased with him.

Dristan sat next to his wife and finally leveled his gaze upon Ian, who did all within his ability not to squirm with the thought of telling the fierce warrior afore him he had handfasted with his wife's sister. He gulped, trying to gain his composure when all eyes fell upon him, yet again. The hostility in this room was high, and 'twas all focused on him. God's wounds, but he felt as if the world had been ripped asunder, knowing his wife was missing.

"Well?" Dristan bellowed, drumming his fingers on the edge of his chair, giving proof his patience was at an end.

"I can explain," Ian began calmly.

"Aye, you have said as much, but minutes afore," Dristan replied, leveling his gaze upon him.

Ian eyed the occupants of the room warily. He was not so sure Amiria's dirk would not fly out in his direction once he found his words to justify what he and Lynet had done. "I must needs enlighten you to—"

"I am sure you can give full details as to why my wife's sister was in your tent without a chaperon, which is why, as you can plainly see, we all eagerly await your story," Dristan all but growled like the fierce dragon his reputation proclaimed him to be.

Aiden took a menacing step forward. "And here, I thought Rolf was the one I must needs keep my eye on."

"If she had been with me, she would not be missing now, I assure you," Rolf chimed in.

"Enough!" Amiria added, trying to calm the hot-headed men. "Let Ian have his say."

Deafening silence filled the chamber. Folding his arms across his chest, Ian hoped he appeared in charge of the situation. "I was ill from a knife wound. Although this may have been the reason Lynet was with me, for the most part, I was not coherent that anyone was attending my wounds 'til I awoke from my fever."

"But you're better now, right?" Katherine inquired. His gaze fell to hers, and Ian could see the sincerity of her question. At least someone was concerned for his wellbeing.

"Aye. Luckily I will live to see yet another day, but 'tis only because of my lady's healing touch."

Riorden took a menacing step forward, only to have his wife take his hand to halt his progress. "*Your* lady? When did she become yours for you to make such a claim on her?"

"Yester eve...when we handfasted. Lynet is my wife," Ian stated confidently, "and as such, she is no longer under your protection, Dristan."

"*Your wife?*" Dristan roared, balling his hands into fists.

Ian could have sworn the floor shook as Dristan quickly advanced, but he stood his ground. He had known this would not go over well. Hands again went around his already bruised neck as pandemonium broke out once more in the solar. But Ian's only concern was that he could not breathe for the second time in a matter of minutes. He tried to fight, but was losing the battle as he saw determined steel grey eyes ready to make him pay for his insolence. The world started to darken afore Ian's eyes as he began to lose consciousness. The Devil's Dragon demanded reparation for Ian's trespass, and by damned, reparation he would have.

Ian's eyes flickered open. Bleary eyed, several moments passed afore his vision cleared enough for him to notice he had been taken to Lynet's room. That he awoke at all, must surely be something short of a miracle and a testament Dristan did not wish him dead, after all.

He caught a slight movement and noticed Lady Katherine mending something by the fire. She was most intent on her task and had not as yet noticed he watched her. He was surprised to see her here, let alone without another woman present. Riorden must have softened in his married state if he would allow his wife to be by herself with another man, especially given what had transpired earlier. He was not sure he would be so lenient with his own dear wife, once he found her.

"Shhhhit!" Katherine hissed quietly, putting her finger in her mouth. "I friggin *hate* sewing! Damn inconvenient...that's what it is. Where the hell is a department store when you need one?"

Ian gave an amused chuckle, drawing the lady's attention to the bed. "You really are not from around here, are you, my lady?"

"You're awake!"

"Obviously...but that does not answer my question." Ian put his fingers to his throat. His voice was raspy, and it hurt to swallow. Luckily, he was still amongst the living.

Katherine put down her sewing and came to sit on the edge of the bed. Ian leaned up on one elbow and watched the woman afore him. She sat there as though 'twas the most natural thing in the world to be ensconced in a chamber with a man who was not her husband. A woman who would act so freely, in Ian's acquaintance, was no lady at all.

"You're lucky to be alive. You know that, don't you?" she responded instead, whilst still ignoring his question. "It took Riorden *and* Fletcher to pull Dristan off you. Not to mention, the three of them to keep Rolf and Aiden from taking his place."

Ian shrugged with disinterest and looked her up and down, trying to see the point of her being here.

"What?" she asked, leaning back against the bedpost.

"Riorden would allow you in a room with me alone? 'Tis most unusual," Ian drawled.

"He trusts me." 'Twas a simple answer, but still, unthinkable.

"Does he now?" Ian inquired, sitting up further on the bed.

"Yes...ummm...aye, of course he does."

"But does he trust me?" Ian leaned forward to test this woman he knew very little about. He was curious just how faithful she, in truth, was to her husband.

She leaned forward, as well, and got a strange look in her aquamarine eyes. For a moment, Ian thought she would betray Riorden, for she looked as though she were begging for his kiss. But she surprised him when she gave him a hard push, causing him to fall back upon the pillows.

"Don't even think it, buster! I've come a long way to be with the man of my dreams, and not you, or anyone else, is ever going to come between us again! The fact you're still alive to be having such a stupid conversation with me should tell you Riorden trusts you, you fool!" She began muttering about idiotic, arrogant men, who only thought about what their needs were between their legs.

"You see? There 'tis again! I have never heard speech as yours afore, let alone heard a woman voice such things aloud," Ian proclaimed. "Come...tell me from whence you hail?"

She gave a muffled laugh. "You'd never believe me in a thousand years."

"Try me..." His words lingered in the air, and Ian could see she mulled over the possibility of telling him her story.

"I don't think so, at least not yet." She gave an elegant toss of her head and reached back to pull her tawny tresses together. Swiftly, she tied a ribbon around its length, ensuring its captivity. Folding her hands in her lap, she once again relaxed and watched him. It became a staring contest between them 'til she finally voiced what was on her mind. "So you married her...well...married being a somewhat loose term, since the ceremony wasn't done before a priest."

"'Tis still binding. Besides, 'tis an old custom to handfast."

Katherine shook her head. "Old...yes, I suppose it was...umm...*is* a custom for this time period. I must admit, I've only read about such pagan rituals. Doesn't it usually have a length of time attached to the arrangement?"

Ian peered at Katherine. "If you are trying to politely ask if I will abandon Lynet and a possible babe after a year's time, then nay, we made no such stipulation for our marriage to end."

"A baby? Then your marriage has been consummated."

"I said no such thing, nor do I feel I must needs justify my actions to a woman I barely know," Ian said with a grimace.

"Well, justify them to me, or validate them to Lynet's family. One way or the other, you will still have to confront Dristan. I won't even mention what Amiria has said of you."

He flinched. How could he not? "I would think it more prudent to find out who has taken Lynet, than to worry about how our marriage came about," Ian rose and found his sword lying on a nearby table. Strapping the blade to his side, he turned again towards the strangest woman he had ever met. She was a bold one. He did not know how Riorden put up with her queer ways. "What have I missed?"

Katherine stood, as well, and retrieved her sewing. She squinted whilst she scrutinized her work. "Damn, I'll have to start again. The seam isn't straight. Ugh! I'd rather clean toilets."

"My lady?"

"Huh?"

Ian ran a hand through his hair. "What...have...I...missed?" he reiterated and enunciated each word slowly, as if speaking to a child.

Her brow rose at his tone. "Don't speak to me like that. I'm not dimwitted, you know."

"My apologies, madam. I but wish to find my wife as quickly as possible so I can take her home."

"Her family may have something to say about that. Besides, Berwyck is her home," Katherine stated calmly.

"Not any longer. Her place is with her husband and at Urquhart. If you do not know what has happened since I've been put here, then I will find someone who can inform me of the circumstances surrounding my wife's disappearance," he bellowed, storming towards the door.

"For God's sake, get your head out of your ass, you dope! I'm tired of men with their testosterone levels off the charts. Always ready to go off to war and leave us women behind. It's really very irritating."

Ian was aghast, hearing her words, but had to admit he did not hear most of what she hollered, other than where he should take his head from! "I beg your pardon?"

"As well, you should. I accept your apology." Ian scowled at her, since he was not aware he had offered a request for her forgiveness. She smiled at him, put down her sewing, and took hold of his hand. They went to sit by the fire, and he used every bit of patience he had left to wait to hear what she needed to tell him.

"You'll have to excuse me, Ian," Katherine began demurely with a soft voice. 'Twas a complete contrast to the woman who had raised the hackles on the back of his neck, but moments afore. He just could not figure her out. "Sometimes, I forget myself, and where I am."

His brow rose. At least she admitted she was not from these parts. "Is there word about my wife?"

"I'm afraid not. It's hectic and crazy as hell out there with a multitude of people packing up their camps and heading in too many different directions, if you were to ask my opinion. Dristan has cancelled the remaining games, for obvious reasons. He has already searched the tents of those who are still here and sent off several groups of knights on various routes to find her. So far, they've turned up no sign of her."

"She could be with any one of those who have already left Berwyck," he grumbled.

"That's precisely my point. We just need to be a little patient to see what turns up."

Ian stood abruptly. "You canna expect me to just sit here whilst my wife is at the hands of someone desperate enough to take her from beneath Dristan's very nose. What kind of coward sits back and does nothing?" he shouted.

Katherine stood up and poked her finger into his chest. "Well, you don't want to be running around the countryside in circles, chasing your tail, like someone else we know, do you?" she yelled right back. Her eyes widened from the words that came rushing from her lips. "Umm...I didn't mean to—"

"By Saint Michael's wings! Are you saying Rolf is even now out there, looking for Lynet, whilst I have been for the most part reluctantly napping?" He strode furiously to the door.

Reaching for the handle, he halted when a gentle hand was placed on his arm. Worried eyes met his as he tried to calm the anger threatening to erupt inside him.

"Please Ian, just be careful, would you? I have every bit of faith you will find Lynet. Just don't do anything rash if you come across Rolf. He loves her, too."

"I never said I loved her, Lady Katherine...although, I do care for her." She got such a sad look in her eyes. Ian instantly regretted his words. "I do not wish to cause you distress, but I barely know the lady she has become. I needed a wife. She was someone I remembered from my past. 'Twill take some time with each other for affection to grow into something to be called love, if such an emotion even exists."

"Then, maybe it's best if Rolf finds her first. At least, he has no qualms facing the truth he is in love with her." He watched her whilst she tried to think of something else to say, but she must not have come up with anything, since her lips shut closed in a firm line of disappointment.

Opening the door, he stood in the passageway waiting for...something...but he knew not what. He turned back to Riorden's lady and gave her a bow. She returned it with a nod of her own. "I pray our paths shall cross again someday, Lady Katherine. Mayhap, then you shall trust me with your tale."

She gave him a very lovely smile that reached her eyes and began to laugh. "Oh, I'm sure we'll see each other again, Ian. After all, we're practically family, in a really long distance kind of way."

Ian shook his head in puzzlement at her strange words, the meaning of which only she knew. "Then, I bid you farewell 'til we one day meet again," he said politely.

"Take care of yourself, Ian," she whispered. "I hope someday you realize exactly what you've found with Lynet, before it's too late. I promise, if you let love into your heart, you'll never regret marrying her. Trust me, it'll be worth it."

She left him standing alone in the passageway. He stood there in silence for several moments, staring at the stone walls and pondering her words. He shook his head to get his thoughts in order and began making his way down the tower stairs. He would see what food Cook could quickly provide for him and then see to his horse. He did not relish the thought of Rolf finding Lynet afore him. He had no doubt the man would do all in his power to convince Lynet to forsake her vows she had made to him. He quickened his pace whilst his brow furrowed in anger. 'Twas time to find his wife.

THIRTEEN

L YNET'S FEET FLEW ACROSS THE GROUND as she ran. She cared not that she felt every stone beneath her feet. The shoes she wore offered no sense of protection from protruding objects under their soft soles. Practically out of breath, she continued her frantic need to escape those who had stolen her from her home. She knew she was losing her battle to outwit those imbeciles who allowed her to take flight in the first place. With the sound of thundering hooves right behind her, she knew her freedom would shortly be at an end.

Raucous laughter erupted behind her and she knew they had her in their sight, although she was certain they would no longer be merry once they returned to camp. She had at least one thing to be grateful for. She remained unsullied by the group holding her hostage, but she was not sure how much tolerance their leader still had for her. Given her latest attempt to escape, Lynet did not think she would be allowed alone again, no matter the amount of begging for privacy she asked for. At least she could tell herself she had tried and put up a fight to obtain her freedom.

The sight of the massive war horse beside her quickly blocked her vision. She continued to run abreast of the beast 'til a body leaned low over the saddle. A gasp escaped her lips when she was scooped up into arms she swore were as hard as the solid trunk of a towering oak tree. Thrown against his chest, she began to squirm with all her might, but 'twas of no use. She was captured and pinned to his muscular torso whilst his arm all but twisted around her waist, ensuring her captivity and the loss of whatever brief bit of liberty she had felt.

"You try my patience, lass." With the slightest touch of his knee, his stallion came to a sudden stop whilst she stared into the furious eyes of her captor.

"I am surprised you came for me yourself. Why not allow your lackeys to do your work for you?" she spat out, staring into Calum's furious features.

"They will be dealt with, as will you, my lady," he hissed, turning his gaze to those he rode with. "Well? What are you waiting for? Return to camp!" Abruptly, he turned her around so she sat more securely atop his lap, and she let out a gasp of outrage at the intimacy of her situation with her captor. She dared not squirm, given her current position, for sitting side saddle had her at a disadvantage. At least with her facing on an angle, she did not have to look upon his wretched face if she so chose. Ignoring him would be easy.

They covered the ground quickly and surely much faster than when Lynet had fled on foot. When she saw their campsite, she became instantly aware she, in truth, had not gone as far as she had hoped. 'Twas not hard to miss that his men had been busy during her brief respite from her unwanted reality. Already they were breaking up camp and putting out the fire to continue their journey north.

Calum tightened his hold around her waist causing her to entirely feel every inch of his chest against her shoulder and side. She tried to calm her fears, but they were rising to the forefront of her mind, knowing she had angered her captor.

She felt his warm breath on her neck, but 'twas the underlying threat in the meaning of his words that caused her to shiver. "Stay in the saddle if you know what is good for you. You will regret your rash actions to disobey me if I must needs chase you again this day."

Lynet watched as he slid to the ground in one fluid movement. He gave her only a brief glance to ensure she remained seated afore he left her sitting there with shaking limbs. Her breath left her in an unexpected burst of relief that she remained unmolested. Still, she grabbed a hold of the pommel to steady her frayed nerves, noticing exactly how much her hands were truly shaking from the ordeal she had been facing. Her eyes darted back and forth to see who watched her. Several men stood nearby, but their attention was focused on Calum, whose angry stride lengthened the distance between them.

The reins were within inches of her fingertips. Should she dare to make yet another effort to gain her freedom? Her eyes traveled to Calum's retreating backside, but something inside her screamed out not to test his tolerance any further this day.

Almost as if he sensed where her stray thoughts had led her, Calum called out to one of his men. "Lachlan!"

"What?" the clansmen bellowed, causing conversations amongst the men to become muted.

Calum halted his progress to peer at the man. "Is that anyway to speak to your laird?"

"You were my brother afore you became head of the clan," Lachlan sneered.

"But I am still your laird. Ensure the lady does not get any more ideas of escaping in her pretty little head."

"I am not your lackey."

Calum peered at him. "Aye...you are," he gloated.

Lachlan spat into the dirt afore making his way to her horse. He removed the straps of leather from her reach, but continued to glare angrily as his brother's retreating back. She supposed with the reins firmly held in the grip of a disgruntled man, such an act resolved any further temptation she may have had on her part to pursue another useless attempt to flee her captors...at least for now.

'Twas well she had listened to her inner voice of reason, instead of acting on her chance to leave her abductor far behind. She had a horrible feeling pass through her when she saw Calum reached for a dagger from the back of his belt. He came afore the man whose lapse in judgment had allowed Lynet to, however briefly, escape.

"Me laird, I—"

The soldier's words got no further, as Calum raised his arm and slit the man's throat. A look of disbelief swept briefly across the man's face afore his eyes went blank. Calum carelessly wiped his dirk on the man's tunic, giving him a slight push. Lynet could no longer gaze on the bloody and ghastly scene afore her. Turning her head, she heard the warrior's body fall to the ground with a loud thump. She swallowed hard in an effort not to lose what little she had in her stomach, knowing the cost for her brief chance at freedom had been a man's life.

Calum returned to her nonchalantly, as though he had not just done something so repulsive, but moments afore. His countenance gave her the impression he would show her no mercy were she to attempt to flee, yet again. Lynet took a deep breath and returned his steady gaze with one of her own, hoping her face showed whatever bit of bravery she still held deep within her. Calum continued glaring at her in silence with those intimidating black eyes of his 'til Lynet could no longer stand to look at him. She turned her head away, refusing to give him the satisfaction of seeing her fear.

"He could have still been of use to us," Lachlan said, handing over the reins to Calum. "You did not have to kill him over some stupid woman."

"Would you rather I had put you out of your misery, since you were the one to hire the man for our company?"

"Nay, of course not," Lachlan replied grimly.

"'Twas a lack of judgement on your part to trust the fool who could not keep one slip of a girl from escaping."

"And he has now paid the price of his life for his error. That does not mean he could not have still been of some use, or that I wish to take his place. You always were such a bastard."

Calum took a fist full of Lachlan's tunic, bringing them nose to nose. "I believe, dear *brother*, 'tis not me who is the bastard."

Lynet wondered at the significance of their *brotherly affection* towards one another, since the two brothers hardly looked related at all. Mayhap, 'twas the cause of Lachlan's anger, that he was not a legitimate heir. 'Twould explain the animosity between them.

The two men began a shoving match afore Lachlan landed in the dirt with Calum towering over him. "Never, and I mean never, question my authority again. Especially in front of the men, lest you wish to end up like your friend over there. Now, get out of my sight, and mount up. We are wasting daylight."

Lynet's attention returned to Calum when he put his foot in the stirrup and swung his leg over the saddle. 'Twas unnerving when she became uncomfortably aware of every inch of his body once he settled her upon his lap again and held her close. Calum turned to reach behind them to grab something from the leather bag attached to the rear of the horse's tack. She was hardly surprised when he took hold of her wrists and bound them together with the rope in a tight knot.

"'Tis not necessary to bind me," she declared in a huff of righteous indignation. "Where do you think I will run to on foot that you could not easily catch me, as you did but a while ago?"

"I take no further chances with you, nor do I plan to leave you in the care of others." He leaned forward, causing Lynet to gasp, not knowing his intent. His brow rose as if he knew she thought he would steal a kiss. "Do not think I am not tempted, lass."

She looked at him with enough skepticism to doubt his honor that he would not harm her. She could not for the life of her figure out why he had not already taken advantage of her and lay claim to her maidenhood. "Then why tie my hands? Surely, you can see the meaning of this foolishness if you continue to keep me hostage."

"Precisely why I will leave you unharmed, lest you test me further. Think you Dristan of Berwyck will be lenient if he knows I do not return you in the same exact condition as when you left his keep?"

"Take me home," Lynet demanded.

He paid her no mind as he reached for the reins. With a tap of his heel into the side of his horse, the animal bolted into motion. His men followed close behind.

"Nay," he at last answered her with a tone that clearly implied he would not change his mind.

"I will tell my kin no harm befell me, my laird," she pleaded. "Just take me home to my family."

"I told you, nay. I would have taken you to wife, if I could have won your hand. But I could not stand by, watching you give your affection and dowry to the MacGillivray laird."

"And who are you to tell me where my affections should turn. I never said they went to Ian, or any other man!"

"The fact you speak of him by his first name tells me you cared enough for the man. He won plenty of matches to prove he would have you, no matter the cost. I could not afford to lose what you would bring to fill my coffers. Instead of a dowry, I shall now claim a ransom. I am sure Dristan will pay any amount I ask to have you returned to his protection."

"Only a fool would take something belonging to the Devil's Dragon," she sneered meaningfully, "or are you so witless you are not aware of his reputation?" She gave him a knowing grin that her rescue was imminent.

"Hence, therein lays my need to put as much distance as possible between us. Now, shut your trap, else I will find something to gag you with so you no longer bore me with your ranting."

They rode hard the entire day with only a few short breaks to rest their steeds. With each mile they traveled, she left Berwyck farther and farther behind. The lowlands of Scotland had disappeared hours ago. Dismay filled her as the terrain became unfamiliar to her. She was never left alone, and she cursed her foolishness this morn, for now she was guarded more diligently than ever afore.

Dusk began to fall. Lynet would have marveled at the brilliant color of the sky with the setting sun, but there was nothing to rejoice about, even with the beauty of God's work afore her eyes. She was too tired, and yet, she was anxious, as well, for she knew 'twas only a matter of time afore Ian found her.

They made camp that night beneath the sparkling stars. Her wrists were chaffed from the rubbing of the rough rope. Trying to find some form of relief, she tore strips of linen from her tattered gown to put between her bleeding skin and the irritating cords ensuring her captivity. She was eventually thrown an even rougher blanket made of coarse wool, and Lynet made herself as comfortable as possible on the hard ground. Calum settled himself next to her...as always...keeping her within his reach and never out of his sight.

Her eyes darted to the shadows of the evening air, wondering if Ian was out there, even now, searching for her and hopefully looking in the right direction. She began to pray that once he did, they would remain unscathed from the violence surrounding Calum's demeanor and his cause. He would not take it well that his prize was stolen from beneath his constant vigil and by one whom had already claimed her heart.

FOURTEEN

ROLF BRISKLY RUBBED AT THE STIFFNESS of his sword arm, trying to get some circulation into his numb limb. He flexed his fingers into a fist and felt a renewed anger that he was still incapacitated and not up to his normal standard for fighting. He knew 'twas stupid on his part to be out searching for Lynet whilst still recovering from his injury. With only a few of Dristan's garrison to guard his back, he had left the keep, not caring for his own wellbeing, but to find the one woman who he cared for, beyond all others.

'Twas a pointless endeavor. He knew that, deep inside his soul. The minute Ian MacGillivray had shown up at Berwyck, he had known any chance for Lynet to learn to love him had vanished. He could still remember the exact moment she had espied the man waltzing across the Great Hall, as if he owned the place...and her! Her face had become radiant with joy afore she hid her feelings behind a mask of triviality. She had looked so lovely, and Rolf had become jealous, for she had never looked at him in such a manner. Still, he felt determined to find the lady who had all but stolen his heart.

At least, he could say he had tried his best to win some form of her affection. Yet, fate continued to thwart his desires to have the fair Lynet as his bride. Rolf had not been fooled, nor had he been misled by her kiss, no matter how much effort she had attempted to put into it. He may have been the first to taste her innocence, but he knew who would be her last. Surly, 'twould not be him.

Bloody Hell! What was he doing out here, anyway? 'Twould be sheer blind luck if he came across whoever had stolen Lynet. Dristan and Amiria had tried to reason with him to await further word from the scouts they had scattered across the countryside in search of her. But, no...he let his common sense play no part in his decision to find Lynet himself. Mayhap, he was a fool, after all.

There was no doubt in his mind that another would be fast on his heels in search of the lady, and, perchance, this was the true reason behind his reckless behavior to find her first. He wanted to make an effort to change her mind, no matter how futile such an endeavor would be. Yet, Kenna's prediction continued to haunt and cloud his judgment. 'Twas evident, Ian had more of a claim on the lady than he did.

In frustration, he threw a stick into the fire afore his feet as his thoughts were consumed with the gall of that man. Yet, such a scenario, he had certainly not seen coming. Who in their right mind would have thought the couple would *handfast* to one another? If he had thought Lynet capable of such a feat, *he* would have suggested the arrangement, as well, instead of wanting a proper wedding with friends and family as witnesses to their union. He supposed if he thought about it rationally, there would be no chance in hell Dristan would have ever let them handfast whilst Lynet was under his protection. Small wonder his liege lord had been ready to choke the very life from Ian. He had had the very same similar thoughts himself.

The sound of approaching riders brought Rolf and the guards to attention with hands firmly clasped on the hilts of their swords. There was only one sort who would be out at this hour of the night, and he did not care to waste all his energy fighting off a bunch of worthless thieves.

The outline of the first horse hovered in the shadows of darkness afore the steed moved into the light of their campsite, followed closely by two others. Rolf cursed to himself at whom he espied, for the man who emerged afore him like a vision, had the appearance of an avenging angel righting the wrongs of mankind.

Again...Why was he not surprised? Ian of Urquhart sat confidently in his saddle, all but flaying him alive with his angry, hostile eyes. The unwelcome trespasser jumped lightly down from his steed and came to stand afore him. Rolf refused to back down to the younger man as they stood toe to toe. Nothing would give him greater pleasure than for Ian to make the first move. At least with his fist planted firmly in Ian's face, he would have a moment of satisfaction for all he had lost when it came to the fair Lynet!

Ian could hardly believe he had actually found Rolf. His anger rose to unbelievable proportions as they stood ready to fight each other over a woman. He took hold of Rolf by his tunic, even as his adversary grabbed at his. "She is *my* wife," Ian shouted. "You have no right to be searching for her."

Rolf pushed Ian away and went back to his place by the fire. 'Twas almost as though all of Rolf's energy left him with his sudden appearance. "And she just as easily could have been mine," the obnoxious man grumbled under his breath. "Besides...I am her captain, and, hence, she is mine to safeguard."

"That privilege was taken from you when she came under the protection of my name."

"And yet, you have not been sealed together as man and wife under the eyes of a holy priest of God."

"Our handfast is still binding. Even you must know that," Ian roared.

"Nevertheless, she is, or was, my responsibility, and my honor is at stake. You do know about honor, do you not? If so, you must surely understand my reasoning behind my actions. She was taken whilst under my care. Hence, 'til found, I *will* search for her."

Ian felt some of the hostility leave him, and yet, he kept his guard up. Still eyeing his rival for Lynet's affection, he was surprised when the older man made a slight gesture to join him by the fire.

"You may as well sit, Ian. There are still plenty of hours left of the eve, and we may as well take our ease together and join forces come the morn in our quest to find your lady."

At least, Rolf acknowledged Lynet was his. Surely, that must mean something. Ian came and took a place next to the man on the ground. There had been a time when he had considered Rolf a friend. They had trained together and fought side by side to hold Berwyck Castle in the name of England's king. It did not matter that Ian would be leaving his allegiance to England behind as he took his place as laird of Urquhart Castle. He understood honor and all that went with a code of chivalry for one who has been knighted. He himself had lived most of his life by such a code. 'Twas of no consequence he now wore a plaid and his duty would lay with Scotland and its king. Some habits were still extremely hard to dismiss.

His gaze returned to Rolf, and he noticed the knight wore only his everyday clothing. No armor, nor chain mail. There was nothing to protect him from an inevitable fight that could cost him his life, except the sword at his side. Considering Rolf's injury to his arm and the knowledge he himself was not completely healed, a fight with the enemy to save Lynet did not bode well for a favorable outcome.

Ian massaged the wound still mending at his side. Truthfully, he was not in much better shape than his old comrade-in-arms. "You ride light, I see," Ian mentioned the obvious, "and with only three guards. What were you thinking?"

Rolf shrugged. "I see you travel the same, so I think we were both idiots with like minds. I am sure Dristan will be appalled we thought so little of ourselves to travel thusly. He will think he failed in our training."

"I am sure we will get an earful when next we meet."

"Is not that plaid a little drafty?" Rolf inquired with a smirk as he turned the conversation to Ian's attire.

"One becomes used to it."

"I shall have to take your word for it."

"The plaid gives one a certain amount of freedom, and it keeps me warm on a chilly night. Those Irish were clever when they came up with such a garment. Although, most times, I still wear hose with it."

"I have no idea how running around half naked or possibly showing your arse to the world during a good wind can possibly give you any form of comfort or protection. You hardly look like a knight of old, Ian."

"Times change, but I still adhere to our code of honor," Ian muttered as he stretched out his long legs whilst attempting to get comfortable. He grabbed his plaid and wrapped it around his shoulders for warmth. "I will assume you will remember such, once we find my wife."

"You do not have to keep reminding me you have claimed her, Ian. I have taken your point."

"Just stating the obvious, old man, in case you had forgotten."

"'Tis hardly likely I could ever forget Lynet cannot be mine. You do not have to continue to rub my nose in it," Rolf declared with a hint of bitterness in his voice.

"I will concede then and expect no further argument that you will try to claim her."

Rolf took a stick and began stirring the embers of the fire. "'Tis not as if I, or anyone else, for that matter, even stood a chance, once you arrived at Berwyck."

Ian tossed his old friend a glare. "What is that supposed to mean?"

"Do you not have eyes inside your head, or are you merely daft? Do you really have no inkling how the lady has always felt for you?"

"She had a childish fascination with me, but hardly knows the man I have become."

"Think you that means anything to Lynet when her feelings ruled her judgment?"

"What do you know of her feelings?" Ian asked harshly as jealousy overtook common sense.

"I am the person who has guarded her, not the one who left her grieving for what she could not have for six years. I was the one who watched her grow into the beautiful young woman she is today. I would be blind if I had not realized where her affections lay, despite my best efforts to let her know another loved her. Given that, I think I know her feelings better than most people, including you." Rolf made no further comment as to his knowledge of Lynet. Instead, he found his own blanket to keep the cool night air away. Throwing another log on the fire, he at last relaxed and closed his eyes. "Wake me afore the dawn," Rolf ordered quietly. "We should make an early start to find Lynet."

Ian harrumphed under his breath, feeling as if he was being likened to some youth who did not know better than to rise early to make the most of the day. He noticed Angus and Connor returning from scouting the area. "Take turns with Rolf's guards, and continue to keep an eye open to the lurking shadows. I do not wish to be taken unawares whilst I sleep. We ride with the dawn."

He watched his men meld into the gloom of the evening night. Uneasiness descended around Ian's soul, as though in forewarning of something dreadful to come. Nervous about what the morrow may bring, Ian had enough of a concern that he took another moment to look at the perimeter of where the campfire light shone beyond the darkness of the trees surrounding them. Seeing nothing noteworthy or any signs of imminent danger, he shook off such an unsettling premonition, thinking he had spent too much time of late with Kenna.

He closed his eyes, thinking of Lynet and how she would view her new home on Loch Ness. He would be most pleased to show her where he had grown up and watch in fascination as she made Urquhart a place to raise their family. He stifled a hearty yawn and settled down for the night. Falling fast asleep, he dreamed of how happy their marriage would be and of the woman he would claim as his lady wife and finally be able to call his own.

FIFTEEN

CALUM TUGGED SHARPLY ON THE ROPE, causing Lynet to hurtle forward with enough force that she sprawled face first in the dirt. She was a stubborn wench, he would give her that, but he was tired of dallying this day. They needed speed and a fair amount of distance from Berwyck afore he would feel any sense of safety for his sorry hide. They must make haste. He could almost feel the heat from the Devil's Dragon breathing down his neck!

Momentarily ill at ease, with thoughts of having to come up against such a powerful foe, he tugged again for the girl to pick herself up off the ground. Calum listened to the gasp escape her lips. Her eyes met his in a furious display of animosity. She hated him, not that he cared. 'Twas not hard to miss her loathing look of contempt she so unabashedly tossed him. He knew 'twas because of the uncontrollable situation she found herself in. Lynet was not good at masking her feelings, for what she felt for him was written all over her beautiful visage. A visage that now bore the signs of several scrapes along her cheek and chin.

He offered her his hand, but she only slapped at it, as if repulsed to even come this close to him.

He could see her wrists were raw and bleeding from the burns of the coarse rope, yet, he would not loosen the knots, in fear of her escaping. She had gotten past his guards more times than he wanted to admit in the past few days. Such an act had already cost one man his life. At this rate, he would be lucky to reach the Highlands with anyone left other than himself and this troublesome girl.

"If you wish to take care of your personal business, I suggest you pick yourself up post haste," he growled. "We have wasted enough time this morn with your attempts to dawdle the day away."

Slowly, she arose from the ground and spit out the dirt that had landed in her mouth during her fall. The glare she tossed him was like the sharpest of daggers thrown in his direction. If she had had a blade, Calum knew her dagger would be protruding, even now, from his chest. *God's blood she has spirit.* Perchance, he *should* keep her for himself after all, and to hell with asking for a ransom. He always did prefer a woman who could stand up to him, instead of some meek little mouse. The more he pondered his alternative, the more he decided against such an action. Keeping her would not fill his depleted coffers and ensure the safeguard of his estate. He needed coin, and he needed it fast. He must needs stick to his plan.

"Untie me," she snarled.

"Nay, I will not."

"How am I to see to my needs then with my hands secured like this?"

He studied her for a moment, understanding her dilemma. He went to her. She did not back down, but held out her arms for him to loosen the rope. He considered her request and again noticed the bleeding flesh at her wrists. 'Twas a sharp contrast to the creaminess of her skin. She gave a sigh of relief when the coarse ropes left her abused wrists. But such a freedom was short lived when he refastened the rope quickly around her waist.

"Nay!" she cried out.

He tossed her a smug look, as if he had already read her thoughts. They were mirrored clearly on her face. "Your hands are free. 'Twill have to suffice."

"But, I need my privacy!"

"I've lengthened the rope, lass. 'Tis all the privacy I will allow you, seeing as you canna be trusted. You best be about your morning ablutions and keep the rope taut, else I will be seeing more of your very delectable body than you would no doubt like."

"You are a brute," she shouted at him.

"A brute, I may be, but I am also a man who is losing what patience I have left. I care not if you piss in the woods or do so right here in front of me. Make your choice, lass, afore I take it from you and set you back upon my horse," Calum warned, waiting for her decision.

She stomped her foot. 'Twas a clear indication he spoiled yet another idea in her pretty little head about an attempted escape. He crossed his arms on his chest, giving the rope a flick, almost as if he was putting his mount into motion. His action of treating her like an animal had the desired effect.

"Damn you to hell!" she cursed. She made her way to the nearest tree afore she gave him another glare of those brilliant blue eyes. "The least you could do is turn your back."

Chuckling, he gave her this one concession, even as he heard her muttering further oaths on his early demise. *God...what a woman!*

Lynet peeked around the tree and saw her captor had indeed turned his back. She would have sighed in relief, but instead, cussed him further, much to his amusement, since he was still within hearing distance. How was she to obtain her freedom on her own? She could not fathom another option she had not already tried in the past several days. Now she had this blasted roped tied about her waist. She still agonized that her antics had already cost one man his life, and she choked down the bile threatening to rise in her throat. Yet, she had no doubt in her mind, she would still risk everything to return to her family.

She felt an impatient flick of the rope that became an instant reminder she must needs hurry. Quickly taking care of her business, she at last dropped her skirt and made an attempt to smooth out the material that was fast becoming a rumpled, torn mess. Giving a weary sigh, she gave up any effort to make herself look more presentable for when Ian at last found her. He had seen her at her worse afore. She supposed now would not make much of a difference, considering her current circumstances.

Leaning her back against the bark of the tree, Lynet brought her hands together, closed her eyes, and took a quick moment to offer up a heartfelt prayer to God to save her. Her mouth silently moved feverishly in her attempt to complete her petition afore she was interrupted yet again by her troublesome abductor. With a hasty amen, she waited with bated breath for some sign her prayers had been heard. But, there was nothing to show that her efforts had pleased God above, no matter how rapidly she had been forced to say them.

She tilted her head, as though listening more intently would give her some form of an answer. Lynet thought it oddly strange the forest was eerily silent. There was no whisper of the breeze rustling the trees, no sound of the birds calling to one another from the treetops, no sounds of small furry animals as they scurried from bush to bush to hide against intruders. Complete silence...something was not right. No forest was ever this still.

"I grow annoyed, Lynet. If you know what's good for you, then you had best make haste," Calum called out, only this time with a more forceful tug on the tether that kept her within his reach.

"I am coming," she replied and made her way around the barrier protecting her from his prying eyes. She was almost surprised to see he still had his back turned. When she neared him, he at last faced her to take hold of her elbow, as if the rope was not enough to ensure her captivity.

"I pray you do not request another reprieve from our course this day, my lady, for I am done stopping every five minutes with another sorry excuse passing from your lips," he all but mocked her, and she knew, without any doubt, he had divined the game she had been attempting to play. 'Twas too bad she had obviously failed to execute her part well enough to outwit him.

"Let go of me, you brute," she sneered. She could tell her ruse to slow down their every move would no longer be tolerated. Looking into his eyes, she could have sworn he had a look upon his face that appeared as if he was indeed impressed with her stamina to keep trying to escape. It quickly changed, and she liked not the gleam that entered his black, menacing eyes.

Afore she could make any form of protest, Lynet was shocked to feel herself harshly yanked up against his body as he captured her arms at her sides in a steely grip. Her head barely met his chest. Her hands hung useless at her sides so she was unable to do anything other than gasp at the contact of their bodies. She tried to calm her breathing, since the last thing she needed was to have her chest heaving in and out, further tempting his arousal. She was afraid to even move, lest he have other ideas in mind than just holding her. She already could tell where his thoughts had led, considering she could feel his rigid manhood pressed intimately against her.

Her mouth opened to voice her displeasure only to snap shut when the unmistakable sound of a snapping twig echoed in the quiet air. 'Twas not hard to miss such a crunch, given the atmosphere around them afore such a racket had been thick with noiseless tension.

She abruptly found herself tossed behind the giant wall of Calum's back. She gasped when his fist dug hard into her belly as he made a grab for the rope at her waist. She began to squirm to try and look around him so she, too, could see what had caused such a clamor.

"Be still," he hissed, giving the rope a hard tug and almost causing her to lose her footing.

"I will be more than happy to, if you would but release me and take your leave. I am more than capable to find my way home," Lynet purred with sarcasm.

"Shut your mouth, and be silent, else I will be obliged to stuff a rag in your trap. I have had enough of you this day."

She shoved at his back. He barely moved as he continued to listen intently to their surroundings. And then, she heard it. Slanting her head, Lynet strained to ensure 'twas not just her imagination playing a cruel jest upon her. But, nay...she heard it, yet again, and there was no mistaking the sound this time. 'Twas the softest whistle, sounding much like the trill of a nightingale. How many times in her youth had she heard such a familiar song? 'Twas the most beautiful melody she had ever heard, for the tune practically called out her name.

She tried not to show her eagerness when she raised her head to view Calum. He appeared as if he heard nothing out of the ordinary with the staccato sounds of the chirping bird, even though he roughly grabbed her arm, forcing her to follow him at a brisk pace.

For the first time since her capture, Lynet's face lit up with pleasure, for she knew something that, apparently, her abductor did not. Male nightingales generally sang out their song to call and attract a mate or to protect their territory. The birds generally only warbled in the eve, or just afore the break of dawn. Since the sun was still up, and night had as yet to descend upon them, it could only mean two things. God had answered her prayers, and, even more importantly, Ian was at last near.

Sixteen

IAN TOSSED CONNOR A SILENT GLARE. If he could have pummeled the man for his stupidity, he would have done so, but he knew how the sound would carry in the air like the sharpest clap of thunder resounding across the land.

"I am verra sorry, me laird," the Highlander muttered.

"Do ye ken what ye are doin' wit' yer feet, ye clod?" Angus replied sharply.

Ian raised himself from his crouched position behind the tree as he watched his lady from afar. The element of surprise quickly vanishing afore his very eyes, he watched in dismay when Lynet's abductor began a fast pace to return to his encampment. Calum of the Duncan clan...he would not have expected him, of all people, to be the ruffian to have stolen his wife. He had thought the man to be determined to win himself a bride, but never foolish enough to take someone from the care of Dristan of Berwyck.

"We must needs hurry if we are to catch them afore they return to his camp," Rolf voiced what was already running rapidly through Ian's own thoughts. The older knight flicked his wrist towards the three guards who had followed him from Berwyck and gave a motion towards his eyes for them to be on the lookout.

"Aye," Ian agreed with a grim expression. "He is sure to have plenty of reinforcements to thwart our plans to free Lynet. Let us away."

Seven men against who knew how many? The odds of success were certainly not in their favor this day. The urge to follow and protect Lynet surged through Ian's veins like fire as he moved rapidly across the forest floor. They had not gone far when a disturbing shriek rent the air. Ian charged ahead. All thoughts of remaining silent were now gone, hearing the distressed cry of his wife.

He came upon them, but Calum was too busy to notice he was no longer alone. He held Lynet by her wrist whilst she was doing her best to try to pry his fingers from her bleeding limb. A trail, formed from her slippers, showed in the dirt beneath her feet where Calum had been dragging her against her will.

Ian burst from the cover of the trees into the small open area, despite the fact he could hear Calum's men in camp within close proximity. All patience he may have had was gone seeing another touching his lady, and he could no longer hold back, nor make any further attempt to remain unheard whilst he rescued her.

"Get your damn hands off *my* wife!" Ian yelled as he drew his claymore from behind his back. The blade gleamed, as though Ian's anger were reflected in the shining silver metal.

Calum gave a menacing glare, although, he let his guard down momentarily, to show he was surprised Ian claimed the lady in such a final manner. "*Your wife?*" he asked and turned his attention back to the woman at his side. "It appears, you have not told me all, my lady."

"'Twas none of your business," she announced with a defiant toss of her beautiful head. Ian had never seen her look so glorious in her state of fury, and he thought on how he would not wish to be on the receiving end of such a gaze.

Her blue eyes displayed her resentment of her captor 'til she turned her attention to Ian, and her whole countenance transformed to one of pure joy. Ian's heart gave a little flip, knowing such a look was for him alone. The distance separating them ceased to exist in his mind whilst they had eyes only for each other. Lynet gave him a smile that silently spoke she had all the confidence in him that he would free her, and, by God, he would not let her down.

"Eh gads, I have no desire, or time, to watch two lovesick fools," Calum said gruffly. "It seems, I have nothing left to lose, and you leave me no choice, but to fight for the coin you would bring me."

Afore any could stop him, Calum pulled Lynet most unwillingly into his arms, and Ian watched as the man's mouth ground onto the lips of his woman. His control snapped at their contact as though 'twere an erupting volcano spewing hot molten lava high into the air. Lynet began squirming in order to free herself. Their brief kiss over, Calum let out a fierce battle cry to alert those nearby that aid was needed. Ian lunged ahead with only one thought in mind. He was going to kill the miserable whoreson for taking such a liberty with his wife!

"*Bloody hell!*" Rolf swore afore he, too, joined into the fray. Men seemed to pour from the woods like an army of ants attacking a food source. Clearly, they were outnumbered.

Rolf saw the chaos breaking out all around them, even whilst Lynet was shoved violently to the ground. She scurried out of the way as swords were raised and clashed with sparks flashing about like dancing stars in the twilight. She might be bruised, but she was safe...at least for the moment.

Any further thoughts went racing out of Rolf's mind as the will to live took over every other instinct in him. His blade rang out as he met one adversary after another. He may have done his fair share of attempting to even out the odds when his present opponent fell in front of him, but the man was just as easily replaced by another. 'Twas more than apparent, they would in no way win such a battle with the small number of forces on their side.

Ian was holding his own, along with his guardsmen who were making a small measure of headway reaching their laird's side. Rolf could tell Ian was doing everything in his power to reach Calum to prove his point he was the better man. Currently, their foe was fighting with one of Rolf's men, who had accompanied him from Berwyck. Alas, he saw the man fall with an empty look in his eyes as he dropped like the weight of a bolder, at Calum's feet. The man cared nothing for the loss of life, as he kicked the knight in the stomach, once he lay upon the ground.

A slice across his arm drew Rolf's attention back to the highlander who raised his sword again to inflict another such wound, if not a fatal one. He ducked just in time to miss the sharp claymore that had been aimed at his head and parried with his own sword, thrusting the blade into the man's back. His gaze caught Ian's across the field of the dying where a river of blood began to seep into the ground. He could tell they were of like mind.

With no thought to the value of his own life or the outcome, Rolf leaped over the man he had just cut down and began running the distance to reach Calum first. Their swords met, and even Rolf had to admit the man was a towering mountain of strength. He could feel the muscles in his wounded arm quiver each time he raised his sword against his opponent.

He looked for Ian who was closing the distance between them. "Get her the hell out of here!" Rolf shouted and watched in satisfaction as Ian's purpose was to now reach Lynet's side.

Rolf's attention returned to the matter afore him. His sword sang out, yet again, but he could tell he was tiring. Calum gave him a shove, and Rolf stumbled back from the force as he attempted to regain his footing.

He stepped forward to challenge the man, yet again, but got no farther. Shattering pain exploded from behind him when he felt the hilt of a sword slam into the back of his skull. Dazed, he began to collapse, even as a blade was thrust into his body from behind. Just as speedily, the sword was withdrawn with a sickening sound. Falling to his knees, he began to choke on the blood rising in his throat, knowing he was not long for this world.

Everything around him began to move in a slow, hazy motion. Rolf's gaze searched out the area 'til he at last espied Lynet. She had a look of horror etched upon her beautiful face, along with a silent cry for his fate frozen upon her lips. Still...she never appeared lovelier, and in his humble opinion, she had the face of an angel. Sadly, he realized he had failed in his vow to keep her safe, along with the trust Lord Dristan had sanctioned him with as her captain.

A quick prayer formed in his mind that God would not judge him too harshly for his trespasses whilst here on earth. His eyes rolled in his head, and he felt himself pitching forward. Afore he fell to the ground, peacefulness began to wash over him, and he could have sworn he heard a heavenly choir singing in the air. Never had he heard such a gentle, sweet sound as their song surrounded his entire body. A calming light appeared afore his vision, beckoning him onward. With a sense of soaring through the air, Rolf willingly reached out for one of the Lord's beautiful guardians who took ahold of his soul as she gently guided him to the heavens above. He was going home.

"*ROLF,*" Lynet screamed out. "Nay!"

She watched in shock when Lachlan pulled his blade out of Rolf's back, even whilst Calum smiled at their deed of defeating the knight.

All the life drained out of the man who had been such a significant part of her existence. Rolf had risked all to come and save her. She could tell the moment his soul left him when his green eyes became vacant, and he tumbled to the ground with a heavy thud. In her despair, she attempted to stagger into the mayhem to reach his side. She did not think of the consequences of her actions, but forced her feet to move forward, step by step. She did not care of the danger she placed herself in. She only knew she must needs see what she could do to help him, whatever the cost might be.

She thought she had made some progress, dodging highlanders and knights as they fought with their blades of steel. Hearing her name called out above the ruckus of battle, she came to the harsh revelation she had not even crossed half the distance to reach Rolf's side. Then, she felt her arm grabbed roughly, and she whirled to suddenly find herself staring into Ian's worried hazel eyes.

"Run, lass, run," he urged, trying to force her to come to her senses and realize their situation.

"My God, Ian, we canna leave him here," she yelled at him through her tears. "We must go back to save him."

"He is past saving, Lynet," Ian replied gravely, pressing her to quicken her pace. "Now hurry, lest his death be all for naught."

Ian gave a short whistle, and a moment later his horse, along with two others, came galloping up through the woods. Ian leapt into the saddle and reached down to hoist her up in front of him. She was barely settled in the saddle, afore Ian kicked his horse into flight. There was no mistaking the sound of Calum's curses ringing out for his highlanders to take up the chase.

Tears coursing down her cheeks, she took one last glance at Rolf's lifeless body lying motionless on the ground. He had made the ultimate sacrifice on her behalf, and his service to her had cost him his very life. She took note that two of Berwyck's own were close by and also dead upon the earth. The third, she had witnessed during the altercation, was nowhere to be seen.

The forest obscured any further witness to the fallen guards who bravely went against enough men to turn away anyone, who had any common sense, from a battle they were sure to lose. Lynet's lips moved in a reverent prayer for Rolf's soul to find peace. After everything the man had done for her over the years, 'twas only right she should offer up her petitions on his behalf. 'Twas done out of respect and the love he had felt for her. To honor his memory, she would keep a part of him in her heart, forevermore.

Seventeen

IAN TIGHTENED HIS ARMS AROUND the napping woman in his lap. Her crying had torn at his heart strings 'til she had at last fallen into a restless slumber. Even then, her dreams continued haunting her as she cried out, now and again. He supposed there was some consolation, whilst he listened to her torment as she slept, that she called out his name alongside of Rolf's.

The sound of pursuit had faded as the miles passed swiftly away. Ian did not give any sign of false hope that Calum was not still following them. He knew his kind and was determined to put as much distance between them as he possibly could. He prayed the third guard who had been accompanying Rolf would make it safely back to Berwyck to alert Dristan of all that had occurred.

Ian made a motion of his hand to alert Angus of his plans to change their current direction. Giving a slight pull to the left on the reins, he directed his horse to move out of the riverbed they had been wading through in order to cover their tracks. The clip clop of their hooves sounded out as they met the rocky bank. Steering their horses up a small rise in the landscape, Ian peered down at the ground. They would need to do something about the impressions of hoof prints the heavy animals left on the grassy soil beneath them. Even though night had descended upon them, anyone with even a limited amount of tracking ability would be able to easily read their trail they left behind and locate them.

They needed to give the horses a rest, for they had done their duty this day by furthering the space between them and the enemy. Ian peered ahead and decided the best course of action would be to head to a grouping of nearby trees. There wasn't much cover here on the open Scottish moors. But, he knew he could not push their steeds further this night to get them into the Highlands and the mountainous terrain that would be of greater benefit in hiding their whereabouts. Unfortunately, Ian realized Calum would know, without any doubt, which direction he planned to take.

Reaching the trees, Ian shifted Lynet in his arms. Her hand reached up and wound its way around his neck. For the briefest instant, he took delight of at last feeling her warm body pressed intimately against his own. Whilst the battle had raged on, he had had his doubts any of them would make it out of there alive. Yet, here she was, a little battered, both emotionally and physically, but at least she was safe.

"Ian..." She said his name in a breathless whisper, causing a slight shiver to traverse its way through his senses.

"Awake, Lynet. Let me help you down for we must needs rest the horses awhile," he replied, brushing his knuckles lightly across her bruised cheek.

Her eyelids began to flutter open, and, for a moment, he saw a brief glimpse of the nightmare hidden in the depths of her eyes as she hovered between sleep and wakefulness.

"Ian?" she repeated, although the tone of her voice did not have the same lilting quality it had but an instant ago.

"Aye."

He swung his leg over the saddle and dropped to the ground. "Connor," he called out quietly as the man made his way to his side. "Double back and cover our tracks, and do it well. I have no desire to be back on the run 'til we have given the horse's adequate time to recuperate from traveling at such speed and distance this night."

"Aye, me laird," he replied and hurried off in the direction from whence they had come.

Satisfied his instructions would be obeyed, he returned his interest to his wife, who was weaving in the saddle. He stretched out his arms towards her, and Lynet leaned down, placing her hands upon his shoulders to slide down the length of his body. Luckily, he was prepared when her knee's buckled beneath her as he continued holding on to his lady. He grasped her firmly around her waist to offer her the support she stood in need of 'til she regained her feet.

Her forehead rested upon his chest, and, for the first time, he realized just how small his lovely wife truly was whilst she tried to reclaim her breath. Her hands rose up onto his torso, and he felt her fists grasp the edges of his tunic. He was about to lean down to place a tender kiss upon her head when she reacted as though he were in truth their enemy and not Calum.

"Get your hands off me!" She all but condemned him with her tone as she gave him a push to distance herself from him.

He rocked back on his heels only to stare down into her mutinous, angry blue eyes. "Whatever is the matter?" he retorted.

"How can you even ask that of me, given what happened back there?" She pointed her arm into the air, but the direction she tried to draw attention to was the wrong way, not that it mattered. Ian knew what she referenced, but there was not much he could do about what had transpired. He did what he needed in order for him to save her, although the price had, indeed, been high.

"You know what the cost of war can be, Lynet. I should not have to explain to you the sacrifice that sometimes must be paid," Ian murmured.

Her eyes betrayed the true extent of her emotions, as though she had written them out on parchment for the entire world to read. Her hand shakily pushed away a lock of blonde hair that had fallen across her brow. She attempted to smother her cry of despair, but instead choked on the sob that tore from her lips in a gasp of sorrow.

He continued to observe her, and he had the distinct feeling she would blame him for Rolf's death. She clutched at the plaid he had thrown around her to keep the chill away, but as she raised her face to him again, her eyes confirmed his worst fears.

"You just left him there," she whimpered so softly with tears running down her cheeks that he barely heard her voice.

"Lynet I—"

"*You left him there!*" Her voice echoed in the air as she yelled out in misery. "You left him there with his blood seeping into the cold, hard ground amongst strangers and for the crows to come and pick away at his body!"

"You are being unreasonable, Lynet."

"Do not tell me I am being unreasonable," she spat out angrily. "You have no notion what I have been through since I was taken from Berwyck."

Ian sighed and ran his hand through his hair. "Aye, you may have that aright, but you must surely know we were outnumbered. Or have you not thought of that, as you accuse me of leaving behind a comrade whilst I tucked my tail between my legs and ran away like a coward?"

"I never said you were a coward. Only that you should have returned to save him."

"He was past saving, Lynet. Rolf knew the dangers we were facing. He and I both did what we needed in order to secure your freedom."

"He was my friend!" she cried out. "I thought he was yours, as well."

He discounted her words, knowing she was hurting, but he began to also wonder what her true feelings had been for Rolf. "You make me believe from your speech you loved him," Ian said brusquely. "Did you?"

"Of course, I loved him, but—"

"Then mayhap you should have handfasted with him, instead," Ian blurted out. "It could just as easily have been me who lies dead in the forest, instead of him."

"You did not let me finish," she returned harshly.

"I am sorry for the loss of the one you declare to have loved," Ian continued on bitterly whilst ignoring her last statement. "If I could switch places with him in order to make you happy, then I would. 'Tis an impossible task for me to change what is done. I hope you will be able to surmise such a fact for yourself, once you can think clearly again."

"Now who is being unreasonable," Lynet fumed. "You automatically assume I wish 'twas you instead of Rolf who is in need of burying. I never spoke such to you, did I?"

He did not answer her, since he did not know how to calm her rising temper. "How are we supposed to live as man and wife if you harbor feelings for a man who is dead, Lynet?" Ian asked harshly.

A snort escaped her, and she shook her head then gathered the tartan over her head. "How little you truly know me, Ian."

"I know you well enough," he began 'til she held her hand up. He clamped his lips together with a snap.

"Nay, you do not, for you were not there, were you? You kissed me after the siege to Berwyck six years ago then left without even a backward glance. I am sure you gave little thought to what such a kiss would mean to me," she said with a catch in her voice. "With a wave of your hand, I watched you leave Berwyck, never to return again, as you proclaimed, even though I wished differently."

"You know why I could not stay."

"Aye, you were in love with Amiria. How could I ever forget for even the briefest of instances that I was a poor substitute for my sister?"

"That is not true, and you know such talk to be a falsehood, Lynet." Ian watched her in the moonlight. He had the distinct feeling he was losing another battle as he saw her slipping away.

She had a far off look in her eyes as she continued on. "Rolf was the captain of my guard since I was but a girl of ten and four. He was more than just a protector who Dristan assigned to safeguard me night and day. He watched me over the years as I languished away for a man who gave me no further thought 'til he needed a bride. He saw my tears and wiped them away. He saw my broken heart and tried to heal it with laughter. He made me try to forget you, but 'twas not easily done. In his heart, he knew he could never be the replacement of what you meant to me, even though he wished differently."

Ian leaned a shoulder up against the tree, trying to not let the ugly emotion of jealousy get the better of him. "Yet, still you profess to love him."

"You mistook my words when I said I loved him, since you did not allow me to finish my thoughts."

"Then finish them now," he said abruptly, but fearing what she might confess.

"Aye, I loved and cared for Rolf as my friend, but I was not *in* love with him. There is a difference, as you well should know."

Ian pushed off the tree and crossed the distance between them. He reached out for her, but she swatted his hand.

"I told you not to touch me," she reiterated.

Renewed anger flared inside Ian. "You are in shock from all you have been through, but you are still my wife," he declared.

"Mayhap, we made a mistake," Lynet said solemnly.

"We made no mistake. You *are* my wife," Ian growled.

"I want to go home."

"We *are* going home...to Urquhart. I am needed there, and as my bride, your place now resides in the Highlands, alongside your laird. You spoke our vows just as willingly as did I with no time restraint to our agreement." Ian heard a low curse pass her lips.

"So, now I have become a prisoner again, only with a different master, is that it?" Her eyes flashed in fury, and Ian had to admit he liked this side of her more than when she had been weeping, even though he understood her grief. Such emotion gave him hope that, perchance, all was not lost between them.

Ian gave a casual shrug. "If that is how you wish to look upon our lives, then so be it. Master or laird, husband or enemy, you will resign yourself that you belong to me."

He left her there as she blasphemed his name for not taking her back to Berwyck. His previous thoughts of how happy their lives would be flashed afore his memory, even as he realized he had a long road ahead of him in order to win Lynet's heart. He prayed 'twould be worth the journey.

Eighteen

Mile upon mile of Scotland's endless landscape passed afore Lynet's eyes, like the never ending grains of sand that counted time in an hour glass. She had been bounced and jostled in the saddle for hours 'til she could no longer even remember what day it was. Each step of the horse beneath her took her farther and farther away from Berwyck and her family. 'Twas the only place she had ever called home.

She supposed her marriage would have been inevitable come the end of the games, and as such, she would have, in truth, traveled to wherever her new husband's place of birth was located. That she moved at such a hasty speed because it may cost the lives of those she journeyed with, complicated that which troubled her most deeply.

She had put the rift in place between her and Ian. She could not blame anyone other than her own self for the silence that cracked like thunder between them. She had been furious with him for not attempting to return for Rolf, and for his claim of ownership over her. But as the day's swiftly passed by whilst they continued to outrun their pursuers, her voice of reason began to at last take precedence over her accusations of him. He certainly was not a coward and had made the right decisions in order to save her life. She just had a hard time forming the words *I am sorry* whenever she saw the stubborn expression in his eyes. Apparently, he had no plans to yield first and apologize, any more than she did.

Ian had been polite, if not downright unreachable, ever since. Lynet had tried to keep herself distant from him but that surely was near to impossible, given they were sharing a horse together. Every bump against him was a constant reminder this was her Ian, the man she had been in love with for almost her entire life. Her resolve to stay furious at him may be trying to rule her head, but her heart was a constant betrayal of her own feelings as it flipped end over end with his closeness.

Lynet had never been this far from Berwyck, and she watched as the scenery and terrain changed from rolling open moors to green mountains and valleys. She was taken aback when they at last came upon a large lake. Ian had whispered softly in her ear as they rode 'twas called Loch Ness, not that she had ever heard of such a place. The water stretched out for nigh unto fifty miles, or so he guessed. He appeared to be familiar with the territory, as he showed an unexpected eagerness whilst he began speaking of the place that had once been his home.

The sun had been lowering in the distant horizon as they traversed the shoreline when she finally espied it. Against a backdrop of a resplendent pink and orange sky from the setting sun, there stood a keep, rising majestically from the shore of the lake...Urquhart Castle. She sat up straighter in the saddle, as if this additional bit of height would give her a clearer view of the place she would now call home.

Lynet chanced a glimpse at her husband and noticed how he had been watching her most intently. A smile formed on her lips, and he returned her gesture with one of his own, as he was obviously pleased by her reaction upon seeing the castle for the first time. He halted his horse, and they sat in silence for a few moments, taking in the sight of the estate. She saw the keep was reflected in the water, adding a hint of mystery for what was to follow as her life now moved forward.

She reached up, trying to tame her unruly locks into some semblance of order. "I must look a fright," she said hastily, feeling vain for the first time in her life. "What will our people think of a mistress who looks as if she has been dragged through the muck of life?"

Ian took his gaze from the castle in the distance to peruse her more intently. Reaching out, he took a lock of her hair and began rubbing the length between his fingers afore tucking it behind her ear. "I am glad to hear you make the reference of saying *our people*. 'Tis most pleasing to my ears, Lynet," he answered.

With a cluck of his tongue, the horse began to clip clop its way over the rocky riverbed. Towering trees lined the lake across from the keep, but those that may have been found surrounding the castle had been cut down to ensure anyone approaching the area would be easily seen.

The keep was not as large as Berwyck, by any means, for Lynet could tell that right away with just one look. 'Twas still of adequate size, reaching perchance five floors high. The battlement walls were not as tall as those at Berwyck, either, but she could still see them weaving steadily around the keep. The rooftops of several buildings peeked out beyond the walls encompassing the estate. The sound of steady hammering told her they had a blacksmith, and surely, a stable would be found close by.

Lynet was surprised to see the fields lay barren. She would have thought they would be filled with sprouting stalks of wheat rising in a golden display of color at this time of year. She took note of only two cows chewing their cud nearby and wondered where the rest of the herd and other livestock could be found. She began to quickly ponder just what the circumstances were surrounding Ian's return and of him taking over as laird and chief of the clan. They never had taken the time to talk of such details, since their conversations had been limited to sparring with one another and his need to wed.

Why had there been such an urgency and need for him to marry? Surely, a fair amount of time would be needed for Ian to become adjusted to returning to his family after being gone so long. She could only guess on the number of years it had been since Ian departed from beneath the shadows of his birthplace. She knew he had been a younger son and had ended up at Berwyck to pledge his fealty to her father, but other than that, she knew nothing of his family, nor what to expect as he returned with a bride not of their choosing. He never talked of his past, preferring for it to remain unspoken.

As they approached, she heard a shout overhead, and Lynet saw the point of an arrow protrude from one of the narrow slits used for protecting the inhabitants of the keep. Angus and Connor moved their mounts forward, raising their hands 'til they were recognized, and the drawbridge was lowered so they could proceed over the dry moat into the interior of what she would consider the baily.

As Lynet looked around, she observed the normal activity of castle life going on all around her. Chores were busily being attended to, people hurried to and fro, and they did not have long to wait afore three young lads came running from the stables to take hold of the halters of their steeds. Ian jumped down from the saddle and once again held out his arms to assist her.

Her hands actually shook as she placed them upon his broad shoulders, and she felt his own reach up and grab hold of her waist to help her down. They stood thusly whilst she tried to calm her nerves that suddenly felt as if they were colliding together with all the emotions of her fate of late.

"'Tis alright now, little one, you are safe," Ian murmured, as though he, in truth, read her very thoughts. Staring up into those alluring hazel eyes, she felt much of her anger melt away and tried not to sigh in pleasure when he gently cupped her face and rubbed his thumb softly across her cheek.

"I do not know why I feel so frightened all of a sudden, Ian. What will your family think of me and our hasty marriage? I just know they will hate me." Her voice portrayed her uneasiness at her precarious situation, so she took a deep gulp of air, trying her best to remember to breathe.

Ian muttered something beneath his breath that she could not make out. "To be honest, I do not give a damn what they think," he at last declared.

"But what kind of a reception do you feel we shall receive?" she asked hesitantly as she heard the door to the keep squeaking open. In unison, they both turned their attention towards the sound. An older woman came to an abrupt pause at the top of the stairs once she saw them and waited there with hands folded in front of her. She looked displeased, as her brows furrowed, and, from where Lynet was standing, 'twas not a good sign.

Ian took her fingers and brushed his lips across them. His eyes sparkled whilst he gave her a timid smile. "We are about to find out," he whispered, afore raising his free hand in acknowledgment to the woman, who scowled and began tapping her foot in impatience 'til Ian called out to her. "Hello, mother."

Lynet's hand trembled beneath his fingers. He gave them a slight squeeze of reassurance. "All will be well, my lady," he told her as she acknowledged him with a slight nod of her head. "Wait here."

His stride was confident as he went towards the keep, even as the briefest of visions passed quickly afore his eyes of a lad being tossed down the very same steps he was fast approaching. Viewing the mother who had given him his very breath, he saw she did not appear as if life of late had been treating her well. Given his view of the fields as he had approached the manor, he was not all together surprised to see them fallow, nor the absence of serfs cultivating the soil.

Her disapproval of him was etched upon her face in the fiercest of frowns. Ian mentally wondered where his mother, who had begged him silently with kind eyes to apologize to his brother so long ago, had disappeared to. Surely, the woman he remembered still lingered somewhere beneath the surface of what she now showed him.

He fell to his knees once he stood afore her and bowed his head. Silence was met with the shuffling of feet as he could feel the stares of those who came out of the shadows to witness his return. Yet, still he waited for his mother to acknowledge his right as the next in line to claim the lairdship of the MacGillivray clan.

He was about to give up and stand when he felt it. Her hands came to rest upon his head. "I give you my blessing, my son," she said loudly for all to hear. "Rise, and greet those who will now serve you."

Ian stood and walked up the remaining steps to stand next to his mother. Taking both her hands, he leaned forward to kiss her cheeks. Turning back to the crowd who gathered afore him, he was startled to see the condition of his people. Their ragged appearance confirmed the situation was indeed dire and far more troubling than he thought 'twould be. He could only pray there was something left in the estate coffers. Though, he would not be surprised to learn his brother had spent what precious little coin he had on drink and women.

The clan began to press forward with the declaration of *my laird* voiced by each person who came and knelt afore him to pay him homage. The creaking of the keep door again sounded, and a woman with dark brown hair came to stand beside his mother, who suddenly began to smile. Inwardly, Ian groaned, knowing what was about to occur.

He reached out his arm to beckon Lynet to come forward. Her eye's widened 'til she gave a slight shake of her head, denying his silent request. His eyes narrowed as he all but called to her. Ian knew she understood his meaning, and yet, still she refused to stand with him as his wife.

"Excuse me," he muttered.

"Ian!" his mother called out. 'Twas obvious he was about to incur her wrath one way or the other, so he might as well get it over with. He cared not that his mother was angry when he left her side. Instead, he continued forward, passing those who still waited to pay their respect whilst they opened up a pathway straight to his wife.

He held out his hand to his lady. The moment he looked into her eyes, he knew she was scared to death. "Come, Lynet. Take my hand. Your place is beside your husband."

"Ian...I am n-not presentable," she stammered hastily. "I canna stand afore our people looking like this."

"I am not much better, if you but care to look," he said, trying his best to put her at ease by lightening the mood between them.

Her eyes raked over him, and she betrayed the slightest amount of interest when she did so. A slight smile broke out afore she remembered herself and covered it again with a show of disinterest. But he had seen her response and knew her feelings for him were still there, no matter that she tried to hide them from him.

Ian took her chin and raised her face. "Your place is next to me, Lynet. Now, come...introductions must needs be made so everyone will know their place in our household."

"Our?"

Her voice sounded surprised, and he could not resist the grin that escaped his lips. "But of course, my sweet. I would not have it any other way."

Her smile was answer enough he had pleased her.

NINETEEN

THIS TIME, LYNET DID NOT even attempt to conceal her smile of delight his words had given her. Still hesitant to be brought afore his mother, looking as she did, any further protest she may have given ended the minute Ian leaned down and placed an affectionate kiss upon her cheek. A gasp echoed through the crowd at his gesture. Lynet was unsure exactly who had been the person who was not happy with such a public display of affection. She only hoped 'twas *not* his mother.

Numb to almost everything around her, Lynet merely followed as Ian took her hand and placed it in the crook of his arm to lead her through the crowd. Voices rose in intensity as whispers from those gathered wondering who she was rushed like the wind through the treetops. A quick peek through her lashes confirmed Lynet's gravest trepidations. The woman standing still as stone at the top of the stairway was unmistakably annoyed with what was transpiring around her, evidenced by the fact her face was turning an unsightly shade of red.

With a deep calming breath, she climbed the stairs, feeling as though she was attempting to scale the tallest of mountains. She fell into a deep curtsey and waited, much as Ian had done, for his mother's acknowledgment. 'Twas not to come.

Ian took her elbow to help her rise, but 'twas the look on his face that told Lynet of the true emotions running amuck inside her husband's mind.

"You do my lady a disservice by ignoring her, madam. This is my wife, Lady Lynet of Berwyck. As such, she deserves your respect as mistress of this clan, if nothing else," Ian said through clenched teeth. His flat tone was low for his mother's ears alone, although 'twas clear the woman standing behind his dame heard his words.

"But, Lady Fiona, how could this be? What of..." Ian's mother paid her no mind, interrupting the perplexed woman with her own query of her son.

"You have wed with an Englishwoman? You must be mad!" his mother snarled.

Ian brought Lynet closer to his side. "She is of Clan MacLaren. Surely, you have heard of her people."

"Harrumph...lowlanders," Fiona sneered, looking down her nose at Lynet. "I heard tell her father married an Englishwoman in order to take over her estate. Rumor has it he would have pledged his loyalty to that English pig of a king if he had not fallen instead."

"You should not slander His Majesty's good name, mother, for even I had sworn fealty to King Henry, no matter that I now serve Scotland."

"Berwyck...'tis quite large, is it not?"

Lynet tried her best not to let her temper flare, even though she swore she could all but hear the chinking of coins being counted in his mother's head. "Why does the size of Berwyck matter, my lady?" Lynet asked, raising her chin and feeling no need to let on she had a considerable dowry. "I am but a younger sister in that household."

Fiona rolled her eyes in obvious disgust. "By the blessed Saints, Ian," she all but cursed him, "could you not, at the very least, even wed with the eldest daughter?"

The old woman might as well have slapped her across the face, although, Ian's mother knew not how much such an accusation tore at Lynet's heart. She began to fidget as Ian's mother made a circular motion of her hand towards her. Lynet looked at Ian, and he shrugged his shoulders, so Lynet proceeded to turn around so this obnoxious woman could inspect her, as though she were a piece of livestock to be closely inspected afore being purchased. When she had completed a full circle, Lynet once more looked directly at her husband's dame and waited for her pronouncement.

"I am Lady Fiona," she declared proudly. Nothing in her expression led Lynet to believe they would become friends anytime soon.

"Madam," she replied with a slight nod of her head.

Lady Fiona turned her back on Lynet and whispered something to the woman behind her. She then had the gall to give a most annoying laugh that was anything but flattering when she peered again at Lynet. Her steely glare returned to her son. "Really, Ian, could you not do better than take to wife some woman who appears as if she has crawled out from beneath a thistle bush?" she sniggered.

The hair on the back of Lynet's neck rose in indignation. How dare this woman speak to her in such a manner! Her mouth was poised to open a sharp retort, but instead, she remained silent, as Ian spoke on her behalf.

"She does have a prickly temper, of which I must say, I approve," Ian softly chuckled, bringing her cool hand again up to his lips. Their eyes lingered one to the other, causing Lynet's heart to quicken. "'Twill keep things interesting, will it not my dear?"

"Most assuredly, my laird," Lynet calmly replied. She watched as Ian's brow rose in amusement at her acknowledgement he was indeed her lord. 'Twas almost as if they shared a private jest between them, and a laugh escaped her mouth. "Do not get used to that, Ian."

He threw his head back in merriment. "And yet, you have now used my proper title twice, dear lady, despite your vow to not let it pass your lips."

Lady Fiona cleared her throat and abruptly brought them back to the realization people were still watching their every move and listening intently to their conversation.

"Has the marriage been consummated?" his mother all but jeered.

"I beg your pardon, madam?" Lynet was aghast she would ask such of them with all of Urquhart looking upon them, waiting for an answer.

Could such a smile be construed as anything else but malicious? "Ah...I see," Lady Fiona said with satisfaction. "Then, there is still hope."

"Hope for what?" Lynet murmured, almost afraid to hear where this woman's thoughts were going to lead.

Lady Fiona's face lit up in happiness as if all was going to right itself in her world. "Why there is hope this misunderstanding between the two of you can as yet be undone, of course. My son can then marry a proper Highland lass of the clan's choosing."

Lynet actually gasped at what she was hearing. Never had she thought her and Ian's handfasting was anything other than a true marriage, no matter that they had not as yet carried out the act of truly becoming one. An embarrassing blush began to creep across Lynet's face. If Ian were to denounce her, she would be returned home to Berwyck a ruined woman. No man of any standing, be he titled or not, would have her then.

Once again, Ian came to her rescue, saving her from any further disgracing remarks by his mother. Leaving Lynet's side, he quickly strode to Lady Fiona to take her upper arm in a firm grip.

"Hear me, and hear me well, madam. There has been no misunderstanding. Lynet is *my wife*, and you will not, under any circumstances forget such a fact," Ian snarled. "Now get inside. Once I have my lady settled in our chamber, I will summon you and finish having speech in privacy where conversations of this nature belong!"

Lynet saw the older woman cast a mutinous gaze upon her son 'til she turned to take her leave, grabbing the arm of the younger lady at her side. Ian's voice halted her progress and her shoulders jerked when she heard the tone of his speech. "Have you not forgotten something, mother?"

Lady Fiona turned back towards them and gave the briefest of nods afore picking up her skirts and hastily retreating into the castle. Already the air, which had only moments afore seemed to be stifling all around them, brightened like the sun peeking through the clouds after a heavy storm. Ian put his arm around Lynet's shoulder and embraced her.

"People are staring, Ian," she whispered, even whilst her arms went around his waist.

"Let them..." he replied, reaching up to cup her cheek. "I am most sorry for her treatment of you. Are you all right?"

"Aye. She does not even know me, and already she hates me."

"I cannot fathom what has gotten into her. She was never like that when I was a lad."

"I am sure all will reveal itself in time, Ian."

"She is just displeased I have gone against her wishes and wed without consulting her."

He took her arm and led her into the Great Hall of the keep. Lynet did her best not to cough from the hazy smoke filling the chamber. A quick glance at her surroundings told her the estate had been in disarray for some time. The hall was sparsely furnished. The walls had but one tattered tapestry hanging from a bent metal rod. Two large grey dogs lounging by the fire appeared as though they were in need of a meal. She could only ponder if, mayhap, everyone at Urquhart was in need of such sustenance.

As they made their way across the filthy rush covered floor to the stairs, Ian called out for water to be brought to his chambers for bathing. Several serfs scurried off to do his bidding. Lynet lost count of the number of stairs they climbed 'til they reached the fifth floor. The passageway seemed eerily silent, with only the occasional torch lit to help them find their way down the dark corridor.

They came to a portal located near a corner of the keep, and Ian pushed the oaken door open. Lynet tried to hide her dismay at seeing the condition of the chamber that was obviously made for the laird and chief of the keep. 'Twas apparent Ian's brother had not spent many hours here afore his demise.

"*God's wounds,*" Ian cursed.

She could understand his sentiments regarding the room. Lynet tried to envision the chamber for the possibilities 'twould offer, thinking of a large bed with lush velvet hangings instead of pelts of fur thrown carelessly upon the floor and up against the wall. A small table that served as a desk would never do, but a larger one would be a nice addition near one of the windows. Colorful cushions in the rounded corner would brighten up the seating space and would add a nice touch to the area where one could gaze at the loch below. There was one chest located on the opposite side of the room, although Lynet was almost afraid to open the lid. She had no doubt she would find within a nest of mice, given there was a considerable hole chewed open at the bottom.

She went towards the window and almost ran into a cobweb that housed a very busy spider as it spun its silken thread around its latest meal. With a timid smile, she turned back to Ian, who still stood rooted and frozen in place. "It could be worse," Lynet said brightly.

He came back from wherever far off place he had traveled to in his mind. "Surely you jest, madam?"

She walked over to him and placed her hands upon his arms. Her thumbs roamed over his skin and she could feel his muscles flex with tension. "We shall make the best of it," she declared cheerfully.

Ian pulled her a step closer, and Lynet's heart leapt as she felt the heat of his body next to her own. She realized this was the man she had wanted all her life. Ian...her knight...her husband...and she could at long last call him her very own.

"Are you, perchance, attempting to make me laugh?"

Lynet gave a slight shrug. "I thought a light heart might be best given the circumstances."

"Do you always have so much hope and faith all will work out?"

Ian brought her fully against him, and a gasp escaped her. She had never willingly been this close to another man in her life. "I am here, am I not?" she replied, as she tried to find breath to fill her lungs, although this in no way answered his question. "'Twas, mayhap, not how I envisioned our marriage starting out, but that does not seem to matter now, does it? We are wed. You have your inheritance—"

"Such as it is," he finished glumly, filling in words she would not have spoken.

"Aye...such as it is, and yet, I know all will work out, for I have faith in *you*. That is more important than anything else, Ian."

A lazy grin formed on that perfect mouth of his, and she waited for the touch of his lips on hers as his head began to lean down towards her. But fate had other plans in mind when a loud knock came upon the door. They broke apart, and Ian called out to the serfs to enter.

An army of clan members, both men and women, came into the chamber bearing a tub, along with bucket after bucket of water. Drying cloths were laid on the table, along with a change of clothing Lynet prayed would fit. A young girl stood meekly by to assist with her bathing, once she was ready.

Ian leaned down and gave her cheek a quick kiss. "I will leave you to see to your bath, my lady. There are matters I must needs attend to, but I shall endeavor to return as quickly as I can so we may finish our...discussion."

She just knew a rosy blush heightened the color of her face from his words, especially when she heard his chuckle. She watched him leave, bellowing orders to ensure the room's furnishing would be made more to his liking. Not knowing how much time she had, Lynet scurried to make herself presentable. After this night, she would be a maid no more.

TWENTY

B Y THE FIRE, WHICH HAD BEEN MADE for him, Ian sat in a chair that could only be termed uncomfortable. His hazel eyes peered at the interior of the chief's solar. It did not take much to envision what this room used to look like afore his brother had run the estate into the ground. He had already dismissed the steward, who had given him a grim report of the clan's state.

Not much was left. Even Ian could have surmised this himself, for surely, he had eyes in his head and had already witnessed the people were almost to the point of starvation. He had foreseen this outcome years afore, knowing his brother's nature. Ian would not be surprised to learn he had spent his last coin on ale and wenching. 'Twould have fit with the brother he had known all those years ago when he had left. He could only pray some woman would not try to claim her bastard child was his brother's, and he would need to find means to feed another soul.

His mother had become bitter over the years, although this, too, should not have startled him. He only awaited her arrival to continue their conversation in privacy. Ian assumed the younger woman who had been at his dame's side was to have been his potential bride, and this was an additional reason why Lady Fiona was displeased with him. He had already been told the lady was packing her belongings to return from whence she had come. It mattered not to Ian where she lived, only that she arrive there safely.

There was only one knock upon the door, and Ian called out for his mother to enter. The portal was pushed opened by a servant. His mother entered with her head held high. She was followed closely by her brother, who leveled his steely gaze at Ian with an open display of contempt. So even this had not changed over the years.

"Uncle Edric..." Ian murmured, barely acknowledging the Scotsman who would like nothing better than if Ian were dead so he could take over the clan as its laird and chief.

"I see you still canna show respect for your elders, boy."

"Surely, I am no longer a mere lad, and as I am clan leader, 'tis you who should be showing me the respect I deserve. Did you, perchance, forget I am my father's son and next in line?" Ian proclaimed as he relaxed back in his chair with his fingers drumming the arm, awaiting his uncle's decision.

"Bah...look at you. You may be wearing a plaid, but everything about you proclaims you to be more English than Scot!"

"And yet, here I am, after being summoned by your own sister, to claim my place as the rightful heir of Urquhart."

"You do not deserve to be laird!" Edric sneered.

"Enough!" Fiona interjected. "I will not have you squabbling about who should rule. By right, Ian is chief, and I will not hear another word of who is worthy or not on the running of this clan."

Ian's brow rose at hearing this unexpected declaration from his mother, and yet, still he waited silently for his uncle's recognition.

"My laird," Edric said through clenched teeth, giving the slightest nod of his head. The older man's glare told Ian he must needs watch his back whilst his Uncle's lips sealed in a firm line of displeasure. Such a display told Ian this was far from settled.

Ian rose from his chair. "Now that such a matter has been established, I see we are in dire straits here. You should have sent for me sooner, mother."

Fiona slumped down into the vacated chair and rested her hand on her forehead. "We sent runners in every direction. How was I to know your whereabouts, since you never bothered to keep me informed if you even yet lived, all these years?"

Edric went to stand behind his sister and put his hand upon her shoulder, as if to offer her some form of comfort. Personally, Ian did not think his uncle held affection for anyone, so this bit of display surprised him. A look passed between the two siblings, causing Ian to wonder at their ploy. Perchance all was not as it appeared, since they turned their attention back to him with a surprising display of welcome. He almost felt as though he were a mouse being led into a trap with a tidbit of tasty cheese as the jaws of death clenched and snapped tightly around his neck.

"So you are wed," Fiona said as she patted Edric's hand, who then moved to the hearth to casually rest his arm upon its mantel.

"Aye," Ian replied warily.

"She has monies to aid in the estate, then?" Edric said, as he began to examine the nails of his fingers as though he had nothing better to do. "I assume this is why you have but recently married."

"I am sure I will be able to collect Lynet's dowry, once I send word to Berwyck. 'Twas the least of my worries at the time of my leaving without it," Ian replied.

"What, pray tell, could be more important than ensuring the future of our clan with coin to fill our coffers?" Fiona's scornful reply dripped with greed and her obvious need of wealth.

Ian crossed to the desk near the window and leaned up against the wood, folding his arms across his chest. "I would think my lady's life more important than a bit of coin madam."

"Explain yourself?" Edric demanded.

"She was kidnapped by another who sought her wealth. I thought it prudent to retrieve my wife afore he defiled her."

"Then she *is* wealthy! You must consummate the marriage and quickly." Fiona smiled and began rubbing her hands together in satisfaction. "'Twill ensure her monies can provide for the estate, and we can return to living in the manner to which we were accustomed afore your brother depleted your inheritance."

"I did not handfast with her for her dowry, mother. I care for the lady."

"Handfast? You were not even married afore a priest?" Edric interrupted.

Afore Ian could answer, his mother rose from her chair, as if he was not even in the room. "'Tis of no import now, Edric. 'Tis still binding. But, we must bear witness they have in truth finalized their union. Then there will be no question Ian has the right to claim her fortune."

"Aye, you have that aright, sister. Come, nephew, and let us see the deed done."

Ian was appalled at where this conversation had led. "You must surely be jesting if you think I would allow you to watch as I take my wife?"

Fiona gazed at him, as though he were but a lad in need of a scolding. "Do not let sentiment play a part in this. You must think of your people."

"I am thinking of my people. Why else would I be here if I did not care for them?" Ian bellowed.

Edric came to stand next to his sister. "Then there is no need for speech about how you must provide proof she is a maid, else you must needs marry another."

"I am already wed, and I will hear no more talk of another taking Lynet's place," Ian retorted hotly. "I stand by my handfast with her, so I will hear no more of such speech!"

Fiona came to point her finger at him again, as she had in his youth. "To hell with the handfast you made with her! As head of the clan, you know of our ways and what is demanded of you, or have you forgotten such customs whilst you were on English soil?"

"I have forgotten nothing, including my duties to Urquhart. Hence, my appearance here."

Edric opened the solar door and motioned with his arm for Fiona and Ian to follow. Ian stood where he was 'til his uncle shut the door once more. He would be damned if he would embarrass Lynet by having his family observe them whist he made her his wife in full.

Ian casually made his way behind his desk and picked up quill and parchment. He would do this in his own time, and not at the whim of an uncle and mother he had not seen, nor heard from, in many a year.

"I have matters to attend to, and you may await me and my decision on how to handle such a delicate matter in the Great Hall. I am hardly fit to run upstairs and take my wife in my present condition, wearing the stench of sweat and blood from battle," Ian informed them.

He dipped the tip of the quill into the ink and began to write a message to Dristan, scratching the words across the parchment. Still not hearing that he was at last alone with his thoughts and the emptiness of the chamber, he looked up with raised brow. He leveled a stern gaze upon the two older people who stood next to one another with open mouths. "You are dismissed 'til I call for you."

Ian heard a low growl emit from Edric, but he ignored such an outburst, knowing the war between them had only just begun. He continued writing his missive 'til he at last saw from the corner of his eye the leaving of his uncle and mother. The oaken door slammed shut with enough force that the sound resonated down the passageway. Putting down the quill, Ian folded the parchment and leaned back in his chair with a heavy sigh.

Why was nothing ever simple? All he wanted to do was come home and begin his life with Lynet. He could see, even that would be denied him, as matters of the estate must needs come first. 'Twas not how he had envisioned the beginning of their lives together. Mayhap, 'twould have been better if Angus and Conner had never found him at all.

Reaching out for a bit of red wax, he held it over the candle 'til it dripped onto the parchment. The heavy seal of Urquhart felt unfamiliar in his hand, but he pushed the stamp down over the wax, sealing the document.

Leaving his solar, he made his way down through his barren hall and out to the stable in search of a runner to take his missive to Berwyck. Once he saw a horse saddled and the man on his way, he felt some small amount of satisfaction that at least Dristan and Amiria would soon know Lynet was safe. Remorse consumed him with his words to them of Rolf's fate. He wished there were more he could have done, but the only other option available for him was to now pray for the soul of the knight who had so willingly sacrificed his own life for that of Ian's lady.

Looking down at his attire, he went to his saddle, sitting nearby on a bale of hay. 'Twas still packed, and he took out fresh clothing bundled in cloth. He began making his way down to the loch. He needed to clean the filth off him afore he presented himself to his wife.

With thoughts of the next obstacle he must needs now confront, he tore off his shirt and plunged himself into the frigid waters of the loch.

TWENTY-ONE

"THANK YOU FOR YOUR SERVICE to me, but that will be all," Lynet stated quietly with a need to be alone in her thoughts.

Her maid bobbed a short curtsey and, with a mumbled, "Milady," quit the room.

The chamber had made a dramatic change since the completion of her bath. The maid who had been assigned to her had placed a screen to shield from view the many people entering the chamber whilst Lynet sat afore the fire to keep warm. 'Twas clear the servants began to set the room aright according to Ian's specifications. Lynet was not privy to what had been going on whilst the young woman began drying her hair and bandaging the wounds at her wrists.

Once the door had closed behind those who had noisily busied themselves to see to their laird's comfort, she was amazed at the transformation that had occurred in such a short span of time. A bed of some size she would soon share with her husband had filled the corner of the room. Instead of covers of cloth, pelts of fur had been placed upon it to keep them warm. A small repast had been laid out on a serviceable table so they might eat their fill, along with goblets filled with wine. Even the tattered trunk had been replaced by another made of heavy oak with sturdy leather straps to close it.

Apprehension filled Lynet, not knowing what was to be expected of her. She fingered the flimsy material of the robe gowning her trembling body. She wished she had been able to spend some time with Amiria so she would be better prepared on what was to come this night, but alas, 'twas not to be. She could only pray she would not fail in her naïve efforts to please her husband.

She rose from her seat by the fire and went to the alcove to peer out towards the loch. 'Twas a beautiful view with the blue and purple colors of sunset skimming across the exquisiteness of God's canvas of life. A slight smile lit her face as she thought of how she would love to capture the scene afore her, if only she had some thread to work with.

A movement caught her attention, and her eyes drew to the person rising from the waters of the loch. She reached her hand to her throat as if to catch her breath that threatened to escape her. All he needed was a trident in his hand, and he would have completed the mental picture she had in her head of the Greek God Poseidon rising from beneath the depths of the ocean.

His reddish brown hair hung in thick wet strands to his shoulders as water ran like rivulets down the firmness of his bronzed chest when he emerged and strode onto the bank. Lynet tilted forward in order to gaze more fully at the vision making his way from the coldness of what she assumed had been his bath. His hose clung to the muscles of his thighs and she marveled at the sheer strength of the warrior who unknowingly tempted her from afar. She felt her maiden heart flip end over end inside her chest, knowing he would soon be at her side.

Watching his every move, she observed Ian reach down to grab a cloth, but halt within inches of the fabric touching his fingertips. Of a sudden, his head slanted upwards, almost as if he suspected her presence. Lynet scooted back from the window and into the shadows of the chamber, hoping she had not been found out, staring at the all but naked man. With her heart hammering away in her chest, she feared Ian surely could hear its beating, even at this distance keeping them apart.

She left the window, frantically searching the chamber for something to occupy her thoughts, yet there was nothing here familiar to her. Even a bit of thread to mend something...anything...would have been preferable to idly sitting with her nerves on edge, awaiting Ian's pleasure.

Her footsteps led her to the table. With unsteady hands, she took a chalice of wine. It took every effort just to raise the cup to her lips. A small sip of the heady brew slid down her throat then down into the pit of her belly where it warmed her considerably. Lynet put the cup back into place in fear she might lose her wits if she continued to drink the spirits that were sure to cloud her thoughts and judgment. She needed a clear head for what was about to happen. She certainly did not wish to forget such a momentous occasion as when she and Ian became man and wife in every sense of the word.

Treading slowly back to the window, she attempted to glimpse yet another view of Ian, but he was nowhere to be seen. It gave her pause to wonder how much time she in truth still had afore he came to her.

She would not have long to wait, but the noise she heard outside the bed chamber was not one she was expecting. The sound of arguing reached her ears and caused goose bumps of anxiety to race down her arms. The door was rudely pushed open by a huge Scotsman who Lynet did not recognize. She gasped and clutched at her robe, wondering if they were under attack. She watched in fear as his eyes raked her from head to toe as though he was stripping her clothes from her body for his viewing pleasure.

Ian pushed past the man at the door and came to her side. She was enveloped into the warmth of her husband's embrace whilst he used his own body as a shield from prying eyes.

Afore she could ask what was going on, another entered their chamber. His mother stood glaring in their direction with her lofty disposition, as if Lynet was far beneath her own exalted station in life.

"I can now see why you wished to attend your wife with all speed, Ian," the stranger muttered in a low seductive tone. "Once clean, she is quite lovely. Mayhap, 'twill not be such a horrendous task you must perform, after all."

"Enough, Uncle Edric," Ian grimaced. "I will not have you besmirch my lady's reputation, nor her tender hearted feelings."

"Bah...her feelings are the least of your worries, boy. You must openly fulfill your obligations to the clan, lest you plan to relinquish the title. I have no issue with such a choice if your decision is to surrender your rights of Urquhart. Such an honor can then pass on to me, as your next of kin."

Lynet peeked around Ian's body and saw a servant come into the room. A white cloth was laid down in the center of the bed, causing Lynet to once more let out a gasp of surprise. Surely, this could not mean what she thought, or could it? From the amount of people, who she assumed were other leaders of the clan, hovering outside in the passageway, she knew her assumptions were correct.

"Ian, please..." she whispered, trying to keep from crying out at the cruelty he would inflict upon her that others were to witness their union. "Do not do this to me...to us."

"Merciful heavens," Fiona said as she went to open the door wider, "just get it over with, Ian, so I may return to my solar and resume my stitchery."

"Aye, nephew, hurry along now, and do your duty," Ian's uncle all but prodded, trying to force him into action.

"Everyone out!" Ian shouted to the group and took a firm grip on his mother's arm to usher her from the chamber.

His mother raised her arm to slap his face, but her son easily took hold of it. "You dare to defy me?" she fumed.

"Aye...mayhap, you should get used to it," Ian replied. "I am my own man and will not be led about by my nose just because you gave birth to me."

"We demand evidence of her—"

"By God's blood, you shall have your damn proof. Now, get out!" Ian roared.

Edric was the last to leave as he gave Lynet another leer. "We shall listen at the door and await the substantiation of her virginity." He left leaving the heavy oaken door slightly ajar.

If Lynet had been trembling afore, 'twas nothing to how she was currently feeling as she listened to the voices of clansmen loudly whispering amongst themselves in the passageway. Her hand rose to her mouth to choke back a sob of dismay. She turned towards the fire, attempting to hide her shame. Her hair hung in her line of vision 'til she saw her chalice of wine thrust afore her.

"Are you all right, Lynet?"

She grasped at the cup and took a large gulp of the liquid that went straight to her stomach. Coughing, she practically shoved the goblet back at Ian in her effort to find some way to control her nerves.

"All right? How can you ask such of me, when we have an audience just outside our door, waiting for us to perform like animals at some village faire?"

"'Tis common enough practice, Lynet, although 'tis not to my liking."

"Then put a stop to it and ask them to leave us in peace." Lynet looked pleadingly into those hazel eyes she had loved all her life. He did not give her the answer she had hoped for.

"'Tis expected...I am most sorry."

A sigh escaped her lips as she resigned herself to her fate and how their marriage would proceed. "Very well...then let us be about this. After all...your mother has important work to do. She should not have to put off her stitchery, waiting for such an insignificant event as the two of us becoming man and wife, should she?"

She kicked off her slippers next to the bed and threw her robe from her shoulders to the floor where it floated in a discarded heap of silky linen. Careful not to disturb the cloth that would be the ruin of the beginning of their lives together, Lynet gently lay atop of it and folded her hands upon her stomach, not knowing where else to put them.

She closed her eyes and waited with baited breath for Ian to join her, yet, still there was no movement on his part. She glanced at him timidly beneath her lowered lashes. He appeared as though he were struggling with some inner demon attempting to take possession of him. His fists clenched and unclenched at his sides 'til he, too, took a deep sip of his wine. His brow was furrowed, showing his disgust at what he was about to do. Lynet was unsure if the act of consummating their marriage was repugnant to him, or the fact the mutterings of those just outside the door seemed to rise in volume.

Lynet surmised he had come to his decision when he made his way to the bed. It dipped with his weight as he sat on the edge to remove his boots. Yet, still, he made no effort to touch her, and Lynet refused to give in to the fear that all but consumed her. She felt his hand upon her cheek as he turned her head so she had no choice but to look upon him. 'Twas such a tender expression on his face it touched her heart, and, for one fleeting moment, she thought he would relent in the course set afore him to prove his worth to his family.

"Kiss me, wife," he whispered, leaning closer towards her as his arms made their way along both sides of her tense body.

She turned from him. "I will gladly do so once you close the door and tell them to go away."

"You would refuse me?"

"How can I not, when you put them and their ways afore me...your wife?"

"'Tis not fair you would make me choose between my duties to my family and you, Lynet. You know this is the way of our people, so why do you fight me on this? We can make the best of this situation. I promise 'twill be better the next time."

Another sob caught in her throat. "You should not make promises you may not be able to keep, Ian. 'Tis not very chivalrous of you, nor does it speak highly of your knightly vow you swore to protect me."

Ian cursed beneath his breath and dug the heel of his palm across his eyes as if to rid himself of his dilemma afore he came to rest on top of her. He tried to kiss her, but she refused to let him soften what he was about to do to her. "Lynet..."

Tears racing down her cheeks, she gazed at him directly. "I shall hate you for this 'til my last dying breath," she swore.

"*Damnation!*" All the fight went out of Ian as he hastily checked the door and sat up. "Be quiet and lift yourself up."

Confused, she did as she was told and felt as he grabbed at the cloth beneath her. Taking a dirk, he ran the blade across the palm of his hand. The slice quickly pooled red with his blood that he dripped onto the whiteness of the fabric.

"Cry out, as if you are in pain," he demanded of her and she let out a small scream. It must have satisfied those out in the passageway and served as justification she was no longer a maid. Lynet swore she even heard one person clap his hands in glee. She could only assume their happiness was for thoughts of her dowry filling the coffers of the estate. Lynet knew there was nothing inside of her to be pleased about, since she had denied her husband his rights to her body.

Ian continued sitting there on the edge of the bed, not moving. Lynet was still in shock of what he intended to offer the crowd outside their chamber. She lifted her hand towards him, and yet, afore her touch could ease the tension between them, he stood. Grabbing the fabric, he quickly strode to the door.

"Here is your proof," he tossed the cloth out of the portal and slammed the door in the faces of those murmuring their words of encouragement.

Grabbing his boots, he made his way to the hearth and proceeded to don them. Ripping at the edge of his tunic, he tore the fabric 'til he was able to tie the cloth around his injured hand using his teeth to tie the knot. Lynet could only pray none would question the bandage.

Ian pulled off a chunk of bread and placed a piece of cheese between it. He came to the bed only to stare down at her 'til a rosy blush flushed her face. She clutched the fur at her side to cover herself from his roving eyes.

Still, he stood there in silence, 'til Lynet could take it no more. "Ian, I—"

He held up his hand to halt her words afore she could utter her apology. When he spoke, his words were layered with anger as tense as the air between them. "Do not ever question my honor again, Lynet, or so help me you shall regret it. I may not be as accommodating the next time."

He gave her a brief bow and left their chamber, without another word. Alone once more with her thoughts, she could only ponder how she had had the nerve to stand up to him, but more importantly, how she would breach the rift she had knowingly put between them. 'Twas more than she had ever dared afore. For the second time in a matter of days, she shed tears for what she had lost. Gone was any respect Ian felt for her, as was evident in his parting look at her. She had the sinking feeling the love that had only just begun to bloom between them had suddenly vanished, and 'twas all her doing. What had she done?

TWENTY-TWO

HAD IT REALLY BEEN OVER A FORTNIGHT ago that Ian had stormed out of their chamber? He had made a decision that eve, and he would not go back on the promise he had made to himself. He had vowed he would not dare touch Lynet, lest she willingly came to him of her own accord. He should have known making such a vow would be a huge mistake.

Every night he came to their chamber in the hope she would reach out to him. Allowing her only a few moments to make some form of an effort, he would quickly come to the conclusion he was wasting his time. Each eve, he gave up waiting for a signal she would welcome him into her bed. Defeated, he would grab a pelt to lie down in frustration upon the floor near the hearth. 'Twas not the first time his tired backside had spent an uncomfortable night upon the ground, nor apparently would it be the last. The stone flooring was no different, except at least he did not have to worry about rocks digging into his sorry arse. And yet, furs and his plaid were a poor substitute for warmth when his wife lay but inches away from him. He must be the biggest fool in all of Scotland and England combined.

Wiping the sweat from his brow, Ian took up the rake and again began the tedious task of tossing fresh hay into the now clean stall for his horse. 'Twas a mindless chore for the laird to be shoveling manure and mucking out the filthy stable, but he gladly put all his energy into such a menial job. At least the chore did not give him time to ponder the misery of his own failure when it came to his marriage bed.

"Ye would make a good stable lad," Angus said with a chuckle from the doorway. "I have not seen the place so clean in a long while."

"I am sure the horses will, at the very least, appreciate my efforts, seeing as no one else appears to care for the steeds' wellbeing," Ian replied. Finishing his task, he leaned the tool against the wall with the others. He picked up a rag and began cleaning his hands afore tossing it into a pile needing to be laundered. "I would ask why they have been so neglected. I could also ask the same with regards to the rest of the estate, but can most likely figure out the answer for myself."

"Yer uncle has been busy."

"Aye, as I said, I guessed as much. He does not leave me a great deal to work with, that is, if there was even anything of some miniscule value after my brother's greedy ways."

"Ye should not speak ill o' the dead, even if he deserves it." Angus pushed off the door frame and held out a flagon. "Here...this may help. We willna go lacking fer wine and ale. Food is an entirely different matter."

Nodding his thanks, Ian pulled the cork and took a long hard drink of the cool brew to quench his thirst. "Any other words of wisdom you care to impart?"

"Ye wish me tae speak freely?" Angus asked with a raised brow.

"I believe you earned that right after aiding me with freeing my lady."

"Ye know, we have not seen the last from the Davidson laird. He willna like that ye bested him, no matter the woman is yer wife."

Ian stretched his sore muscles. "Tell me something I do not know, Angus. We will keep our eyes open and be on the lookout for trouble. 'Twill surely follow Lynet wherever she may go, and I suspect being my wife will not change that." He sat down on a bale of hay and motioned for Angus to do the same, offering the man a drink from the flagon.

Ian watched the Scot's indecision, giving him a moment to take a good look at a man who had traveled far just to find him. It appeared Angus was not much older than Ian himself, if they were not of similar age. Ian could see the man spent many an hour training with the broadsword he had strapped to his side, considering his fit appearance. This led Ian to have nothing but respect for the Highlander, since Ian was not one to live an idle life, either. Dark brown hair hung loose to his shoulders whilst brown eyes peered most warily at him, almost as though he dared not speak his mind. He also sprouted a full week's worth of whiskers, hidden underneath was a square jaw.

Ian continued to hold out the leather flagon towards the clansman, who finally took ahold of it and sat, even if 'twas done with considerable hesitation. "Go on, Angus, tell me what I am up against that others will not dare say to my face. I am not even sure who I can trust here," he urged, relaxing back against the wall to await the worst. "How bad can it be, other than from what my own eyes have already shown me?"

"Aye, ye have that aright, me laird," Angus said, after wiping his mouth and handing the brew off once more to Ian. "Yer Uncle has done a fine mess o' things tae further burden yer people after all yer brother did tae start the clan's ruin. We are almost tae the point o' starvin', we are, especially when Edric has done nothing tae cease the raiding o' our cattle and sheep."

"What else?" Ian's words were clipped. All he wanted was confirmation of what he had already assumed. His Uncle had run the estate further into the ground, almost to the point of annihilation.

"There's not much left," Angus stated, coming straight to the heart of the matter. "Yer coffers are empty, and the fields are fallow. The livestock is almost gone tae the point o' being non-existent, and winter will be upon us sooner than we would like. 'Tis why yer mother sent fer ye in the hope ye had some coin tae spare in order tae save us."

"You have been here all this time and never thought of leaving?"

Angus shrugged his broad shoulders. "Where else am I tae go? 'Tis the only home I have ever known, even though there is not much left tae it. Besides, I have a wee bairn on the way and would not risk movin' the little woman in her condition."

Ian slapped the man on the back. He barely shifted. "I had not even thought to ask if you were wed."

"'Twas hardly time, considering yer desire tae enter the tournament tae win yerself a bonny bride. Then, there were more important matters needing attending, besides chasing after yer abducted wife."

Ian stood, and yet, Angus remained where he was. "What could be of more import than my lady?"

"Yer own health, fer one thing, or had ye not thought on having the lass have a look at yer wound tae see if the injury festers?"

Ian busied himself with tidying up the mess he had made by gathering the cloths he had thrown upon the floor. "We have not had time for much speech of late," he grumbled, "nor have I made the effort to see what she does with her day."

Angus did not hold back a low chortle. "As newly wedded, I would not expect a lot o' talking tae be going on between ye, at least during the midnight hours. Not that I am one tae council ye on how tae handle yer wife, but ye should make the attempt tae have speech with her. It tends tae make life a little easier, not tae mention keep ye warm at night, if ye take my meaning."

"Speaking from experience, are you?"

"Aye, that I am."

"I will consider talking to her soon. However, I do not feel Lady Lynet desires my company."

"She was making her way towards the dock when I passed her. She dinnae appear too happy, not that I am an expert on reading neither a woman's mind, nor their moods. Go have speech with her," Angus urged.

Ian began making his way from the stable with Angus following closely behind. He squinted from the daylight, even though 'twas another typical cloudy day that was not entirely different than his time spent in England. He saw Lynet was indeed sitting on the edge of the dock near the loch, tossing rocks into the calm water. Still feeling put out that she had no desire to fully become his wife, he let his pride and anger get the best of him and refused to make the first move. Angus must have read his thoughts, as he began tsk tsking.

"Ye willna go tae her, then?" he asked tersely.

"Nay," Ian muttered, "I must needs see the blacksmith and attend other duties."

"Do ye mind, then, if I have speech wit' yer lady?"

Ian was not sure what possessed the man to ask this of him and, yet, could not say him nay. "You may as well see to her. After all you have done for us, I put Lynet in your care as her guard to protect her when I am not able to do so myself."

Angus gave him a slight nod. "I am honored, me laird."

Ian watched the slightly older man make his way towards his wife not knowing why, for the life of him, he was not making the effort himself.

Her mood could only be termed gloomy, at best. She did not fit in here, and any of her attempts to become mistress of the castle were continually thwarted by Fiona's meddlesome ways. Lynet had all but given up, since 'twas clear she did not have Ian's support. She surmised, once her dowry was received from Berwyck, she would be all but sent to some obscure dwelling to live out the rest of her life. She might as well have joined the nunnery, as she had threatened to do so many times in the past. At least her life would have been a worthy sacrifice as one of God's brides, instead of being seen as a useless annoyance and always being told she was under foot.

Lynet had tried to take charge of the hall, the kitchens, and even to see if anything could be salvaged from what remained of the gardens. Time and time again, Lady Fiona had made it clear her assistance was not needed, despite the fact the condition of Ian's hall was atrociously filthy. She was shocked the dogs would even sleep upon the flea ridden floor, but it explained much of why those that walked across the room scratched at their legs.

She had angered him that night, which almost seemed as if it had happened a lifetime ago. 'Twas an eve that constantly played inside her mind 'til she wanted to run screaming from the keep. Ian had made no attempt to soften her wounded heart that he would take her in front of others, notwithstanding the fact that he did indeed honor her request. The evenings were the worst torture she had ever encountered, for she would have no choice but to listen intently to his steady breathing as sleep overtook him whilst he slumbered upon the floor.

Lynet picked up another stone lying next to her and tossed it into the waters to watch the rippling effect of the wave 'til it dissipated into nothingness. She wiped at a tear, wondering where the sassy lass of Berwyck had gone. Sometimes, she felt like such a child, and knew not in which direction she should now turn. Going back home to Berwyck did not seem like a possible solution to her problems, not that she had the means or energy to travel the length of Scotland to reach it.

"Ye should be careful about throwing stones, lassie. Ye might awaken the monster lying far beneath those murky waters o' the loch."

Gathering her skirts, she rose quickly, only to espy Angus standing some distance from her.

"Hello, Angus." Her words were soft, and she supposed their tone echoed her feelings, since a sad look appeared upon his face. She tossed her head in the direction of the now calm surface that seemed as smooth as glass. "Is there really a creature living within?"

"So the legend goes, if ye believe such things. Why so forlorn, milady?" He came to stand next to her as they both turned to stare back over the water. "It canna be as bad as ye think."

"Aye, it can," she whispered. "Nothing is how I thought 'twould be from my youth."

"Weel, sometimes bairns tend tae not think o' anything other than dreamin' and wishin' on what could be. Usually, the reality o' the situation is a far cry from what their life will become."

"I serve no purpose here, Angus. I am not even mistress in my own keep," she fumed afore she remembered herself and shyly looked up at the man beside her. "I am sorry. I barely know you and should not be confessing my thoughts so openly."

"I am honored ye think yerself comfortable enough around me that ye would do so. Should ye not be admitting such tae our laird? He seems a most reasonable man tae make things aright between ye and the lady Fiona."

"We have fallen into disaccord."

Angus gave a heavy sigh. "He said much the same thing, not that he told me any details."

Lynet inwardly gave a sigh of relief that Ian had not confessed to another she withheld herself from her husband. 'Twas embarrassing enough for her to be living with the knowledge of her foolishness. 'Twould be a hundred times more so if others knew, as well.

They stood there in silence for several moments, lost in their own thoughts. 'Twas a beautiful place she had hoped to call home, but now her uncertainty welled up inside her 'til she knew not which direction she should turn. She rubbed at her temples, hoping some answer would come to her. There was nothing, but all the questions of what she could have done differently. With a polite clearing of Angus's throat, Lynet turned towards him and saw 'twas clear he had been attempting to gain her attention.

"Was there something you wished to speak to me about, Angus?" Taking her eyes from the loch, she gave the highlander her full attention.

"I was pondering that, mayhap, ye should see just how far ye can push our laird into giving up some o' his pride and making things aright with ye."

A very unladylike snort escaped her lips in surprise. "I hardly think pushing him to whatever limits of patience he has left with me will do our relationship any good."

"Bah! Such an effort canna hurt," Angus scoffed. "Besides, I believe yer own willful determination tae remain immune tae Ian's charms is precisely what drew the man tae ye in the first place."

"Hmmm. I still do not know if 'tis a good idea, Angus."

"Let us start with going for a ride. I shall plead that ye ordered me tae take ye or ye'd go off on yer own."

"He shall be furious," Lynet stated, but beamed in delight with the thought of escaping the stifling confines of the castle for however long such a reprieve should last. She would not mind being away from Ian's mother, as well.

"Aye, that he will. Although, we shall take several men with us fer extra protection."

Lynet clasped her hands behind her back, trying to hold back her excitement of going for a ride. "I believe your idea does have some merit. Let us away, and you can show me the lay of the land."

And that is how Lynet escaped the ever watchful eyes of the Lady Fiona and Ian's uncle for the afternoon. As she raced across the countryside under close guard, she enjoyed the small amount of freedom she had been granted. She knew her return would be turbulent, and for the first time in the past several se'nnights, she was looking forward to the storm.

Calum watched the procession of horses as they made their way back behind the security of the walls of the castle. The man was a fool to let Lynet go beyond the one place she would be safe from his clutches. He would have never been that careless. He squinted afore raising his hand to shield his eyes from the brightness of the sun peeking through the ever persistent clouds.

He began making his way back down from the mountaintop to rejoin his men. His scouts had done a fair enough job tracking his lady, despite Ian's attempts to hide their trail. Yet, Calum knew where they were headed, for 'twas no secret where MacGillivray would make his home.

He called out his orders to make camp for the night, even whilst he began to formulate how Lynet's fortune would soon be his. He had lost the fair damsel once due to his own stupidity. When he at last got her in his grasp, he would not make the same mistake, ever again.

Twenty-Three

IAN STORMED HIS WAY PAST HIS KINSMEN, who apparently had nothing better to do then stand around staring aimlessly at the party who had just ridden into the outer bailey. His angry stride proved he had only one purpose in mind, and that was to reach the woman who sat prettily upon a chestnut mare with bubbly laughter upon her lips. If he was not so furious with her, he might have noticed how beautiful she appeared. With blue eyes sparkling with uncontained joy, 'twas apparent she had enjoyed her outing, along with the company of others.

As he drew closer, she must have felt his nearness, for the smile that only seconds ago graced her face, now fell into a grim line of displeasure. Her delicate brows drew together in a fierce scowl that rivaled her brother-in-law's. Ian all but dismissed her foul temperament as insignificant, considering Lynet's actions this day were the cause of his own unpleasant and foul mood. He felt as if his wrath was about to explode. Seeing as she was the one to have erred, he had no notion as to what she had to be so upset about.

Calling out to the lad about to take the reins of her horse, Ian stepped forward and all but wrenched them from her grasp. Tossing the leather aside, he raised his arms towards his errant wife. "Get down," he ordered through clenched teeth. Lynet glanced over her shoulder in the direction of Angus, but the highlander merely plastered a smile upon his face that could only be termed as one of satisfaction. Ian was not sure what was going on between the two, but he did not care for it, at all.

His wife nonchalantly rested her arm upon the pommel of her saddle. "I do not need your help, Ian. I am perfectly capable of getting off my horse, with or without your unwelcome assistance." Her words dripped dangerously close to all but insulting him.

Stunned she would shun him in front of others, he tried again, but to no avail. "You are my wife," he stated firmly. She did not take his meaning, only furthering his annoyance with the lass.

"Really?" she snapped with raised brows. "I was not sure you remembered, since I have all been but forgotten since our arrival." Slapping away his outstretched hands, she dismissed his attempt to be chivalrous whilst she slid to the ground in one fluid and graceful movement. Adjusting her skirts, she dared to look up at him as though she had done nothing wrong.

He leaned forward, causing Lynet to move 'til her backside rested against her horse. "Do not test me further this day, lass." His whispered words were meant for her ears alone, but Ian swore he heard an amused chuckle coming from Angus whilst he led his horse in the direction of the stable. "Who gave you permission to leave the castle?"

"I was not aware I must needs ask your consent," Lynet replied with a sweet smile. Skirting around him, she casually began taking off her gloves as though she had all time at her leisure. "I was well guarded." Turning her back on him, she began to make her way towards the keep. He quickened his pace to catch up to her.

"That is not the point," he declared, scowling. Reaching for her arm, Ian made the mistake of pulling Lynet closer to him. Her flowery scent assaulted his senses like a rich, heady wine. Just to feel her standing this close to him was intoxicating.

Inhaling deeply, Ian sensed her very essence capture his soul, and he felt as though he were a man starving for food. Their eyes met. For just an instant, Ian swore he witnessed such longing hidden in the depth of blue that swam afore his vision. Lynet quickly changed her expression to mask the emotions Ian knew for certain she had been feeling. Once again, she portrayed a lady who was cool and unresponsive to his charm.

"Then what *is* your point, Ian?"

"Have you so easily forgotten the danger that could be awaiting you? Or, perchance, you do not care if you are captured, yet again?"

"Do not be so ridiculous," she answered confidently. "I was perfectly safe with Angus and the men he had to guard me."

"I will advise you to not be a fool, thinking you are safe outside of these walls. I do not feel my trying to keep you protected is unreasonable."

"I am not the one being unreasonable," she shouted.

Ian hid a smile as he watched his wife's face become flushed in her efforts to remain in control of the situation they were discussing. "Then, we are in accord. You will not leave the grounds again, lest I give you leave to do so," Ian replied, taking her elbow to escort her, whether she liked it or not.

"I never agreed to such terms."

"You may not be in agreement to my directives, but you will obey them just the same, if you know what is good for you."

"I am not a child to be ordered about," Lynet fumed.

"Then stop acting like one," Ian answered. Leading her through the hall, they made their way up to their chambers. Opening the door, he gave her a gentle push. When she sat with enough force to break the stool afore the fire, he gave her a look that he would not tolerate further arguing. She snapped her lips shut, not giving voice to the sharp retort she was most likely about to spit out at him. "I will send a maid to help you change and will see you at the evening meal."

Giving her a formal bow that would have rivaled any gentleman at court, he left her sulking in her seat and closed the door quietly between them. Ian could only ponder on what object met the door as the sound of it shattering ricocheted throughout the passageway.

⚬⚬⚬

"That insufferable, pig-headed lout!"

Lynet paced the width of the chamber, feeling as though the walls were closing in around her. "How dare he treat me as if I were a misbehaving child? Who does he think he is?"

She made her way to the window seat and sat to enjoy the view of the loch. Taking several deep breaths to calm her nerves, she began to feel better. A giggle escaped her after she realized her plan may just work, after all. Ian had been furious. She supposed he had every right to be, given the circumstances. He also was not immune to the connection between them. She could hardly miss the look of desire that flashed momentarily in his eyes when he held her close. It had taken everything within her power not to lean in to rest her hands upon his muscled chest. She had been so very tempted, but that would have been giving up the game too quickly.

Aye, Ian needed to see for himself she was a worthy companion as his wife, and 'twas past time for her to assume her role as chatelaine of the castle. Only when the keys to the keep were on a chain around her waist would she begin to feel like a wife. Perchance then, he would at last take her to his bed. Her face flushed with heat at the thought of them trysting beneath the covers.

A discrete knock sounded upon the door, and Lynet called the servant to enter. A devilish idea came into her mind when the woman pulled out a dress of pale blue linen. Lynet had marveled at the garment afore, since 'twas indeed perfect and would bring out the color in her eyes. Someone had taken great care in constructing the cloth with stitchery that would rival her own. She would save it for a special occasion and not wear it this eve.

"I believe something a little less formal is in order this night, Lorna," she said going to the trunk and digging down to the bottom. Her fingers came in contact with material of soft wool, so she carefully pulled, trying her best not to disrupt her remaining dresses. She gave the garment a shake and a pair of leggings fell into her awaiting hand. A gasp escaped the maid.

"'Tis unseemly, milady," Lorna replied, covering her mouth. She began to turn red in the face from shock.

"This is precisely why I will dare to dress accordingly."

"You do not wish to incur the wrath of Lady Fiona and Sir Edric. Surely, if you plan to wear such attire, they will be displeased." Her pleading tone more than begged Lynet to rethink her choice in attending the evening meal dressed as a boy.

"I thank you for your warning, but am I not the laird's wife?" Lynet stared at the woman, who wisely snapped her lips shut. "I shall do and dress as I please. If you would help me get this dress off, I think I can manage the rest."

Lorna did as she was bid, grumbling beneath her breath. She may only be a maid, but she certainly was an opinionated one.

Lynet could hardly berate the woman for the good intentions on her behalf. Still, Lynet ignored the serf's urging to change her mind, for she was determined to push Ian to the brink of whatever held him back from making her his wife in every way. If this did not do the trick, she would need to think of something else.

Not sure what could be more daring than attending the evening meal dressed in men's attire, Lynet dismissed Lorna, thanking her for her help. The door shut. Left alone with only her thoughts to occupy her, Lynet pulled at her hair and began braiding its length. 'Twas a tedious task, and perhaps she had been too hasty in dismissing Lorna. Finally reaching the end, she tied a leather strap to hold it together and stood. Moving about the chamber caused the long braid to swish back and forth, much like a horse's tail. She gazed down upon the dark green tunic that reached just below her hips. Mayhap, she should have found one longer, but 'twas too late now to find another, for she heard the bell ringing to call those in the keep to sup.

She took another look over her shoulder and down the length of her body. The leggings hugged her bottom far tighter than she thought they would, showing off every curve God had graced her with. When she had found the clothing in the trunk that had been brought to her chamber for her use, she had never dreamed she would be wearing them for anything other than tending to those who may have need of her healing touch.

She waited several more minutes to ensure the hall would be filled with hungry clansmen afore she left her room. Practically skipping down the passageway, a cheeky laugh escaped her. Lynet's only thought was of Ian dragging her back to their chamber posthaste to make love to her, lest of course, he clobbered her first.

TWENTY-FOUR

HIS EVER VIGILANT EYES SCANNED the Great Hall to view the mayhem afore him. Boisterous voices grew in volume as the chamber began to fill. Scowling, Ian remembered this room from his youth. The large chamber had always been meticulously clean, at least as much as was humanly possible, given the number of clansmen who came to sup here. He was not sure how his mother had let the place become what he now beheld.

Barking dogs ran between the tables and the legs of the clansmen who came to fill their hungry stomachs and partake of whatever bounty could still yet be found at Urquhart's table. One beast even dared to lift his leg upon an unwitting recipient afore receiving a swift kick from a serf, sending the hound scurrying for cover. The rushes were a mess, and Ian would not dare to wonder when the last time they had been changed. Even the dust and grime marred, tattered tapestries hanging upon the walls were a disgrace to his ancestors. Things needed to change, and quickly.

Ian had taken what coin he had when he left Berwyck so abruptly, but he would need far more than what he currently held. Not only would restoring the castle to its formal glory require what he had in Edinburgh, but the dowry Lynet would bring must be secured, as well. He would not rest 'til he saw his home brought back from the mess his brother had left behind. Such an undertaking may just cost him every shilling he owned.

A platter of meat was placed in front of him. Ian took one look at it, and his stomach churned in protest. He knew he should be thankful there was at least food for his table, but there was nothing appetizing about this meat swimming in a sea of grease he was supposed to sup upon. He grimaced. Even the smell that reached his nostrils held little appeal. Another servant came bearing bread then left quickly after a short curtsey. Ian tore off a chunk, hoping against hope that, mayhap, something could be salvaged of the meal.

Taking a bite, he almost choked on the coarse bread as he spat out a stone that had escaped the process of being sifted properly from the flour. He rubbed at his jaw, thankful he had not lost a tooth. Gazing around his hall, it appeared he was the only one having an issue with the meal that was supposed to curb his hunger. Even his mother and uncle appeared eager to fill their trenchers. He must needs speak to his cook, or else replace him. Starving might be preferable than having to endure another meal such as this.

He stabbed at the meat and watched the fat drip from what he could now smell was boar. Taking a bite did not improve his thoughts on what would make it edible. The food barely held any flavor. He began to chew the tough pork and wondered how long 'twould take afore he would be able to swallow what was in his mouth. Taking his cup in hand, he drained the wine and held out the chalice for it to be refilled. At least there was something to be said about the flavor of his drink.

Mayhap, if he ate his fill fast enough, he could enjoy what was left of the eve. As he began to devour his meal, he caught the sound of several gasps afore conversations in the room faded to a deafening silence. Ian wiped his mouth upon his sleeve and looked up, wondering what was going on in his hall that drew everyone's attention.

To say that she captured every member of the clan's interest was a complete understatement. Sauntering across the room, Lynet portrayed enough confidence of an entire invading army. Her tunic barely covered her very fetching arse, causing parts of Ian to stir. Her blonde braid swung behind her just begging for him to reach out and take hold of it. She was so reminiscent of her sister Amiria, that for an instant, Ian was lost in the memories of what he had lost years afore. He was brought back to the present when his mother snarled in anger.

"How dare she come to my hall dressed in such masculine costume," Fiona hissed furiously whilst she began to rise to apparently further voice her displeasure.

"Sit down, mother," Ian insisted. "'Tis her hall now, and she may dress as she damn well pleases."

Edric leaned forward on the table, nearly putting his sleeve in the trencher he shared with his sister. "Do you presume to usurp your mother's authority, after all she has done for Urquhart?"

Ian's eyes narrowed, taking in the pair. Considering all their ranting with the need of coin for the place, 'twas evident from their garments such was not the case when it came to donning their finest, each day. "And you will not tell me how to run my estate, including how I deal with my mother. If you do not like my hall, I am sure you can find suitable lodging elsewhere.

Mayhap, such a dwelling will be more compatible with your discriminating penchant for having the finest of life's offerings."

Fiona's face began to turn red with rage. "You forget yourself, Ian," she fumed.

"As do you, mother. The both of you should refrain from irritating me so I may enjoy my meal, if that is even humanly possible."

"How dare you speak to me thusly?" Fiona stood, looking down at Ian as though he was still but a lad. But he was a boy no more, and 'twas time his mother learned she could not control him any longer.

"If you do not care for my company, than by all means, you may take your leave of the hall and eat elsewhere, along with your brother."

Conversations resumed at a booming level, as everyone in the room had an opinion of what was transpiring in the Great Hall. Yet, Ian continued to wait, as if he had nothing better to do than for the pair to come to some decision. 'Twas a near silent exchange between mother and son afore Fiona's words sputtered to a bare murmur. She once again took her seat.

Satisfied that he would not have to listen to his dame besmirch his wife's name, he leaned back in his seat and called for Lynet's chalice to be filled. Returning his attention to his meal, he gave no further thought that Lynet would not make haste to join him at the table.

He waited, refusing to consider the unthinkable alternative that she would dare to eat elsewhere. That was his first mistake, among many, where the lass was concerned. He swallowed hard, feeling the gristly piece of meat make its way down his throat, inch by inch. It seemed as though even the food was to disagree with him as he attempted not to belch. He grabbed at his goblet to help hasten the grub's journey to his protesting stomach.

Where was she? His eyes flicked through the crowd of men 'til his gaze fell irritably upon his wife. She stood next to Angus, who pushed the man next to him with his elbow to make room for her. How she could appear so demure and angelic dressed in those tight fitting hose was beyond his ken. Surely, there was a bit of the devil in her that she would actually attire herself in the garments of a man. Yet, there she was, sitting at a table full of clansmen as if she had done it a hundred times afore, listening intently to Connor's ramblings.

Ian's eyes narrowed as he viewed the display afore him. Was it done on purpose? Even she would not dare to be so blatantly ignorant that she would knowingly snub her laird afore the entire clan by sitting at one of the lower tables. She was his wife. Her place was by his side.

His hands clenched the arm of his chair whilst a hundred pair of eyes watched his every move. He tried to calm down, and yet, she made it hard when he heard her laughter from across the chamber. She had made a statement by ignoring the vacant seat at the high table. Ian would not let himself lose face with his people with a disobedient wife.

She raised her head slightly to look at him from beneath her lowered lashes. The slightest smirk began at the corner of that luscious mouth of hers afore she took up a linen and pretended to wipe her lips. But Ian knew without a doubt what her scheme was about. He stood. With a determined stride, he made his way towards his mischievous bride. He would prove to her, once and for all, who was the master of the game in her little contest of wills. He would not be the loser.

Lynet swore beneath her breath for her mistake. She should not have set her gaze upon her husband, but she could not resist the small smile of satisfaction from seeing Ian's attempt to remain calm when she decided to sit elsewhere. The situation became worse as she heard the chuckle of the man next to her.

"A job well done, lassie," Angus whispered to her, "but dinnae lose yer courage. Ye will need it now, more than ever."

She took a bite of the ghastly meat that had been set afore her knowing her time for nourishment was quickly going to end. She was surprised Ian's chair remained upright, given the amount of force of his rising from the table. His stride was furious, and she could see for herself that his temper flared as he quickened his pace across the hall. How could it not, with all the ribbing he was receiving from his clansmen as he strode ever closer. Their message was clear. If Ian could not control his wife, he was certainly not capable of leading the clan.

She knew the instant he stood behind her waiting for her to acknowledge his presence. His uneven breathing practically called for her to calm his simmering temper. She waited. He did nothing, and yet, she experienced the sensation of his every move. She knew she must finish what she started and would not give him the gratification of reacting to his impending furious outburst that was sure to come. Was there truly a need to do so? From the amount of heat radiating from his body, Lynet made every attempt not to throw herself into his arms. She never wanted the man more than she did at this very instant. Again, she hid her smile. She would not be won over so easily, nor would she yield the game.

"Get up," Ian insisted with more control in his voice than she thought possible. Yet, the tone of his speech practically scorched her where she sat with the angry undertone those two little words implied. He must have made some motion to signal his men she could not see, for those seated next to her quickly scrambled from their seats to leave her alone to her own fate.

He made to pull out her off the bench, but she just as firmly took hold of the edges to slide it forward. He tugged. She pulled. *Let the battle begin!* "I have not as yet finished my meal." She kept the pitch of her own voice flat, as though she barely had the inclination to recognize his order. Since she could not see his face, she could only assume her answer did not please him.

"Aye, you have."

"Nay, I have not. As you can plainly see, if you but look at my trencher." She moved her body so he could view her meal that had barely been touched. She pointed to the food as though she were speaking to a child. "See you here? Barely a morsel has passed my lips and I am most famished."

Lynet made to ignore him and took another bite of the tasteless meat. It stuck in her throat, but she was determined to show her husband he would not deter her from her meal. A growl of outrage erupted from him, as if the beast within him had at last been unleashed. She had not expected such a backlash, and yet, she should have known 'twas a possibility. She had been pushing him to the very edge of the civility left between them all this day.

Not only was she pulled from her bench that fell to the floor with a loud clatter, but she was lifted clear off her feet and turned towards him in one swift motion. Crushed against the solid wall of his chest whilst Ian held her with a steely grip, Lynet became level with those mesmerizing hazel eyes that had always been her downfall. She gulped and prayed he did not hear the noise that was as loud as bagpipes inside her own head. He grinned, quite handsomely, the damn rogue. His eyes began to sparkle mischievously, and Lynet knew he thought he had won the battle between them. *He should have known better*, she mused, for she was not done with him, as yet.

TWENTY-FIVE

S HE WAS SO SLIGHT AGAINST HIS CHEST, he had no problem
holding her with only one arm. Her pupils dilated, and the
blue of her eyes were more vivid than he had ever seen them
afore. He watched in fascination as the pulse at her neck ticked
in a rapid staccato, and he knew he had affected her with his
touch. She swallowed hard. He smiled, knowing her thoughts.
By God, he had never wanted a woman more than he wanted
Lynet, despite the fact she had done all in her power to irritate
him.

"Yield," he murmured huskily. Her tongue peeked out of
that delectable mouth of hers to moisten her lips.

"Never," she declared, just as firmly.

"You are my wife."

She leaned closer and her flowery fragrance sent Ian's own
pulse to beat madly within his chest. "Not completely," she said
faintly in his ear.

"Is that what you want?" Hope rang in his whispered words
that she would at last ask him to share her bed. She wound her

arms tightly around his neck continuing the torture she was un-knowingly putting him through.

"Aye, that, and more."

"More?"

"Aye."

"What more could you possibly want?" Ian set Lynet down upon her feet. His ill-behaved little imp had the audacity to take the time to adjust her tunic and continue down her legs to smooth the fabric of her hose. It took every bit of strength not to run his own hands along her bottom, since her short tunic brought her very fetching backside to his attention.

She folded her arms across her chest, causing the tops of her bosom to show a fair amount of cleavage in the neck of her tu-nic. Ian's hungry gaze all but devoured the sight whilst his mouth began to water in anticipation of what she unintentional-ly offered. She made no further effort to answer him, but stood, tapping her fingers on her arm and waiting for him to figure out for himself what she wanted of him.

He became impatient the longer she held her silence. "Do you plan on letting me know your desires, or am I to guess?"

She took a step back. Glancing at Angus, the man gave the briefest of nods afore Lynet put her hands on her hips. "Am I, or am I not, your wife and the lady of this keep, Ian MacGilli-vray?" she declared so loud that silence again fell as those in the keep endeavored to listen in on what had, but an instant afore, been a private conversation between just the two of them.

"You have doubt of this?"

"Aye!"

"Why?"

"Why?" she shouted out and began shaking her fist at him. "You have done nothing to allow me to make this my home. Everyone treats me as if I serve no purpose here, other than to bring a dowry to fill your empty coffers. You have not given them any reason to believe I am your wife and our handfast is binding. If I am to remain here, then I must have their respect. Such a feat will not begin 'til you have made it known that I am the laird's wife, and therefore, mistress of this household."

"Our handfast was binding and will not be undone," Ian answered, taking a step towards her. She moved away and furthered the distance between them.

"Prove it," she dared him with mocking eyes.

God's wounds, but she was magnificent standing there with her fiery MacLaren temper pouring forth like the richest of wines. She wanted him, and she had announced it for all the clan to hear. He would not disappoint her, but 'twould be on his own terms. "So be it," he answered gruffly.

She smiled, but not for long. Reaching out, he took her by the hand, only to grab her about the waist to lift her high afore tossing her roughly over his shoulder. She began cursing and pounding on his back. It had little effect other than to earn her a swat on her bottom, much to the amusement of the male members of the clan who began to egg him on. She became more enraged than afore, hearing their laughter.

Grabbing a firm hold upon her legs, Ian swung around to address the clan. "Everyone, follow me," he ordered, and then he began making his way out of the keep.

"Where are you taking me, Ian?" Lynet demanded, smacking his back once more.

He retaliated with another swat to her bottom. "Keep quiet. You shall know soon enough."

Striding across the hall, he pulled open the massive door and a blast of cool evening air met his face. He felt her shiver. Whether 'twas from the cold, or in anger, mattered not. Ian was on a mission to have this settled once and for all, not only between himself and his wife, but for the clan, as well.

A rush of humanity began filing out of the hall. They followed their laird closely so they did not miss the next spectacle that would surely occur. As Ian overheard the banter going on behind him, 'twas clear it had been some time since anyone had had anything to laugh over, and they were enjoying the entertainment their laird was providing.

Ian did not have to carry her far. 'Twas but a short distance to the destination he had in mind as he listened to the rantings of his very irate wife. With each step he took, her head bounced on his back afore she caught took hold of his waist to steady the rocking of her upper body slung over his shoulder. He muffled a laugh, thinking of the sight they must surely be making. She continued to curse him to hell.

Pushing open the door, he held the entry wide, allowing his people to precede him through the portal. The once empty space began to fill within the chamber. His mother and uncle were the last to arrive, with grim expressions marring their faces. Ian motioned for them to follow him to the front of the chapel.

"Father Michael," he called as the man appeared from a side door of the now overflowing chapel. He set Lynet down and held her about her waist 'til she gained her feet. When she saw where he had taken her, an O of surprise lit her features.

"Laird MacGillivray, 'tis a pleasant surprise to see ye." He looked around with a furrowed brow. "I have already performed the evening mass."

"Aye, I know and apologize for missing it," Ian answered.

"What do ye require of me?" the priest asked.

Ian brought Lynet close to his side and urged her to kneel beside him at the front of the altar. "I ask you to wed us in the sight of God and these witnesses so that no one will ever again question my marriage to this woman."

Father Michael's brow rose in surprise 'til he leveled his gaze upon Lynet. "Will ye have him, milady?" the priest inquired, going straight to the point.

"Aye." Lynet's answer was simple, and Ian could see for himself he had pleased her.

"Then let us begin," Father Michael said. He stretched out his arms, motioning for those in attendance to take a seat as their voices lowered to a bare whisper. Since he had a large audience, the priest took advantage of a full house and began a short sermon.

With bowed heads, Ian and Lynet clasped hands whilst Father Michael at last pronounced them man and wife. Ian stood holding out his hand to assist Lynet from the floor. She took it, and he could feel her fingers trembling within his. Cupping her face, he leaned down to seal their fate with a gentle kiss.

Turning to his people, he expected to see some reservation on the faces of the clan. To his delight, most were in accordance with the match, or so it at least appeared. Only Edric looked as though he was about to yell out in protest 'til Fiona put a hand upon his arm. Even his mother did not appear pleased.

Tucking Lynet's hand in the crook of his arm, he strode the short distance to stand in front of his mother. His gaze leveled upon hers 'til she gave the slightest of nods. 'Twould have to be enough, for now.

Ian held out his hand. "The keys, mother."

Fiona's lips pursed closed in a public display of unreleased fury. A low murmur of approval raced through the chapel, as even the clan was aware her reign as chatelaine was over. Her fingers reached for the chain about her hips, she reluctantly unfastened the clasp, and the keys jangled as she turned them over to Ian.

They did not remain long in his possession. He took the chain and put it around Lynet's waist afore turning back to the clan. "From this day forth, let there be no doubt that the Lady Lynet is indeed my wife. Obey her, as you would obey me. Now, if you shall excuse us. I have some unfinished business with my wife."

If Lynet was expecting her departure from the chapel to be anything other than her arrival, then she was mistaken. Once again, Ian picked up his wife and carried her in the same manner in which she had arrived for their brief wedding ceremony. Boisterous laughter followed the couple out of the chapel and back into the Great Hall. Ian called out for a barrel of ale to be brought up from the cellars to celebrate their union.

Neither Ian nor Lynet would indulge in such festivities going on in the Great Hall, and he took the stairs two at a time, still lugging his cursing wife. He had other ideas in mind. 'Twas long overdue that he must needs deflower his young virgin bride. He would put himself wholeheartedly into such a task.

TWENTY-SIX

L YNET FELT HERSELF BEING TOSSED from Ian's shoulder to
land softly on their bed. Their bed. She had actually done
it, and no longer would Ian find his place on the floor to rest his
weary head. He would be hers from this night forward. Yet,
there were still matters that must needs be set aright between
them, whether he knew it, or not.

She would not give in so easily to his charm. 'Twas practically radiating from him as he all but swaggered over to the hearth
to add several logs to the low flames. The smell of burning oak
filled the room, making Lynet's nose twitch. She would ensure
the chimney had a proper cleaning come the morn.

She scooted off the bed, refusing to become such an easy
conquest for him. Ian said not a word, but stood staring at her
with a cocky grin plastered on his handsome face. One arm was
placed upon the mantel of the hearth whilst he casually leaned
against it, standing there with those sparkling hazel eyes. Eyes
that never left her own and observed her every move.

Unbuckling the belt at his waist, he slid the scabbard holding his sword from the leather and leaned the blade up against the wall. His sash came next as he placed upon the mantel the crested brooch that had held it in place upon his shoulders. His fingers took hold at the edge of his tunic, and, in one fluid motion, he removed it from his chest, flinging it to a nearby chair. Her eyes freely roamed the bared muscled skin touched with a hint of red hair. Her fingers burned in reaction. 'Twas as if she were already skimming them lightly across the hardness of his chest.

The thud of his boots hitting the floor brought her out of her short-lived daydream of touching his body. But this was no hallucination, and, from the look on his face, Ian was more than willing to accommodate her demand that she become his wife this eve.

"Come here," he murmured. 'Twas not exactly an order, but, in Lynet's mind, it seemed as though it might as well be one.

"Nay." She lifted her chin in defiance, determined he not treat her as property, but as an equal.

He crossed the room, backing Lynet up 'til she was trapped against the wall. Her hands balled into fists to prevent her from doing the unthinkable. She knew without any doubt that to touch his scorching hot skin would doom her to fail in getting him to admit his love for her.

Memories of their conversations at Berwyck when he had returned for her came rushing to Lynet's mind. They stood but inches apart. Her chest heaved as she made some small attempt at catching her breath. 'Twas of no use. She loved him. Her heart had always belonged to him, from the very beginning, whether he had known her feelings or not. He had continuously had her love, even though he had thought her nothing but a mere child, all those years ago. She would hear his declaration she had longed for, even if 'twas the last thing she did.

Ian placed his hands on the wall above her head. He moved even closer 'til they were almost chest to chest. "By God, woman, you would deny me, yet again? I thought marrying you by our priest and in front of the entire clan would satisfy whatever schemes you had hatching in that pretty little head of yours," he bellowed, pushing off the wall to rake his fingers through his hair in frustration. He turned his back on her and strode to the window to stare with unseeing eyes out into the darkness.

"I do not consider it scheming in order to get what I want out of our marriage."

He whirled to face her. "By forcing my hand?" he yelled.

"'Twas the only way I could think of for you to come to your senses."

"Come to my senses?" he repeated. "Was it your desire to have every man in that room ogle you like some common strumpet?"

Lynet ignored such an offensive comment and shrugged. "I only cared that one man was gawking at me. Were you, or were you not, intrigued having me dressed like my sister?"

A grunted laugh escaped him. "You would bring up Amiria, now, of all times?"

"Aye! I want no mistake that when you bed me, 'tis me, and not my sister, you think of."

"You should not have dressed like her then, if you were looking for a different outcome, for she is exactly who I first thought of."

"I am not my sister," Lynet said firmly and felt dismay, realizing she may have erred trying to emulate Amiria.

"Nay, you are not."

"'Twas meant to get your attention."

"I assure you, lass, you obtained your objective." His arms folded across his chest. He waited for her to continue.

"I want no misunderstandings between us, Ian. I only did what I needed to do in order to earn some respect in this household. Your mother has ruled with an iron fist, as if this keep was still hers to command."

"She is my mother. That will not change."

"Nay, 'twill not. Yet, 'tis time she also learn her place, now you have brought home a wife."

"I am sure there is no doubt in her mind where her place is after handing you the keys to the keep, Lynet. You are now chatelaine, and none shall go against your orders, or they will answer to me."

"And I thank you for it, although it should have been determined from the moment we walked through the front gates."

"There were other matters of more import to attend."

"Not to me," Lynet answered, lifting her chin, yet again. "I wanted some reassurance of my place, along with knowing you no longer have feelings for Amiria."

"The only feeling I have for Amiria is that she is your sister. Anything else that happened in the past is just that, and best left there."

"I'm glad to hear it."

"But what of you?" Ian asked with raised brow. "Will there be the memory of another man in our bed, Lynet?"

Rolf's face flashed briefly in her mind. "Nay, there has been no other holding my heart but you," she declared honestly.

"Then all is settled between us," Ian declared.

"Not quite." Lynet was not sure what sound emitted from the man who was holding his temper in check by the barest of minimums.

"What more do you want of me?" he jeered.

"I want everything." Lynet willed herself to remain where she was, instead of going to him. 'Twas one of the hardest things she had ever done, besides defy him.

He was upon her faster than she thought humanly possible. His breathing was ragged, as though he tried to control himself from what only he knew for sure. She put her hands upon his chest to hold him off. 'Twas a mistake, she knew, but she would tell him her heart's desire and pray he felt the same.

"What is that supposed to mean?" he asked with furrowed brows.

Lynet reached up to smooth the wrinkle upon his forehead afore placing both her hands upon his cheeks. "I want to be *your* everything, Ian, just as you are mine. When your eyes behold the beauty of a sunrise, I want you to think only of me and the love we share. I want to be the air in your lungs when you take a breath, the blood in your veins as it goes rushing to your heart to pump the very life into you, the tingle in your fingertips when we touch, the sweetness tasted upon your lips and tongue. I want my kiss to be the one that puts your soul at ease."

"You ask much."

'Twas a quiet statement, and yet Lynet could tell he was pleased by her words. "Not really, for is that not what love is all about? I do not wish to be treated as your chattel, Ian, but to stand proudly next to your side, knowing I am loved."

"I took you to wife," he whispered.

"Aye, you did. Yet, that does not mean you love me."

He reached out to pull at a lock of her hair and began rubbing the tresses between his fingers as he considered her words. "Surely, you must know I care for you, Lynet."

She gave a brief laugh, for she was not sure what to believe as he took another step closer. Air rushed from her lungs. She tried to find her next breath, but he had stolen it from her, along with her heart, with just one look into his hazel eyes. "You do?"

"Aye, I do."

"Prove it," she challenged him with the same words she spoke in the hall.

He leaned down, placing his forehead upon hers as he made his vow. "I shall do so, even if it takes all of my days, my lady," he whispered huskily, caressing her cheek.

"And what of the nights, my laird?" she murmured in return.

"They belong only to you."

"Forevermore?"

"For forever and a day."

"Then love me, Ian," she said, wrapping her arms around his neck, "and make me your wife."

His lips breathed life into her with his kiss. 'Twas gentle at first afore it became demanding. 'Twas her own doing, since she urged him on by molding herself into his body. She had waited a lifetime for this very moment, and she would not deny herself the pleasure of his touch.

Ian's hand snaked around her legs and he scooped her up in his arms. He walked over to the bed where she slowly slid down the length of his body to rock on wavering legs. How she was able to stand on her own was beyond her ken, once he touched her. Her skin felt both hot and cold at the same time. 'Twas as if 'twere not her own. Every nerve felt alive as her body's inner cravings heightened with her need to be close to him.

His mouth brushed lightly down her neck 'til his tongue flicked its way even lower to her breasts showing above her tunic. 'Twas in the way of the bountiful treasure he now sought, and Ian made quick work of removing the fabric from her body. She gasped when he took one nipple in his mouth, raising it to a

· 232 ·

peak afore turning his attention to the other. She had no notion where to put her hands, so she interlaced her fingers with the reddish-brown tresses of his hair whilst she took a firm hold.

He gave an amused chuckle afore he continued his exquisite torture. Surely, there would be no doubt left in what little was left of her mind he cared for her after he had his way with her. His hands slowly caressed their way down the curve of her hips then brushed against the flatness of her stomach. She had no idea what he would do next 'til her hose puddled at her feet, and the coolness of the air hit her skin like an icy cold blast of awareness.

Ian threw back the pelts from the bed whilst his plaid quickly disappeared from his glorious body. She had never seen a man nude afore, but this specimen afore her eyes surely must have been carved in God's image. He was beautiful, and he was hers.

Climbing into the bed, Ian seemed in no hurry whilst he propped himself on one elbow to feast his eyes upon her body. She felt a blush starting from the tips of her toes and rising everywhere in between. She reached for the covers, but his hand grabbed hers to stop its progress.

"Nay," he murmured, stealing yet another kiss. "I will not have your beauty covered. I have waited long enough to see you, Lynet. Even my dreams were tortured with wanting you."

"They were?" Was that actually her voice? Those raspy words that were part moan, part question, and part innocence?

"Aye." His fingers began playing with her own as her nerves were pricked with anticipation of the unknown.

Lying side by side, Lynet studied his eyes, marveling at the emotions that fleetingly swept across his visage. "I do not want to disappoint you," she declared honestly.

"I cannot imagine how you would," he answered with a small smile.

"I do not know what to do, or even what you like."

"I shall show you."

"You will?"

"Aye, my lady, I will, indeed. But that will be for another eve. As I promised, tonight belongs to you."

She may have mumbled some answer, and yet he did not wait for one afore he began to leave a blazing trail of kisses down the length of her body. She gasped when he touched her where no other had ever dared afore. Embarrassed to the very core of her being, he only continued his loving assault on her senses 'til pleasure replaced all her inhibitions.

Her back arched. Her hands clenched in the bedding. She wanted more of...what? His name came rushing from her mouth whilst she teetered on the brink of her sanity. He stopped and looked up at her. Everything surrounding her in a swirling heat of sensations halted in an instant. Time passed slowly, as though the days and nights had of a sudden all become as one whilst their gazes held one to the other. He moved atop her as he took her legs to wrap them around his hips.

"I am sorry, lass," he whispered almost reverently like she was his most prized treasure, "but there is no easy way to do this that will not hurt you."

He plunged inside, breaking the barrier that was the proof of her virginity. "Ian!" His name left her lips, yet again, even whilst she clung to him. He held her, unmoving. Stroking her hair with fervent soothing words, he murmured to her in both English and Gaelic. His murmurings were meant to lessen her pain. And lessen it did. Slowly, he began to show her the rhythm known to couples throughout time itself. If she had had an inkling of what she had been missing, she would have asked him to take her sooner.

Onward and upward he took her, to heights she had never thought possible. Lynet knew not what force overtook her own body, but she lost all control as a startling energy consumed her like the burning of the sun. Every piece of her very soul tightened. With one final thrust, Ian called out her name, and she shattered like a piece of fragile glass breaking into a million fragments. She would never be the same again. She was at last his.

TWENTY-SEVEN

A PIERCING WHISTLE SLASHED THROUGH the quietness of the morning air, much like an ax descending upon a piece of dry wood. Calum opened his eyes to peer into the mist surrounding him. The morn was chilly, giving a clue nature would not be cooperating with his plans for fair weather. 'Twas only summer, and yet, this morn gave the impression winter would be upon them sooner than expected this year, or so Calum surmised.

Standing, he wrapped his plaid closer around his shoulders to find some remnant of warmth. Another warning signal echoed, alerting Calum someone was fast approaching. He attempted to determine from which direction the sound originated, but 'twas difficult to ascertain, given he could not see far in front of him.

The shadow of a horse with its rider began to take shape on the outer edges of the clearing. He kicked at Lachlan, who repeated the gesture to the man next to him as the rest in camp began rousing from their slumber. Lazy louts! 'Twas no small wonder he had not been cut down whilst he slept, whether by an assailant or Lachlan, who would like nothing better than to replace him as laird. The camp finally began to come to life when they realized they were not alone and had an unwelcome visitor in their midst.

Calum's hand reached for his sword 'til the stranger pulled on the reins, halting his steed, and held up a gloved hand in surrender. Calum relaxed, but kept up his guard. There was no sense in losing more of his men than he already had from the fiasco of losing his prisoner.

The rider dismounted. Calum's sword sang out as he pulled the heavy steel from its sheath and pointed the blade in the direction of the intruder, who began to advance towards him. "That is far enough. State your business," he ordered loudly.

An amused chuckle emerged from the depths of the cloaked figure, who swept back the hood of his cape. "I mean you no harm and come unarmed," he answered snidely.

"Is that wise?"

"I take my chances that the proposition I have for you will be to your liking."

Calum nodded to one of his men. "Search him."

A grin split the man's features as he again held up his hands whilst his body was patted down for weapons. "I spoke no falsehood."

"Then you will not be surprised if I ensure you come here in good faith," Calum replied knowingly. "I take no chances with strangers who enter my camp."

"I would do the same, if I was in your position."

His man completed his inspection, and Calum returned his sword to his scabbard. "Why are you here?"

"Direct and to the point, are you not? You are a man to my own liking. No reason for us to indulge in idle chit chat then, eh?"

"I have little time, nor patience, for such things. Again, what do you want of me?"

"I have, or shall I say, Urquhart has, something you desire. I want to help you get it."

Calum folded his arms across his chest. "And just how do you think you know what I want, or who I am, for that matter?"

The man pointed to the log near the fire. "May I?"

"Suit yourself."

"My thanks," he said, taking a seat and holding out his hands to the fire.

Calum stood where he was but his patience was wearing thin. "Comfortable?"

"Aye."

"Who the hell are you?" he roared with a scowl, wanting to get down to this man's business.

"My name is Edric, lately of Urquhart," he answered with a sly grin. "I've been holding on to the estate and running it for my sister."

"From what I can see, you have not been doing a very good job of it."

"And therein lies my problem, and hence, my reason for seeking you out, Laird Calum."

"You surprise me by knowing who I am."

"I knew the exact moment you rode across our borders and who you were. Only a fool would not be vigilant in protecting what is his."

"I believe that is no longer your right, if you could claim such ownership prior to MacGillivray's arrival to lead his clan."

An animal-like snarl erupted from Edric as he lost his composure. "The lands should have been mine, and would have been if Fiona's brat of a son had continued on his path, looking for glory abroad."

"How unfortunate for you he has returned to claim his birthright, including bringing home a bride," Calum smirked meaningfully.

"And therein lays the root of my proposition to you."

"Go on. You have my attention."

Edric stood. "I need monies to see myself settled where I can live out my life comfortably. You need the same in order to ensure Clan Davidson's survival through the coming winter. Split Lynet's ransom with me, and I will ensure easy passage into the keep. You should have no trouble capturing the girl, once inside."

"Why should I trust you?"

"Do you think it wise not to? I could have just as easily sent out our own guards to lead you on your merry way back to whence you came without so much as a shilling for your troubles."

"'Tis still no reason to take you up on your offer of helping me obtain that which I need."

"I would think we would both benefit from such a scheme."

"What if I want more than mere coins to fill my coffers?"

"Pilfer whatever you can find from Urquhart, for all I care. There is not much left for the taking. Believe me, I have looked. Why do you think I wish to leave?"

"What if I desire to keep the girl?"

"Give her to Dristan of Berwyck, keep her for yourself, or drown her in the lake. Think you I care what happens to her?"

"She is part of your family."

"Bah! All I want is my fair share of the coins she will bring. I will then bid good riddance to the place, along with my useless sister."

Calum considered Edric's plan, including the drawback of sharing what he could easily get done by himself. Had he not been scoping out the lay of the land, including the routine of the castle guards, for some time now? Then again, if Edric could ensure easy entry through the barbican gate, then, mayhap, 'twould be just as simple to get rid of the man afterwards. He would not have to share any of the ransom, but keep it all to himself.

Calum held out his hand. "Do not cross me," he warned.

Edric reached out to seal their bargain. "'Tis done then."

"Aye."

Edric gave a satisfied smile. "Let me tell you how we shall go about getting you inside the keep."

Calum listened intently and nodded in encouragement for Edric to divulge all he could on the inner workings of the castle. Afore too long, he had a good handle on the situation, knowing he would indeed easily obtain Lynet, along with her ransom monies from Berwyck. Edric, on the other hand, would quickly become a useless liability and would in no way further aid his cause once the keep had been breached.

Edric droned on about the wealth that would soon be his, causing Calum's head to throb with a horrendous headache. 'Twould give him the utmost pleasure when the time came to put this babbling idiot out of his misery. He called his men to gather around the fire and listen to how they would obtain their gold. Calum smiled. 'Twas time to put his plan into action.

TWENTY-EIGHT

IAN AWOKE TO STARE IN WONDER at the miracle lying next to him. His heart seemed to freeze for an instant afore beating ferociously within his chest again. Was it no small wonder the woman he had taken to wife had slowly crept her way into a place where he thought no lady would ever dwell again?

She lay there beside him, appearing like a picture of innocence. The corners of her mouth were turned up in the slightest of smiles set upon her lovely face. He reached over to brush a strand of her hair from her temple, and the heat of his fingertips caused her to automatically lean into him. Her own hand came to rest upon his chest. 'Twas almost as if she tempted him in her sleep for him to take her, yet again. But she would need time afore her body would be ready for another round of pleasure as they had shared last eve. Kissing her forehead, he moved to leave her side.

"Ian..." He paused at the sound that escaped from her dreams. His name came from her pouting lips in a breathy wave of desire. A hungry craving for her rushed through him, almost causing him to rethink his thoughts of but an instant ago.

"Rest awhile, my love," he replied. Her eyes opened wide at his words whilst she looked upon him as if he had given her the greatest of gifts.

"Come back to bed, Ian," she murmured, snuggling into his chest. "'Tis too early to rise after such a night as ours."

He chuckled at the thought of lounging with her to while away the morn. "Duty calls, Lynet. There is much that must needs be done today."

"'Tis barely sunrise. Surely, you can rest a little longer." She yawned and began to stretch. The cover slid down to expose the creaminess of her breasts, taunting him to reach out and caress them. He gave in to the temptation. His thumb slid gently across one peak, and he grinned, watching her unfold beneath him. She moaned. Arching her back in response to his touch, she reached up to wrap her hand around his neck. "Stay with me," she whispered as she gently brought their heads closer afore capturing his lips in a searing kiss.

Any thoughts of leaving her side swiftly left him when she all but molded her body into his, as if she were an extra layer of his own skin. Heat flooded his senses when her hands began to roam upon his body. She was so small next to his own tall frame, and yet, she behaved as if they had been lovers for years. She may have been a shy virgin the night afore, but she left all inhibitions behind in her eagerness to please him now.

A discrete knock at the door interrupted their play, and Ian reluctantly tore his lips from his wife's. He still did not move as their breaths passed one to the other. Opening his eyes, he stole one glance into the blueness of Lynet's and knew, without reservation, he was lost. Aye, she had indeed captured him, heart and soul, the little minx.

With one last parting kiss, he left their bed to quickly don his garments whilst Lynet covered her lovely self from whomever had disturbed what might have been a most pleasant way to start the day. A giggle escaped her lips, as if she knew where his thoughts had led.

Ian opened the door to peer into the passageway then moved aside as Lorna came into the chamber with a mumbled apology. She was not alone. She crossed the room to place a tray of food upon a table then waved the servants waiting in the corridor forward like a captain commanding her troops.

The room began to quickly fill as a large tub was brought near the fire and bucket after bucket of water was poured into it. The hearth was stoked and wine poured 'til Lorna nodded her approval and began shooing the women from the chamber. With a hastily bobbed curtsey and a knowing grin towards her mistress, Lorna fled the chamber.

Silence filled the air, with the exception of the cracking fire. The wood snapped and hissed once greedily consumed by the growing red hot flames that heated the room. The fire itself was not the only thing in the chamber smoldering, for Lynet followed his every move with longing in her eyes. No woman had ever looked upon him with such yearning, and he was more than pleased she was as eager for him as he was for her. With a sigh, he knew she needed the hot water that would soothe the aches she was probably not even aware would be hurting, once she was fully awake.

He came to her side, but 'twas her delicious tongue moistening her lips that was almost his undoing. He captured her mouth briefly and listened quite contently to the sigh of pure bliss that left her.

"You, dear wife, would tempt a saint to sin," Ian declared softly.

"Then come lie abed with me," she urged. "We can rise later to greet the day." She batted her eyelids and gave him a pouty pleading look, but he would not be swayed in his resolve.

He chuckled and stood to his full height, feasting his eyes on the woman who now belonged to him in every way. "Nay, lass. There is much to do, and we best be about our duties."

She wasted no time flinging back the covers and kneeling upon the bed. He sucked in his breath watching her come to life beneath his gaze whilst a rosy blush crept up her body. *By Saint Michael's Wings, she is perfect,* he mused. His feet suddenly felt as if they had become like granite, and for the life of him, he could not move from her side. With a racing heart, he became weak-kneed and felt a shiver of lust swarm up his backside. He had never felt such a hunger afore and was pleasantly surprised such a wee, young lass could reduce a seasoned warrior like himself to the point of feeling overwhelmed in anticipation of her touch.

His hands shook when he reached out for her, but 'twas not to give in to her demands that they return beneath the coverlets. Instead, he gently picked her up and carried her to the tub. Slowly, she slid down his body. If she did it purposely just to arouse him, he could not say, since holding her naked body against his own had already had such an effect. He swore. She laughed as she sank down into the water.

"Will you join me, Ian?" she whispered seductively. "There's more than enough room for us both, and I should look at your wound to ensure 'tis healing properly."

"The wound is fine, lass. I could not be done in by such a cowardly act as Broderick had planned for me."

"I hate that someone who is kin to me would do such to you."

"We cannot always choose our relatives, my dear."

"Aye, I suppose that is true, but I should still see to the wound. Come join me," Lynet tempted again.

He lean down to kiss the top of her head and proceeded to bring over a small table and the tray of food so she could break her fast. "Another time, my lovely wife. Relax, and enjoy your bath. I will see you later, at the noon meal."

As he began to make his way from the room, a splash of water followed by another blissful sigh captured his attention.

"Are you sure?" she teased, lifting her leg up for his viewing pleasure whilst she began to soap that silken porcelain limb.

Ian groaned. "I shall make you pay for jesting with me once you are up to another round of love making, sweet Lynet. Of that, you can be sure."

She laughed afore resting both arms on the rim of the tub to smile seductively at him. "I will look forward to it, my laird."

He gave her a brief nod of acknowledgement and quickly left the room, afore he changed his mind and joined her in the tub.

Sometime later, he made his way down the turret to the Great Hall, and Angus approached at a brisk pace to meet him at the bottom of the stairs.

"There is trouble afoot," Angus whispered.

Striding across the room, Ian sat at the high table as food was laid afore him. He motioned for Angus to take the vacant seat next to him. Surveying the room, he was not completely surprised to see 'twas mostly empty. He assumed the celebration had continued on, far into the early morning hours.

"Report..." Ian mumbled, taking a mouthful of porridge that for a change did not stick in the back of his throat and actually had some flavor.

"'Tis as ye suspected. A small army is camped approximately four miles away. Calum and his men, as far as I can gather. I did not want tae get too close without giving away that we are on tae him."

"And my Uncle?" Ian tore off a chunk of bread as Angus hesitated with his account. He went on with his meal whilst he pointed the piece of bread in Angus's direction. "Proceed..."

"Again, ye were correct in yer assumptions that yer uncle was up tae no good. He left the castle afore dawn and has yet tae return. I have a scout tailing him, but am sure the two are conspiring against ye."

"I am not surprised. He has become greedy in his old age and a fool to be in cahoots with the Davidson laird. Surely, they must know Lynet is now my wife, and I have no plans on giving her to anyone."

"'Tis obvious they only look fer the coin. Mayhap, ye could offer them a small stipend and send them on their way."

Ian wiped his mouth with the back of his sleeve and sat back in his chair. "Men of their ilk are never satisfied with a mere pittance of monies if they think there is more to be had to line their coffers, no matter how they procure it."

"Perchance, if ye make the offer," Angus urged.

"Nay, I will not. 'Twill only encourage them to find another way to ransom more coin from me, or worse, make an attempt to get to my wife."

"Ye are aware that is what Laird Davidson is most likely planning to do?"

"With a dowry the size of Lynet's, I have no doubt they will do everything within their ability to seize it." Ian stood and began making his way from the hall with Angus walking beside him.

"What if he wants the young lady for himself?" Angus asked.

Ian stopped to turn and stare at the Highlander who had already risked his life for his wife. "My Uncle would not dare such an offense," he fumed.

"Nay, not yer uncle, but Calum."

"*Bloody Hell!* The man would need to step over my grave afore I would let that happen," Ian replied hotly.

"I believe, me laird, that is *exactly* what he has planned."

Twenty-Nine

L YNET HUMMED AN OLD FAMILIAR TUNE her mother used to
sing to her when she was young. 'Twas a fine day, and she
had already made incredible progress on the cleaning of her
hall. The floors had been scrubbed clean and fresh rushes with
dried lavender made the room pleasant smelling. 'Twas a vast
improvement of its earlier condition, and everyone was more
than eager to help her now that Ian had married her afore the
clan's priest. She had found her place amongst them.

After giving her directives on how she would expect the same
meticulous care to be given to the kitchens, she had called to
Nessa to join her in the gardens to see what she could do to
help the plants that were suffocating between the rocks and
weeds. Nessie, as she preferred to be called, was a young wee
lass of ten summers and had been more than willing to head
outdoors, instead of staying in the unyielding heat near the fires
in the kitchen. Lynet could hardly blame her and had spent her
own childhood in much the same manner.

There was something incredibly soothing about taking care of the earth beneath one's feet. She had always enjoyed the task of making things grow and bloom into the thriving gardens found at Berwyck. A fleeting memory of her mother as they tended the flowerbeds together flashed in Lynet's mind and made her homesick for her family. A sigh escaped her, knowing she would soon be making her own family here within the walls of Ian's birthplace. 'Twas her home now, as well, and she doubted she would see Berwyck anytime soon.

Moving aside her basket, she took out another tool to dig at a rock that had no business being in a garden. It seemed even a place that would provide the much needed herbs for their food or medicine was just as neglected as the rest of Urquhart. At least, she now had free reign to put things aright.

Consumed with her task at hand, she hadn't realized Nessa was chatting away, and she had no clue as to what the child had been saying.

"...and we ne'er 'ave tae worry about the cattle raids again," Nessa said with innocence.

Lynet stopped tugging at the weed surrounding what must surely be a boulder hidden underneath the dirt. "What cattle raids?"

The girl gave a carefree shrug, but continued on with her work. "They been going on fer years now. Neighboring clans steal our livestock from us. We steal 'em back. 'Twill change, now that the laird is 'ere."

"You have such confidence in your new laird, then?" Lynet surmised, hiding her grin.

"Oh, aye, he's verra bonny, isna he?" Nessa got a far off dreamy look afore coming back out of her daydream. "Beggin yer pardon, milady..."

Lynet laughed and watched as a pretty blush crept up the child's face. "No need, Nessie. I agree with you, completely."

A look of understanding passed between them afore they continued on in silence. Lynet saw they were starting to make some progress when her eyes alit briefly on a figure hovering near the entryway of the garden just afore the person disappeared. A frown crossed her features afore she put herself back into her work.

They had been making a significant difference in their surroundings, if the growing pile of weeds was an indication, when a voice behind her caused Lynet to flinch. She had been wondering how long 'twould take afore she was confronted.

"Leave us," Lady Fiona ordered.

Lynet stretched and laid a hand on Nessa's shoulder. "Why do you not go over near those roses, Nessie, and see what help you can give the poor things. They are in much need of your loving care."

"Aye, Mistress Lynet," the girl whispered afore quickly gathering her things and heading out of hearing distance.

Lynet stood and turned to face Ian's mother who had a grim expression on her visage. "What can I do for you, my lady?" Lynet asked quietly whilst wiping her hands on the apron tied at her waist.

"You could leave Urquhart and return from whence you came, but I have no doubt that is not an order you would care to follow," Fiona huffed with a frown marring her otherwise wrinkle-free complexion.

"The only orders I plan to follow are my husband's." The audacity of this woman astounded her. "Do you really believe I would leave Ian to suit your whim, because *you* insist that we are not man and wife? I would think the ceremony last eve afore your own priest and the entire clan would have settled such an issue."

"I am his mother. Ian will listen to me and my council."

"Aye, you are the woman who gave him life. Give him sound advice, and I believe he would listen to what you have to say...within reason, of course."

"You do not belong here," Fiona declared. "There are others here, who would be far better for our clan and to our way of life in the Highlands than a woman who is obviously more English than Scot!"

Lynet eyed the lady and was thankful her upbringing at a border castle had prepared her for this type of confrontation. She considered herself more than capable of handling this woman, much as she had seen her sister do as mistress of Berwyck.

"And yet, here I am, and by Ian's own words, sworn to him in the eyes of God that we are wed. I have no plans on going anywhere, madam, so you may as well get used to having me around." Lynet watched as her words sank in with the woman standing afore her. Did it appear some of the fight left her as the reality that she was unable to control the situation finally registered?

"I only wanted what was best for Ian," Fiona whispered afore she rubbed at her eyes as though to clear her vision.

"What makes you think I will not be good for your son? I have loved him for as long as I have known him, even when he thought of me as only a child. I cannot think of a better reason than such a devotion as love to be good enough for another to hold dear."

"Love? You are so young," Fiona surmised, looking Lynet up and down as if assessing her worth. "What do you know of love, or what a mother would do for her child?" Fiona went but a short distance away to sit on a lone stone bench. Since she left enough room for another to sit next to her, Lynet did just that and watched as the woman began wringing her hands in uncertainty. "I suppose, since I caused you such ill will, that you will now have Ian send me away."

Lynet surprised her when she reached over to take hold of Fiona's shaking limbs. "I may be young, my lady, but I know what love is. One day I, too, will know a mother's love and will no doubt protect my bairns just as fiercely as you yourself have done. My children will need their grandmamma near so they can learn from her. I would not think of sending you away, but we must needs find a common accord. Do you not think the love we both bear your son is enough for us to begin again?"

"You willna send me away?"

"Nay, I will not." Lynet watched the resolve in Fiona's face and gave Ian's mother a timid smile that she hesitantly returned.

"Then let us begin, again," Fiona proclaimed.

For the first time, Lynet saw the woman give her what appeared to be a genuine smile. Perchance, there was hope for them after all. "I would like that, my lady."

They sat in silence with clasped hands, listening to nature's song. The chirping birds in the treetops, the rustle of leaves within the branches overhead, the feel of the soft breeze caressing their cheeks as they sat side by side in thought and enjoyed this moment together. But 'twas the sound of a distant thunder that began rolling over the hills that caused both women to look up to the sky in puzzlement. 'Twas unusually sunny, considering Urquhart's location so far north, and the sky did not appear as though a storm was in the vicinity that they would need to worry about rain.

A warning shout from a guard posted upon the battlements was repeated by another. Lynet and Fiona came simultaneously to the same conclusion.

"Nessie!" they called in unison.

The girl looked up as Lynet grabbed at her skirts and ran in her direction.

"To the keep!" Lynet yelled.

The girl took off like a jackrabbit bouncing away from a hungry fox intent on devouring its next tasty meal. She obviously knew the routine and was used to raiding clansmen intent on stealing whatever was available on MacGillivray land. Lynet could not say the same, since she was as yet unfamiliar with the complete inner workings of this particular keep.

"Go on, now," Fiona urged, "follow her, and get to your chamber. 'Tis the safest place for you."

"I have to find Ian," Lynet protested.

Fiona took hold of her arms. "Ian will know where to go to find you and will expect you to keep yourself safe. The laird's wife would bring quite a high ransom, and we cannot risk you being captured in the event the gate does not hold. Run!"

Lynet's eyes widened at the thought of being apprehended, yet again. With a nod of assent, she hitched up her gown and began running towards the keep. She was unprepared when she rounded the corner of the garden wall to meet a shovel that was well aimed at her head. Once again, she fell backwards and watched as the sky swirled around and around 'til her vision turned fuzzy. An unexpected face loomed afore her with an evil leer.

"You are mine now, my lady," the face afore her jeered in satisfaction.

"Nay...not you," she managed to whisper.

She tried to yell out, but she could not form any words as she began to lose consciousness. His arms stretched out towards her and something heavy was thrown over her head, suffocating the air from her lungs. Lynet had no energy to struggle. Her last thought afore she blacked out was to wonder why on earth this kept happening to her, for 'twas becoming a most annoying occurrence!

Calum was disgusted that he was reduced to climbing his way up through a garderobe just to gain access to the keep. The stench alone permeating from his clothes would alert the entire MacGillivray clan that something was afoot. The chute was narrow and slick with...well...piss and shite. He knew he needed coin to refill his coffers, but he was beginning to rethink the methods and lengths he would go to get it. He was not entirely sure, at this very moment, if 'twould be worth it.

Perchance, he should have sent Lachlan to achieve this part of his plan, instead of entrusting him to lead their small contingent of men towards the castle. He was unsure Lachlan would have been capable of taking the lady without her screaming her bloody head off and alerting the entire castle, even though they had infiltrated the keep's defenses with the help of one of its own. But he knew he could not trust his brother, and with good reason, given all their past arguments they had had throughout their entire lifetime.

With one hand after the other, he pulled himself up by clawing at the rocks to ensure a firm grip to get out of the hell he had put himself in. It could not happen soon enough. Looking up, he was satisfied to see for himself he was almost to his goal. His two men, who were below him, grumbled, cursed, and echoed aloud his own thoughts running amuck within his head.

"Shhh, you fools," Calum scolded with a hiss of displeasure, "lest you wish this travesty to be all for naught and get us captured."

Their grumbling quieted, and Calum continued upward 'til he reached the top. He knew the rest of his army would be fast approaching the barbican gate of the castle. Time was of the essence, in capturing the laird's wife to ensure an easy escape from those very same front gates.

Slowly, he lifted the wooden seat to peer into the small closet. There were a few garments hanging from a peg, but that was not what infuriated him. Nay, 'twas the smirking face of Edric that had Calum ready to wipe the amused, annoying look from the obnoxious man's features. He did not so much as even offer Calum a hand to assist him from the confines of the narrow hole, not that he could entirely blame the man.

As Calum rose from his self-imposed temporary prison, Edric took a cloth from his sleeve and held it to his nose.

"Eh gads, man," Edric gagged as he went to the window to get a breath of fresh air. "Mayhap, this was not the best of suggestions."

Calum narrowed his gaze at the fool afore him. "You think?" he growled as fiercely as any angered or trapped animal would. Peering down at his clothes that were covered in filth, he yanked at the cape hanging from a peg and began wiping his hands and face, not that it did much good. He would smell the stench of the garderobe for days, and the disgusting odor was only getting stronger whilst the small, confined space of the closet began to fill with the addition of two extra men. They were in much the same condition as Calum. 'Twas horribly revolting.

Squeezing around his co-conspirators trying to avoid contact with the filth of their clothes, Edric made for the exit to peer into a vacant room. "'Tis empty," he declared, pushing the door wide for everyone to follow.

"Where is she?" Calum asked, reaching for his sword as Edric went to the next door to peer into the passageway.

"She will be in her chamber, as is the standard protocol for the laird's wife, during a hostile siege. Down the corridor, four doors to the right. 'Tis the very last room at the end of the passageway. You cannot miss it," Edric replied as he began rubbing his hands together with anticipation. "I can already feel the ransomed coins in the palms of my hands."

Calum's brow rose. "Can you now?"

"Aye, I can. You are going to make me a very rich man." Edric cackled in glee as he peered into the passageway. "The way is clear. You should hurry afore someone gets a whiff of your stench."

Edric never knew what was coming when Calum pulled a knife from his waist, deftly reached around the unsuspecting man, and proceeded to slit the fool's throat. 'Twas a clean kill, not that the man deserved such, after what he had put Calum and his group through.

Calum gave no further thought to the gurgling sounds of the dying man who toppled over, grasping at his neck. He smirked at the stupidity of men and stepped over the twitching corpse. Edric had served his purpose. The rest would now lie with him.

THIRTY

IAN RACED FROM THE FORGERY and made quick work of stowing the dirk the smithy had made for him into the belt at his back. The inner bailey was a beehive of chaos as the clan ran in every imaginable direction. Women rushed to gather their children and usher them into the keep whilst men hurried to their posts. Even the barbican gate was still wide open to allow more villagers to make their way inside the castle walls to safety.

In the midst of all the activity, a merchant quickly dumped a rolled tapestry into his cart, jumped into the driver's seat, and slapped the leather reins to urge his horse into motion towards the gate. Ian did a double take at the foolishness of the merchant's choice, but assumed the man's only concern was to reach whatever safe haven he thought was far from Urquhart's soon-to-be upheaval.

"Connor," Ian called out to halt the Highlander, who was helping a crying child from the ground.

Pushing the bairn into the arms of her mother, he closed the distance between them. "Aye, my laird?"

Ian pointed his sword to the cart. "Who is that tradesman?"

"Never seen him, my laird."

"Well, see if you can catch the fool. Surely, he and his goods will be safer within the castle walls than outside of its gates. Or does he wish to be ransacked for every bolt of cloth he has of any worth? When you're finished, follow me."

Intent upon reaching Lynet to ensure she was safe, Ian gave no further thought to the trader, who cursed at Conner, waved his fist in the air, and then proceeded to yell at his horse to "*giddy up*" whilst narrowly missing the closing of the portcullis on his cart. Seeing Angus, Ian motioned for his kinsmen to join him, as well.

He had just reached the first step leading to the keep whilst Connor ran to catch up, when his name was called by a small, wee voice.

"Laird MacGillivray!" a young lass bellowed as she ran up to him to tug on the edge of his tunic to gain his attention.

"Not now, lass. I must needs find Lady Lynet. Hie yourself into the keep and get yourself safe," Ian said briskly, dismissing the girl.

"But my laird...'tis about the Lady Ly–"

The sound of her voice faded as Ian hurried ahead into the hall with Angus and Connor close behind him. He attempted to make quick work of dodging servants and villagers alike who were hastily filling the chamber to over-flowing, but 'twas near impossible. Clansmen and women were everywhere, and it appeared most had reached the safety of the keep.

Finally, making his way through the mass of humanity, Ian raced up the turret to reach Lynet's side. He was only half-way down the passageway when he noticed blood pooling from beneath a chamber door. Pulling his sword from the scabbard at his side, Ian carefully started to push upon the heavy oak, only to have to shove harder in order to make the door open. The cause...the dead body of his Uncle with his throat slit had been hindering it opening smoothly.

"Bloody Hell, who would do such a ghastly thing," Angus muttered, making the sign of the cross. "He may have been a greedy fool, but no one should die in such a manner."

"Lynet!" Ian bellowed, leaving the room to head to his own chamber, only to see his door was slightly ajar. Pushing the door wide, it should not have surprised Ian in the least to see Calum and two of his men standing there with a look of bewilderment on their faces.

"By God's bones, the stench," Connor gagged, covering his mouth.

Angus came to stand next to Ian's side, but his laughter only angered the men afore them. "The garderobe? Ye chose the garderobe tae gain access tae the keep? The smell alone would have alerted us all tae yer arrival, ye fools."

"What the hell have you done with my wife?" Ian roared, ignoring the odor that assailed his nostrils.

Calum practically choked on the laugh that escaped him. "I have done nothing with her, as you can plainly see, if you but care to take a closer look. The woman has eluded me, yet again," he sneered with contempt.

"Where is she?" Ian shouted once more, looking about the room, but seeing for himself, his wife was not within their chamber. Angus and Connor moved about the room to guard Calum's men and hold them at sword point.

"Damnation, man, I do not have her! If I did, do you think I'd be standing here in an empty room, contemplating life's mysteries, instead of making my getaway in order to collect her ransom?"

"Harrumph! Have you not seen for yourself Urquhart's condition? I barely have enough monies to see us fed through the coming winter, let alone pay a ransom," Ian retorted fiercely.

"If I canna get coinage from you, I am sure Dristan of Berwyck will pay me most handsomely to see his wife's sister returned safe and sound."

"Dristan no longer has claim upon the Lady Lynet. She is mine," Ian proclaimed, trying to calm his anger.

"And yet, you do not seem to know of her whereabouts, now, do you? 'Tis no fault of mine if you canna keep your wife where she belongs, and you have misplaced her...again," Calum mocked. Ian's fury rose, not only from losing Lynet, but from the audacity of the bastard in front of him.

Ian swung his clenched fist, punching Calum hard in the face. The man stumbled backward from the blow, falling into the men that stood behind him whilst Angus and Connor moved to place their blades in a location that would ensure they would not see another day if they did not yield. Ian turned and pointed his sword at Calum's throat when the man tried to rise.

"Do not insult my wife, sir," Ian snarled.

Calum put up his hands in surrender, but Ian knew better than to trust him. He motioned for Calum's men to help their laird to his feet, which they did after a moment of hesitation.

"Take them to the dungeon," he ordered his men. "But leave him."

Calum smiled evilly as his men were shoved from the room.

"Do you really want to fight me, boy?"

"I am no boy. Draw your sword, and we shall see who wins this day."

"Is this revenge you seek?" Calum said with a shrug. "I did not steal your wife."

"Nay, you did not, but 'twas your intent."

Ian charged forward, but Calum easily dodged him, elbowing him in the face. Ian fell against the wall, facing his enemy who drew his sword confidently. Instead of engaging in a fight, Calum darted from the room like a coward, which was not what Ian was expecting. Yet, Ian was quick to follow, and Calum began swinging his sword like a mad man. Ian's blade rang out as it encountered Calum's. A crossroads perchance, but Ian got the advantage when he pushed Calum away. The passageway was dimly lit, but there was enough light to see every bit of movement.

The battle between them went on down the corridor towards the stairs. With every attack Ian performed, Calum countered it 'til he ducked beneath Ian's arms, leaving Ian dangerously close to the edge of the stairs. Once more, Ian brought his sword forward, and the sound of the metal connecting resounded in the air. He stared into the face of his nemesis.

"Give up," Calum said, pushing Ian closer to the edge of the stairs.

"Never!" Ian shoved him away, but received another blow to the face, leaving him stunned. He collapsed to the ground and spit out the blood that pooled in his mouth. Calum was chuckling as he took a moment to circle Ian, like an animal stalking its prey. Ian wiped his lips and reached for his sword, but Calum kicked it away.

"You have become weak, lad. I expected more of a fight from a knight who has trained with the Devil's Dragon. Has your woman made you so soft that you forget how to battle someone superior to you?" he said with a sly grin of satisfaction. Calum squatted down to face Ian afore grabbing his hair to tilt his head and get a better look at him, as though he knew he had already won. "How did you think you could ever beat me?"

Ian pretended he was seriously wounded from the punches he had received in order to get closer to his enemy. He began to finger the hilt of the dirk hidden from Calum's view. The fool was too focused on a clear victory, and leaning his head back, Calum let out a wicked laugh. 'Twas just the moment Ian was waiting for, as he pulled forth the dirk at his waist and drove the blade into the pit of Calum's stomach with a twist, for good measure. Calum fell backward with a howl of pain as Ian staggered to his feet. He retrieved his sword and stood over Calum's dying body.

"Just like that," Ian spat out his answer. With as much force as he could muster, Ian swung his sword forward in a wide arch, severing Calum's head from his body. He did not bother to look down at the now dead man, or what he had done, but wiped away the remnants of blood from the sword afore taking the stairs.

Ian was panicking about Lynet's whereabouts as he made his way to the lower level of the keep. He saw the girl called Nessa down a deserted hallway. When she saw him, the little girl ran to him immediately.

"Me laird," she squealed. "I 'ave tae tell ye something important."

Ian picked her up and set her on the window seat so he could face her better.

"You said something about the Lady Lynet," he started to say calmly, wishing he had listened to the young lass afore.

The girl nodded. "Aye."

"Where is she, Nessa?" Ian's head was pounding, but he was determined to find out where his wife had gone.

"She was taken me laird," she said, spinning a thread of her shawl around her fingers as she looked at him with big eyes.

"Taken? By who? What did he look like?"

"'e was a tall man, but 'e wore a hood, me laird," she gave a nervous reply. "I did not see his face."

"What else, girl, what else?"

"'e put her in a cart, wrapped in a tapestry."

Ian thought but an instant about Nessa's words afore he realized his own foolish mistake. Unknowingly, he had let that very same man escape with his wife. He had unwittingly, let the culprit walk straight out of his own damn front gate.

Knowing with each moment that passed Lynet was being swept farther away, he strode with a determined purpose. As he reached the Great Hall, he espied Angus coming from the opposite side of the room where the dungeon was located in the lower levels of the castle.

"Angus," he called out as the Scotsman rushed to his side.

"Aye, me laird," he said briskly.

"There is something offensive in my keep, and it can be found in the passageway on the floor where my chambers are located. Fetch it, and follow me outside," Ian ordered.

Angus's brow raised in question. "He is dead, then?"

Ian smirked, waving his hand towards the stairwell. "You doubted my skill? Go see for yourself. But hurry with retrieving what I asked of you."

Whilst he awaited Angus's return, he saw his mother entering the keep. A look of anguish appeared on her face afore she took up the fabric of her dress in order to hasten to him with tear-filled eyes. "Son, I must beg your forgiveness for acting so rashly towards Lynet and listening unwisely to my brother's council. I just learned Lynet has been taken, and we must needs find her."

Ian wrapped his mother within his arms and was thankful to at last see the woman he had cherished in his youth. He laid a kiss upon the top of her head afore he held her once more at arm's length. "There is nothing to forgive, my lady mother, and unfortunately, your brother met his demise at the hand of our enemies. Be at ease, and see to our people. Lynet will be returned to us shortly."

"But what of the throng of armed men about to storm the barbican gate?" she asked in fright.

Ian's gaze took in the people within his hall, knowing they were in his care. With Angus returning and carrying a sack in his hand, he was confident the enemy army would disperse.

"Let me worry about those who wish to take what is rightfully ours," Ian answered with a grim line of displeasure. "Angus...follow me."

Ian and Angus made their way from the keep and into the baily. Standing afore the gate, Ian motioned his men to raise the portcullis. With steady feet, they walked the short distance beneath the metal spikes that would be the demise of anyone foolish enough to fall beneath them. They waited just outside of the gate to witness the small army Calum had amassed. To Ian's practiced eye, there appeared to be just over two score of men.

Ian held up his hand, even as the men prepared to charge. He gave Angus the briefest of nods, afore his man made his way to the end of the wooden bridge. In the sack, he carried Calum's severed head. Angus strode but a few more yards to where he placed the atrocity on a pike afore proceeding to remove the sack. A mighty roar of outrage emitted from Calum's clan.

"This is what is left of your leader," Ian shouted for all to hear his words. "This is the man who chose to trespass into my keep and attempt to steal what is rightfully mine. As you can now undoubtedly surmise, you will not be granted such easy access into the interior of my castle."

The bravest of the lot stepped forward. "Where be our two clan members who traveled with our laird?" he hollered, his anger barely contained whilst witnessing the offense of his dead laird.

'Twas then Ian heard his clansmen take their places behind and above him. They took aim at the intruders from above, upon the battlement walls, arrows knocked into their crossbows. Other arrows appeared through the narrow slits in the walls of the keep. Only someone with no common sense would dare attack, for he would lose more than half of his men in such a foolish confrontation.

"They are enjoying my hospitality in my dungeon. Leave now, and, if I feel gracious, I may release them, as long as you never step foot on MacGillivray land again. Or perchance, you would prefer to suffer the same fate as your laird. 'Tis your choice, of course, but be quick about making your decision. I will not show mercy to those who try to harm my people."

One foolish enough to doubt Ian's words, standing behind their new leader, bellowed out a battle cry in order to vindicate the death of their laird. He rushed forward swinging his blade whilst the rest of Calum's men followed him at a run. Arrows began to fly from overhead, killing those in the front as they all pushed forward. Ian and Angus swung their claymores, even while Ian's own men rushed from the gate to protect him. Swords clashed, but 'twas soon apparent Calum's men were outnumbered. Those who had not fallen quickly regrouped at a safe distance away from the deadly arrows. There were not many of them left.

"Is there anyone else who would care to test my words and the strength of our arms?" Ian stood his ground and stared around at the few men left in front of him. "This is your last warning." He finished his speech as he brought his bloody sword forward.

One man stepped to the fore, as if he might take Ian up on his challenge, but 'twas not to be. He peered at Ian with contempt and spit upon the ground as if to insult him. Common sense prevailed, and with a whistle, the Scotsman signaled the remaining men to retreat. Ian gave an order to send a small contingent of clansmen to escort their unwanted guests past the boundaries of his land.

He watched them go in silence afore taking in the carnage in front of him with a grimace. Gravely, he pondered how long 'twould be afore he himself would feel it safe enough to travel. He did not wish to worry of his own sorry hide being attacked afore he could once again begin searching for his captured wife. With Calum and Edric dead, he could only ponder who in the hell had his wife?

THIRTY-ONE

L YNET BEGAN TO ROUSE with the uncomfortable feeling of being suffocated. Whatever kind of conveyance she was being carried away in, 'twas not one made for comfort, as she was jostled and bounced about whenever the vehicle hit a rut in the uneven ground. The rough treatment of her already abused body did serve some purpose, as she found a slight amount of relief when she felt the confining restrictions of the material holding her give way a bit. At the very least she was able to move, however slightly.

She tried to remain still and not panic, for how was she to know her fate at the hands of the madman who abducted her from her very home. Vague images of his face swam within her memory, memories of seeing that very same face as he had killed poor Rolf. 'Twas obvious Lachlan was in cahoots with his brother and was just another determined man who was bent on having her dowry, despite it rightfully belonged to Ian. Was there anyone who was not chasing her for coinage and dowry left in England or Scotland? Surely, there were other ladies who were just as wealthy?

Since she could see nothing, she felt what she assumed was a cart beginning to slow. Lachlan's voice was muffled, but she could faintly make out her abductor humming a strange tune afore he turned to cursing. He must have led the horse to water, for she could distinguish the sound as the horse drank its fill. She licked at her dry lips, only to come in contact with the material in front of her face. She had never been so parched in her life.

Silence descended, and Lynet began to attempt to squirm loose of the material holding her captive. She began to roll back and forth, and, after much effort, she was at last free to take in great gulps of fresh, clean air. Her head was throbbing, and she carefully lifted her hand to feel the bump on her forehead that surely must be the size of a bolder. She held back a sneeze from the dust that lingered in her hair and clung to her clothes from the tapestry that Lachlan had rolled her in. Not knowing his whereabouts, she was unsure how much time she had afore he returned from taking care of his personal business.

Carefully, she rose up to peek over the edge of the cart in order to obtain a glimpse of her surroundings. Panic struck her as she saw nothing but green landscape and determined the sun would soon set upon the earth. Clearly, she was no longer near the keep. She tried to steady her heart as she quickly attempted to formulate some kind of a plan. With her head fuzzy from being knocked unconscious, she was worried she would not be able to flee far.

But try, she would, and there was no time like the present. Lynet began to scoot her way to the edge of the cart, only to stand on wavering legs once her feet hit the ground. Though her stance was unstable, 'twas now or never if she were to attempt an escape.

With only one step forward, she found herself landing upon her hands and knees and almost planting her face into the dirt. 'Twould not be the first time such an occurrence happened, she thought, as she relived those disturbing memories at the hands of Calum, even whilst she made a fast attempt to collect her breath that had been knocked from her. Yet, 'twas not Lachlan's doing, but her own inability to remain upright from her injury to her head.

Stumbling to her feet, she knew she must make haste whilst the opportunity presented itself. Although the water appeared to offer her what she needed most to quench her thirst, she decided the best course of action would be to run in the opposite direction. Run...if only her feet would cooperate with her need to flee from her captor. She mentally cursed when her bare foot encountered a stone beneath the foliage upon the ground. 'Twas the first time she realized her shoes were missing, but she could not linger on what other injuries she might incur by a bit of rocks. Nay! She must flee and put as much distance as she could between herself and Lachlan.

She had not gone far afore an ear splitting cry of outrage filled the air and echoed throughout the forest. Birds flew from the treetops. Lynet looked overhead as they took flight, and the noise from the flapping of their wings faded into the distance. Yet, there was no mistaking the man who was now trudging his way through the forest, as he made no attempt to lessen the amount of noise he was making in his attempt to find her.

Knowing her brief amount of freedom would soon be at an end, she hastily picked up a fallen branch and clasped it as if this meager bit of wood might save her from an enemy who would surely do his worst to her. Her heart raced as she frantically sought a place of refuge. But given her injury that was more of a hindrance than she cared to admit, she knew 'twas but a matter of moments afore she was once more captured.

Lynet snuck behind a tree, as if hiding behind the oak would make her invisible. The stick she held afore her, as though 'twere the mightiest of blades made of the hardest steel. As she scanned the woods in front of her, she felt sudden dread as his hand gripped her upper arm from behind. She should have known he would find her. Still, she swung her branch and had a brief moment of satisfaction as it made contact with the side of his head. 'Twas short lived as he wiped at the blood where the wood left a scratch from his temple all the way down to his chin. At least, she would live with the knowledge that he would have a scar the rest of his life as a reminder of her defiance, and that 'twould mar his otherwise handsome face.

"You vile, little bitch," he grimaced as he took a piece of linen from his cloak to dab at his bleeding face. "Look what you have done to me."

Lynet could not keep the smirk from her features, even if she had wanted to. "'Tis more than you deserve, sir. How dare you take me against my will and beneath the very noses of my people?"

"'Twill be a long time afore you see the place again. Calum will be busy with the taking of Urquhart, and afore my asinine brother can find me, we shall be far away, and I will claim your ransom as mine."

"I am already spoken for, if you have forgotten. Besides, you have a funny way of showing your loyalty to those who you demand are your kin. Your brother may have something to say about your plans, since he is technically laird of the Davidson clan," Lynet sneered, waving the branch in front of her for protection.

"My *brother*, could care less about his bastard sibling," he spat, and Lynet realized the sibling rivalry went far deeper than just sparring brothers.

Lachlan looked her up and down, as though assessing her ability to remain upright. Considering how she swayed, she saw in his eyes what she herself did not wish to admit. She would not remain standing for long. Her brief respite of freedom was already taking its toll upon her.

He came towards her with his sword raised. Thinking he was bent on killing her, she swung the limb, only to have him easily knock the branch from her hand and send it sailing off into the distance. She rubbed at her fingers, numb from the impact of his sword against the wood. He grabbed her and forced her up against his body. A gasp escaped her lips, and she wedged her hands between Lachlan and herself to push against his chest and force as much distance between them as possible. He laughed. She frowned and watched as his eyes became even darker, in sharp contrast to the fairness of his hair.

He spun her around and gave her a push in the general direction from where she had come. Afore she once more stumbled to the ground, he took hold of her arm to hasten their return to the water's edge. In dismay, she came to the realization she, in truth, had not traveled that great a distance from where they had stopped.

"You best drink, if you are thirsty," he jeered, still wiping at the blood upon his once handsome face, "and leave your comments to yourself in regards to my brother."

Cupping her hands, she dipped them into the cool water and greedily brought a mouthful to her parched lips. The liquid slid down her throat like the sweetest nectar. "Calum is still laird, and I am still wed," she mentioned again whilst dabbing the hem of her gown into the water so she could clean her face.

"Not for long," Lachlan said as he went to the cart and came to stand afore her with a length of rope.

"What mean you by that?" she asked, almost afraid to hear his answer.

"It means that soon you will not have to worry about being a part of the MacGillivray clan, my lady. I plan to take you back to Berwyck where I will receive a fair amount of monies for your return."

"Berwyck is no longer my home," she declared, lifting her chin in confidence that Ian would soon be close at hand. "My husband will find me."

"If he is still alive, then I am counting on it," said her captor, "and when he comes for you, I will kill him."

There was no time for a retort or protest of any kind as he swiftly gagged her and bound her to a tree. She was becoming familiar with a coarse rope that seemed to continually be the choice means of her captors to keep her in one place. She closed her eyes, steadied her breathing, and remembered a time, not too long ago, when she was in this exact same situation, just with another bent on ransoming her for a bit of coinage. She had lost her friend that day, and she regretted not being able to save him.

Giving a silent prayer for Rolf's eternal soul to be at peace, Lynet practically willed Ian to her side and asked God to keep him safe. Her heart could not stand to lose another person she cared about, especially the one man she had loved her entire life. Once they were reunited, she would press the issue for Ian to declare his feelings about her, no matter that thus far she had been a most troublesome wife. She had waited her entire life for him to speak the words she longed to hear, and her faith in her husband that he would soon find her would not waver.

Thirty-Two

IAN TIGHTLY GRIPPED THE LEATHER REINS in his hands all the while attempting to remain level headed. 'Twas nigh unto an impossible task. Worry etched his features, wondering at what Lynet's fate had now become, and who had abducted her, this time.

With the slightest pressure from Ian's knee, his well-trained horse turned sharply into the forest and off the road to follow the tracks of the cart that had taken Lynet from the boundaries of their land. Angus and Connor rode by his side in silence as the miles continued to distance them from Urquhart. Whoever had taken his wife, they certainly made no attempt to hide their tracks. 'Twas almost as if the miscreant was giving Ian ample time and ease to locate Lynet, without much effort on his part. At the very least, he had that much going for him.

Judging for himself that the sun was beginning to set caused Ian to push his steed harder afore the cover of night halted their progress. They rode light to make better time of catching up to the scoundrel who had stolen his wife. With a brief glance at the MacGillivray plaid and the rest of his attire, he barely recognized the knight of old who used to dress in full armor to fight for an English king for many years in his past. He would not need the heavy metal, encasing his body, to see that justice was swiftly served...again.

But English knight or Scottish laird, he was determined to bring Lynet home, and upon her return, if he must needs keep a guard upon her night and day, he would ensure no one would ever dare to steal his wife, again. 'Twas becoming an irritating occurrence, and he cringed when Calum's words about Ian not knowing the whereabouts of his wife echoed in his head. Certainly, he should be able to keep one tiny woman safe within the walls of her own castle.

Ian pulled back on the reins to slow his mount with Angus and Conner doing the same. He knew of this place, although he had not been here since his youth. Memories of his family spending hours upon hours enjoying the warmth of a summer's day near the small lake invaded Ian with pleasant thoughts of happier times. For one brief moment, he relished the visions that danced afore his mind. He could see himself and his brother frolicking in the water whilst his sire and mother laughed in joy at their antics. They were peaceful memories of days gone by when he was young enough to believe his father would live forever, and he would never lose faith in his family's love.

A burst of annoyance almost erupted from his lips as he thought on his brother ruining the clan, but he choked the bitter memories down, not wanting to alert anyone they were near. He shook himself free of the images that quickly faded from his mind. He peered at the landscape with a practiced eye of one who knew what dangers to look for. Ian had no doubt he would find Lynet up ahead, and but a short distance away from where he now stood.

Ian dismounted, and his horse neighed, as if not pleased he must needs stand still. Ian reached out to pat the stallion's neck. The horse's skin quivered afore he began to snort air from his nose, toss his head about, and then proceed to rear his front legs up in anticipation. The beast finally gave Ian a nudge, almost as if to tell him to mount up so they could be on their way.

"Easy, boy," Ian urged with another calming pat. "We must needs handle this matter delicately. We do not want any harm to come to the Lady Lynet, now do we?"

The steed began shaking his head to and fro again, as though answering him. Ian left the horse standing still, knowing the animal would not move 'til called to do so. "Let us away, men," Ian ordered quietly, and they took off on foot to scout out the area, as quietly as possible.

The silence of the woods was deafening, and it took much skill on their part to remain just as quiet. They came to a bend on the narrow path made from the conveyance that had stolen Lynet away when Ian held up his hand to listen intently to the strange melody coming from up ahead. Obviously, someone did not care if they were heard or not, and yet, the tone had an eerie, sing-song quality that did not give Ian any sense of comfort as to the state of Lynet's wellbeing.

Inching their way onward, Ian motioned to his two men, and they made their way up a small hill. The advantage was taken, as they now were able to look down into the camp of the very person who had Lynet tied to a tree.

The man was a complete fool to so openly flaunt his wife for any who would care to come upon their camp, if a camp is what one could call it. His experienced eyes took in every detail of Lynet as she was uncomfortably tied to a large towering oak. Her captor kept his identity hidden with the hood of his cloak covering his face. He appeared as though he had not a care in the world, as he sat on the back end of the cart, humming his queer little tune, and swinging his feet back and forth in mid-air. He was whittling something in his hands and occasionally threw a stick into the fire that blazed like a beacon so they would be found.

Lynet never looked more beautiful, even though she was in complete disarray. Her hair stood on end, her face streaked with dirt. Ian's eyes narrowed, seeing how the simple gown she wore was torn in several places, not to mention her feet appeared battered, for she wore no shoes. She could not be happy, considering she was not only tied to a tree, but gagged, as well. Her eyes were closed, so he had no way of knowing if she slept or was merely resting. There was only one way to know for sure.

He whistled the tune of a nightingale's song just as softly as he had done but recently when Calum held her captive. He had his answer when Lynet's eyes opened wide as she searched for his whereabouts in the darkening forest. Her breathing accelerated as her chest rose up and down, and Ian could tell she was more than ready for him to come to her rescue. She began to fidget with the ropes, and he whistled again 'til she remained still. If only her eyes did not show her fright.

Ian moved forward whilst Angus and Connor guarded his back. They had almost made it to the edge of the perimeter of the camp when the scoundrel jumped off the cart to land near Lynet. Ian dared not breathe, considering the man now held a knife to his wife's throat. Tears escaped her eyes, and he prayed she would remain calm.

"That is far enough, I think, MacGillivray," the man sneered, pulling off his hood so his identity was at last revealed.

Ian stared at the man who had killed Rolf. "I know you," Ian snarled, "but who are you to Calum of Clan Davidson?"

The man laughed. "That depends. Since you are standing here, and he is not, should I assume he is dead?"

"Aye."

The man began to laugh. "Then you have done me a favor, and I now have one less obstacle to hurdle in my quest to gain all I desire."

"You still have not answered my question. Who are you?" Ian asked, taking a step forward, but held his breath as he watched Lynet's captor prick the tip of the knife into her neck. A small trickle of blood began to run from the wound.

"I told you, that was far enough, or did you doubt my words?" he tugged at Lynet's hair 'til she gave a muffled scream of outrage. Ian backed off. "As to your question, my name is Lachlan, not that you will know it for long. Since you have given my brother an early demise, you are now looking at the new laird of the Clan Davidson. I may be a bastard son, but the one person who knew such information as a certainty is now dead. Once I get rid of you, I can collect a handsome ransom for this one here and return to the clan as its leader, since I am next in line to inherit."

"Let her go, and you may yet live to see another day," Ian reasoned.

Lachlan gave another eerie laugh. "Let her go? You must be insane. She will bring a fair amount of coinage from her sister's husband so that I may replenish my dwindling coffers."

"Aye," Angus interjected, "if our laird or Lord Dristan does not kill ye first."

"Shut your mouth, you worthless cur," Lachlan yelled irrationally. "The estate should have all been mine in the first place, since I was the eldest son! But no...my sire has to go and have a legitimate heir, and I then watched all his attention turn from me. I spent years bowing and scraping at Calum's whim, and he never let me forget I was a bastard. I became an outcast from my own family and was only useful as a solider...nothing more. Just another faceless man, who if he were to die in battle, would be easily replaced with another."

"'Tis hardly our fault for your circumstances that have shaped your life," Ian said. "Surely, there are other women you could wed that will bring you the monies you need to replenish your clan's needs."

"Bah! Why should I bother looking for a woman, when this one will suit just as well as the next wench I come across. Besides, I have been to Berwyck, and the Devil's Dragon will have more than enough coinage to spare with the return of a member of his family. Then, and only then, will I have my revenge."

"Revenge? What revenge? What the bloody hell does any of this have to do with us?" Ian inquired with furrowed brow.

Lachlan stood, shaking off his cloak and drawing his sword. Ian pulled his forward as a precaution. He would take no chance with someone who appeared bent on killing him and his guards.

"'Tis an oath I swore to my dying mother that I would one day avenge her when my sire cast us both aside for his wife and legitimate son. 'Twas only after her death that my father took me in, and his lady wife made my life miserable, never letting me forget where I really came from. The bitch called my mother a whore. My revenge will come when I am able to spit on their graves and claim leadership of the clan," Lachlan's smile was confident. "You stand in my way. Therefore, you must die, along with your men."

Whatever bit of control Lachlan had been holding on to snapped as easily as a brittle dried twig. He lunged forward. Everything happened at once. Ian brought up his sword to defend himself, even whilst Angus and Connor flew to Lynet and began sawing through the ropes to free her. Ian heard her coughing and sputtering as the rag was taken from her mouth.

Ian saw his men usher Lynet a short distance away, even as she protested that she was more than safe. Lachlan dove at Ian, once more. With Lachlan's arms wrapped firmly about Ian's waist, the man's anger drove his momentum, and afore Ian knew what was happening, they were falling into the lake.

Lachlan had no issue with attempting to hold Ian's head beneath the water as the man's fingers tightened around his neck. With no thought of wanting to die by drowning, Ian reacted out of sheer necessity to get air into his lungs. Jerking up his knee, Ian hit his mark as he made contact with Lachlan's groin. A dirty ploy, but it did the trick, and Ian came up sputtering for air.

The wind was only momentarily knocked out of Lachlan, for he had years of anger that had built up in him blinding him to anything but, apparently, avenging his mother. He grabbed at a knife hidden in his belt and, with an evil leer, once more advanced towards his adversary in a rush. He was so focused on reaching Ian's side, he did not see Ian reach for his sword beneath the water 'til 'twas too late.

Lachlan's eyes widened in surprise as he all but met his own demise whilst he was skewered upon Ian's blade. A moment of pity filled Ian's face, causing Lachlan to scowl with hatred. "May your soul go to the Devil," Lachlan gurgled in his last breath afore his eyes rolled back into his head, and he fell dead into the water.

As Ian rose, he had no time to think on the dead man floating at his feet, for his arms were quickly filled with the sobbing form of his loving wife.

Thirty-Three

T HE GREAT HALL WAS FOR THE MOST PART DESERTED, with the exception a few serf's milling about finishing their chores. Lynet sat near the fire as Ian rubbed a small amount of a healing concoction she had hastily made on her neck wound. She had fussed that she was more than capable to see to such a tiny wound herself. Yet, Ian would hear nothing of her protest, especially not knowing if Lachlan had used a dirty blade. He had told her on numerous occasions to sit still so he could see to the injury so the wound would not fester. He had already spent a considerable amount of time massaging ointment into her battered feet.

"Do you suppose I shall live," she teased him, with a soft smile.

He dipped his hands to clean them in a bowl of water afore drying them and handing everything to a serf, who then scurried away. He came to sit down next to her on a stool, but said not a word, and only continued to stare at her, as though she were some figment of his imagination.

Still, he did not answer her question, and she finally reached out to cup his face. He quickly took her hand, and she watched in fascination when his head dipped down to lovingly place a lingering kiss into her palm. She quivered inside at such a romantic gesture and wondered how she would ever live with the man if he knew what he could do to her with just the simplest of kisses.

Ian finally raised his face towards her and leaned forward 'til their foreheads touched. "I swear by all that is holy, no harm shall ever come to you again, my lady, even if I have to guard you behind our closed chamber door for the rest of our lives," he vowed solemnly afore capturing her lips in a searing kiss.

Their lips broke apart, and she gave a girlish giggle. "'Tis an interesting proposition you propose, my laird. Mayhap, we should start now," Lynet suggested as she traced his check with the tip of her finger.

"Not as yet, wife," he declared, motioning to Lorna who waited near the entrance to the kitchen. "I will see you fed, if I must needs feed you myself. Surely, your stomach could use some nourishment, by now."

"I am not hungry for food," she pouted 'til her stomach betrayed her by letting out a very unladylike grumble that surely would be heard throughout all of Christendom. Ian tossed her an I-told-you-you-were hungry-and-so-you-shall-eat kind of a look. 'Twas hard to put up much of a protest once Lorna started laying out such a marvelous array of food to choose from. Surely, there was enough afore them to feed the entire clan. "Mayhap, I could eat just a little."

Ian's brow rose as he began filling a trencher of the choicest of meats. He did not stop there, but began to pile on all manner of breads and cheeses 'til Lynet was full just from looking at so much food. "You will eat 'til I am satisfied that you have a full belly. I will have no wife of mine going hungry. Then and only then, will we go to our chamber," Ian began, but wagged a finger at her as if he knew her thoughts, "to rest," he finished.

"That does not sound at all like what I had in mind," Lynet declared in a huff. With a mischievous twinkle in her eye, she began running her toes up the leg of her husband underneath the table.

Ian chuckled and easily caught her foot and began holding it down firmly in his lap. "Behave, you saucy wench, and eat. We can play later, as long as I feel you are up to such an endeavor."

"Oh, I shall be up to the task, Ian, the question is...will you be able to keep up with me?" Lynet looked up at him shyly, considering she just gave him such a bold, seductive invitation.

"I guess we shall see," Ian declared with a hearty laugh. "Now eat afore I forget myself and take advantage of you right here in your hall.

Satisfied her husband would be making love to her sometime soon, Lynet gave in to breaking her fast, for it had been, in truth, a long while since she had last partaken of food. Since they were almost finished with their meal, she was about to ask Ian if he was ready to go upstairs when the door of the keep opened and hit the wall with a mighty slam. She almost jumped out of her very skin 'til her eyes widened in delighted surprise at who was walking through the portal.

"Sir Fletcher!" she cried out. Limping unsteadily across the hall, she threw herself into his arms.

"'Tis a most unusual welcome, my lady, but I am glad to see your knight was able to find you, after all," Fletcher remarked with a roguish grin. "Any problems, Ian?"

"None that I could not handle," Ian replied, coming to greet the new arrival and pulling Lynet closer to his side. "I am surprised to see you this far north from Berwyck. As captain of Dristan's guard, I would expect you to be near its borders, not in the wilds of Scotland."

"Bah! Dristan would trust no one else leading the men he sent with me in the off chance you did not come across his little sister," Fletcher declared and opened the door again.

Several men began to bring in bundles of items for Lynet's inspection. Lynet gasped in startled surprise. "Why, they are my things from Berwyck," she cried out happily.

Fletcher smiled. "Aye, Dristan thought you would want a bit of home with you, along with your dowry and horse. To be honest, I do not think it appeals to him that you are so far removed from his notice."

"This is my home now, Sir Fletcher," Lynet said, marveling that Dristan and Amiria knew how much 'twould mean to have her possessions. A shadow fell across her features that did not go unnoticed by Ian.

"What is the matter, lass," Ian whispered whilst he cupped her face to wipe away a lone tear running down her cheek.

How could she not but shed a tear or two whilst remembering a handsome knight who sacrificed his very life so that she might live. A fallen knight who had loved her, mayhap, more than she deserved. She raised her face to Fletcher, begging him silently to answer what surely he knew what she would ask of him. "Did you find h—?"

"Aye, we found Rolf after one of the guards who had traveled with him returned," Fletcher answered.

"You have him here?" Lynet tried to disentangle herself from Ian's arms. "I must see him," she said, trying to get to the door.

"Nay, Lynet. Rolf's body is not here, my lady, but already in a final resting place at Berwyck," Fletcher answered gravely.

Ian pulled her back into his arms whilst she attempted not to cry a river full of tears. "I but wanted to see him one last time," she whispered into his chest. She felt him place a kiss upon her head.

"My dearest wife, you and I both know Rolf would not have wanted you to see him like that. Remember him in your heart, alive and being the cocky pain in my arse that he was," Ian said, attempting to make light of the situation.

"He is in a place of honor, Lady Lynet, and he is resting in the only place he ever called home," Fletcher said. "'Tis more than some of us ever get a chance at."

"Will you stay with us for a while? You are most welcome for as long as you so wish it," Ian inquired, brushing Lynet's hair back from her face.

"Nay, I will only stay long enough to rest the horses. But also know that Dristan and Amiria will expect you to bring yourself to Berwyck soon. They will want to see for themselves that Lynet is content in her choice of husband. Personally, I am ready to be about the journey. No offense, Ian, but I prefer my feet to be planted firmly on good English soil."

Lynet was only half listening to Ian and Fletcher speaking already of his departure. She was more than thankful they had found Rolf. She gave herself a mental shake to right herself and then peered strangely at Berwyck's captain afore she smiled. "You should be married, Sir Fletcher. I will see how we can best go about finding you a fair lady to call your bride."

Fletcher laughed at the prospect. "That may be a little difficult, my lady, for I am most particular on the sort of woman I would even consider to take to wife. Besides, 'tis not as though she is just going to show up and fall at my feet, now will she?"

A strange gleam lit Lynet's eyes. "One never knows, Sir Fletcher. One never knows..."

Stifling a yawn, Ian and Lynet at last made their way up to their chamber. She did not wish to admit it, but her ordeal had taken its toll on her, and all she wanted was to lie down. Even that was denied her as a tub of steaming water was at the ready near the hearth. She was more than willing to sacrifice a little sleep to sink into the soothing water.

Stripping off her soiled garments, she gave them no further thought as she slipped down into the liquid paradise that immediately began to work its magic. With her head laid back on the rim of the tub, she suddenly felt a soapy cloth being run along the length of her skin. Opening her eyes, she saw Ian, who was just as naked, as he began to wash her.

"I believe you owe me a bath, my dear," Ian said huskily.

"I believe you are right, husband," she answered sweetly. She pulled herself up so he could join her as the water sloshed over the sides of the tub and onto the floor. But such a mess mattered not at all. She came to him and sat down on his lap with a wiggle of her bottom. His brow rose in invitation, and she gladly accepted what he offered. When Ian began to kiss her, Lynet became completely lost, especially whilst he guided her into taking the lead in their lovemaking. 'Twas not 'til the water began to cool that common sense prevailed, and they rushed to climb beneath the coverlets on their bed.

Lying there, face to face, Lynet could only stare in fascination at those hazel eyes that had captured her in her youth. He reached over and tucked a piece of her hair behind her ear, but continued to twirl the end of the length around his finger.

"Any regrets, Lynet?" Ian asked with such a serious expression that she leaned forward to capture his lips.

"Nay, none whatsoever, my love," she replied honestly.

"My love?"

"Aye. I love you, Ian, just as much, if not more, as when I was just a child. There has only been you who has filled my heart for as long as I can remember. You are everything I could ever want and more, for my husband."

"I am proud to call you my wife, little one, and look forward to a lifetime together," Ian murmured, gathering her close within his embrace as exhaustion began to consume them both.

As she listened to his heart beating for her beneath her ear, she thought he might have dosed off. Instead, her heart soared with his next words.

"I love you, my sweet Lynet..." His words trailed off as slumber overtook him, leaving Lynet with a satisfied smile. A vague memory of her brother Aiden asking Amiria if she was content with Dristan as her husband flashed in her memory. Her sister had never given him an answer that day, and, mayhap, there was no need for her to do so, either.

Aye...it may have taken Ian a while to profess his love, but he had undeniably proved he cared for her after all. She, too, was indeed most content...

EPILOGUE

Berwyck Castle
Fall, The Year of Our Lord's Grace 1180

Ian STOOD WITH FEET SPREAD WIDE APART and arms crossed against his chest. His wife had requested some time alone, and he could hardly gainsay her. That, of course, did not mean he would still not stand guard over her, even if 'twas at a respectable distance. There was only so much he was willing to concede to his headstrong wife. Leaving her completely unguarded was not one of them.

She was so young, he still sometimes wondered if she would regret marrying a man so much older than her. He shook his head at his foolishness. They were married in the eyes of God, and he was blessed to call the woman his wife, especially since she carried his child within her. He would not let further thoughts or worries mar their visit here with her kin.

He continued to watch her from a distance, and saw when she placed the flowers she had carried from the highlands on the graves of her father, her mother, and Rolf. Aye, Rolf had indeed been laid to rest close to Lynet's own parents. Fletcher had told the truth when he declared the knight was given a place of honor. Not many guardsmen would be buried within the family cemetery. He saw his wife as she bent her head in prayer, and Ian knew she would not be too much longer at her vigil at the graves.

"Thank you for bringing her home to us, Ian," Amiria said, reaching out and placing her hand on his forearm, "even if the visit is a short one."

"I have a feeling our jaunts to Berwyck may be few in the foreseeable future," Ian said grimly.

"Why?"

"You must needs ask?" When she only raised a brow above those startling violet eyes, Ian sighed. "A Scottish laird will be considered a traitor in the eyes of an English king who he once served."

"I had not thought that far ahead, but I suppose you have it aright. I do not like the idea of not seeing my sister, but we will make do with the time we have."

"Aye, we shall. Besides, I could not keep her away, even if I tried, my lady," he said, giving her hand a pat afore resuming his stance. "Your sister is as tenacious as you are and threatened to bring down our own keep about my head if I did not take her here myself to see you."

Amiria gave a lighthearted laugh. "We are a stubborn lot, us MacLaren's, but the men who wed us, I will add, are also a mite pigheaded."

Ian smirked. "You must be talking about your dragon, for I have never been one to be...pigheaded."

"I believe, good sir, that I would contest such fanciful speech. Have you, perchance, been weaving whimsical tales to keep the children amused like the bards who come to my hall?"

"I am not pigheaded," he repeated with a scowl.

"Oh, aye, you are!"

"I do not know where you and Lady Katherine get such fanciful ideas in your pretty little heads."

Amiria burst out in laughter. "'Tis why you fit in so well with those who live here at Berwyck. Dristan and his guards have the same annoying traits, but you all know how we ladies admire you, all the same."

"Hmmm...I know not how you can say you admire us and then call us names in the same sentence."

"'Tis because we love to tease you all so. 'Tis not often we mere women get the best of our handsome knights who are sworn to protect us, not that I cannot do a fair job of it myself. Besides, we must needs take advantage of such rare occurrences when we can," Amiria answered as she continued to have a mischievous look upon her face.

"Then enjoy your time jesting with me whilst you may, Amiria, for Lynet and I shall need to leave soon. I do not relish being caught so far south when winter begins. I worry over Lynet and the babe."

"I wish you could stay longer, but we understand," Amiria replied somewhat sadly.

Ian grew serious as he continued to watch his wife's sister from the corner of his eye. She began looking over his shoulder 'til she suppressed a girlish giggle. "What so amuses you now, Amiria?" Ian stated with a frown.

She returned her attention to him whilst continuing to hide her smile. She failed and promptly burst into a laughing fit, annoying him further, thinking he was the reason of some jest he was not privy to. "Fine...do not answer me then," he fumed.

"Oh, Ian...do not be so serious all the time," she began. "You must enjoy life and the surprises given to you sometimes."

"I am done with all the surprises I have had of late and need no more of them. I only wish for Lynet and myself to live a happy, normal life."

"Bah! Normal is boring, my dear friend. 'Tis best to live your life on the edge of anticipation that all things are possible," she said, looking around him yet again with a very enchanting smile.

Ian turned to see who was behind him, but saw only the barbican gate. "Who is it you keep staring at? Whoever he is, he seems to be keeping you amused," Ian declared in puzzlement.

"Let me just say that there is someone who is wishing a word with you."

Ian frowned. "Then, mayhap, he should come forth from the keep so we might have speech together."

"He is already here, Ian. Open your mind to the gift that is afore you and enjoy the moment," she murmured softly. She tugged on the sleeve of his tunic, and when he leaned down, she gave him a quick kiss upon his cheek. "I will leave you two together. I am sure there is much you must needs catch up on."

Ian was confused as she left him standing there very much alone. "Daft woman," he grumbled aloud as he watched her depart.

"I heard that," Amiria called over her shoulder afore she continued walking inside the castle gate.

Ian took up his stance of watching over his wife. He had not been standing there long afore a fierce wind blew across the land, causing him to rock on his feet. He brushed back the hair that had fallen across his face and began to rub his eyes from the grains of dirt that had attached itself to his skin. As he began to get his eyesight back, he had a moment of startled surprise when he saw a vague, ghostly, transparent image begin to take shape next to him. "By all that is holy! It cannot be!"

"Hello, my friend," the ghost whispered inside his head.

"Rolf?" Ian at last managed to gasp out. "God's Wounds! What trickery is this?"

"'Tis no trickery, and I will not appear to you for long, so my time with you is short," Rolf answered brusquely. "This state of being takes some getting used to."

Ian's gaze shifted up and down the ghostly apparition in disbelief. "Why are you not resting in peace, Rolf? You did your duty. Lynet is safe. You must needs enjoy the heavenly delights that are yours by right for saving the woman you loved."

Rolf's attention went to the woman who was rising from the ground and hastily making her way towards them. "Aye, I loved her, but she will never see me as I am now. 'Tis the vow I made when I asked the angels to allow me to stay at Berwyck to watch over its people. You may feel that I did my duty, but in my heart, I know I failed in my quest to keep Lynet safe. 'Twill be the penance I will gladly pay to watch over the castle for all time."

"She would want to see you and, at the very least, hear one last time that you loved her," Ian urged, still mystified that he was having this strange conversation with a spirit not of this world.

Rolf gave a cocky smile. "You tell her for me, my friend. You will take good care of her."

Ian watched in amazement when Rolf began to fade the closer Lynet came. "How can you ask that of me? You should know I will protect her to my last dying breath."

Rolf gazed only once more towards Lynet afore he vanished, "'Twas really not a question, Ian, but more of a fact. God Speed, my friend."

Ian stumbled forward after he felt a hearty slap upon his shoulder and upon hearing Rolf's last words to him rumbling around inside his head. The damn ghost surely was most amused, as he listened to Rolf's cheerful laugher. He had no further time to ponder such strange happenings, for Lynet came up to him, and he pulled her into his arms.

"Is all well with you and the babe, Lynet?" Ian asked, kissing her forehead. Her brow was furrowed, and he reached out to smooth the wrinkles.

"I had the strangest feeling come over me when I was finishing my prayers. I looked up towards you, and I thought I saw...someone..."

"Who?" Ian asked quietly as they began to make their way toward the bridge of the castle.

"'Twas nothing, I am sure, and just my imagination. But still, I could have sworn I saw...Rolf," she said with a look of stern concentration on her features, as if she was trying to determine whether her mind was playing tricks on her.

"*I could not resist letting her see me just once, however slight, Ian,*" Rolf's voice whispered inside his head. "*I am certain I will pay for such an offense against my vow.*"

Ian brought Lynet's fingers to his lips. "I am sure, if you think you saw him, then you did, Lynet," he answered reverently.

"You will think me daft afore this pregnancy is over," she said in delight and began twirling around with a brilliant smile set upon her face. 'Twas as though the sun began to shine all the brighter because she was so happy. "It feels so good to be home, Ian,"

"I am glad you are happy, my sweet."

"How could I not be? I always wanted a knight to call my own, and not only do I call him my husband, but he's also a Scottish laird. With your child growing inside me, I would say our lives are just about perfect."

"Aye, I would have to agree with you, my dear wife, for I have my own nightingale to call my very own, as well. I love you, Lynet, 'til the end of time."

"I swear, I will never tire of hearing you say those words to me. I love you, too, Ian. Our souls shall always find a way to each other so we can forever and a day be together."

She pulled upon his tunic 'til he leaned down so she could capture his lips in a searing kiss. He groaned, knowing they had hours yet afore they would be able to excuse themselves and make their way to their bedchamber.

Ian watched her skip ahead across the bridge and under the barbican gate. As he made to follow her, Rolf's ghostly figure appeared standing guard afore the entrance to the castle. He appeared as he always had been, strong, tall, and proud to be part of the Devil of Berwyck's guardsmen.

When Ian drew closer, Rolf withdrew his sword from his scabbard and hoisted it in a salute to his comrade in arms. Honored by such a gesture, Ian gave the knight a courtly bow afore taking his own sword and returning the gesture. Rolf gave one last cocky grin, returned his sword, and disappeared from view.

"Ian? Whatever are you doing, my love?" Lynet called out. "I thought you were going to assist me in the garden?"

Ian sheathed his sword with a flourish. "I am coming," he answered and watched as his wife disappeared inside the outer bailey.

Whistling a merry tune, Ian began to follow her to help her with whatever task she had in mind. Only God knew for sure what He had in store for them in their future together, but one thing was certain. Ian would follow Lynet to the ends of the earth if he needs must. For Ian had indeed found love in the arms of a small slip of a wonderful woman whom he now called his wife. As far as he was concerned, that was not a bad place to spend one's life and all of eternity...

Author's Note

I hope you enjoyed the continuing saga of the MacLaren's, including Lynet and Ian's journey to finding love. I must admit this story was extremely difficult to complete given what had to happen to one of my beloved characters in order for my plot to move forward with the rest of my time travel series, *The Knights of Berwyck, A Quest Through Time Novel.*

As in my other three books, I'd like to clarify several historical aspects of *A Knight To Call My Own*. This novel is a work of fiction and, as such, I have weaved my story around actual places and people.

When deciding on my cover art and a public domain image, I decided to go with one of my favorite artists. The painting *God Speed* by British artist Edmund Blair Leighton (September 21, 1852 – September 1, 1922) depicts everything I wanted for Lynet and Ian. You may recognize Chapter Nine from this scene as Lynet races to meet both Rolf and Ian and ends up given them both a token of her affection. Giving a knight a favor was a medieval custom which assured both parties would be reunited, alive and well.

If you haven't read my previous work, I will briefly mention that Berwyck Castle is a figment of my imagination. Although there was a castle at Berwick-Upon-Tweed at one time, you can find out more information on its existence either in my previous author notes or on the internet.

The first documentary record of Urquhart Castle occurs in 1296, when it was captured by Edward I of England. Edward's invasion marked the beginning of the Wars of Scottish Independence, which would go on intermittently until 1357. Although I have moved the history of this castle back to the 12th century, it was actually founded in the 13th century. The present ruins date from the 13th to the 16th centuries, though it was built on the site of an early medieval fortification (source of information: https://en.wikipedia.org/wiki/Urquhart_Castle).

Today, Urquhart is one of the most visited castles in Scotland, especially for those attempting to spot the famous Loch Ness Monster, Nessie. I couldn't help myself by inventing a fictional character and calling her Nessa, even though she only makes a brief appearance.

Any reference to the Clan MacGillivray being lairds of Urquhart is a figment of my imagination, although their origins date back to the 12th century. Events relating to Clan Davidson and Clan MacLaren are also a work of fiction on the part of this author.

I hope you find these short author notes on my research for my books interesting.

Dear Reader:

I would like to take this opportunity to thank you for picking up *A Knight To Call My Own*. I hope you enjoyed Lynet and Ian's story as much as I had writing it.

If you follow me on social media, and in particular Facebook, you will know that I have a lot in store for you in the future. I am currently working on several projects, one of which will be my subsequent time travel, *To Follow My Heart*, and will be the next in *The Knights of Berwyck, A Quest Through Time Novel* series. If you haven't as yet guessed, Sir Fletcher, who is Berwyck's captain of the guard, will be the next knight who will have his fate determined by a modern woman. This time, it will have a twist and I hope to have this published soon.

I also will have *Under the Mistletoe*, my first Regency era novella, available with The Bluestocking Belles' boxset entitled *Mistletoe, Marriage, & Mayhem*. All proceeds will go to our mutual charity The Malala Fund and will be released November 1, 2015. You can find out all about us on our website at www.BluestockingBelles.com.

If this isn't enough on my plate, including my day job, I will also be working on a full length Regency novel entitled *One Moment in Time* that I hope to publish in early 2016. This novel was actually the very first manuscript that I ever wrote, and I'll be working diligently to rework this story of Edmund and Roselyn.

If you haven't stopped by my website, please do and take a look around. You can sign up to join my newsletter so you can stay up-to-date on what I have going on, sign up for my street team, and also join my member's area so you can discuss my books with other members.

Thank you again for all your support and especially those who have taken the time to write such marvelous reviews for my current work. I get so happy when I hear from my readers about how much they love my books and characters. You are the lifeblood of an Indie author like myself, who is just starting her writing career. I appreciate you taking the time to write reviews, re-tweet my posts on Twitter, or even like or comment on my posts on Facebook. You are very much appreciated and I thank you for all your support from the bottom of my heart!

With Warm Regards,
Sherry Ewing

OTHER BOOKS BY
SHERRY EWING

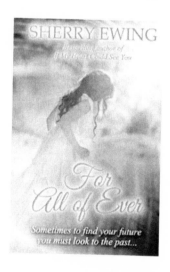

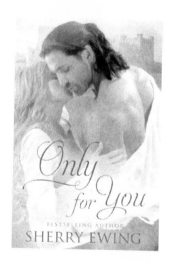

Available in paperback and eBook
At all on-line retailers
If My Heart Could See You also available in audiobook

COMING SOON

UNDER THE MISTLETOE

A Regency novella with
The Bluestocking Belles first boxset entitled

MISTLETOE, MARRIAGE & MAYHEM
Release date November 1, 2015

And

TO FOLLOW MY HEART
THE KNIGHTS OF BERWYCK,
A QUEST THROUGH TIME NOVEL

ABOUT THE AUTHOR

Sherry Ewing picked up her first historical romance when she was a teenager and has been hooked ever since. A bestselling author, she writes historical & time travel romances to awaken the soul one heart at a time. Always wanting to write a novel but busy raising her children, she finally took the plunge in 2008 and wrote her first Regency. She is a member of Romance Writers of America, The Beau Monde & the Bluestocking Belles. Sherry is currently working on her next novel and when not writing, she can be found in the San Francisco area at her day job as an Information Technology Specialist. You can learn more about Sherry and her published work at www.SherryEwing.com.

CPSIA information can be obtained at www.ICGtesting.com
Printed in the USA
BVOW02s1827030516

446594BV00001B/41/P